VIOLENT MIND CANDY

A NULL
&
BOYD NOIR

GARY S. KADET

ISBN: 978-1-955784-97-9

Melange Books, LLC
White Bear Lake, MN 55110
www.melange-books.com

Cover Design by Caroline Andrus

"The more you take away, the bigger it gets. The bigger it gets, the less you have. A cheaper story could never be found. My love for you is like a hole in the ground."

—PLEASANT "COUSIN JOE" JOSEPH

For those who do the hard jobs and get no credit for it—and to Nancy Pepin, née Durocher, who's been there and back.

FORETASTE

It's the same in Boston as in any other city—

The screaming.

It happens in a single second—a debauched moment in time—a secret, jagged opening, a sickening fissure in the continuum of the usual.

Always discreet, this time under cover of a sopping rain.

Now, the rain in Boston is in fact unlike the rain of any other city; thick, heavy, stupid globs coming at you in fits and starts like the clabber of a mad dog shaking its head. Icy, yet greasy to the touch. A Boston rain seems to know in some dumb way just how and when to piss you off the most. It's like it knows precise and predetermined ways to get to you.

Open your umbrella and find it chewed and ruined almost instantly by the brutish wind. Try to turn back and find yourself slammed instead into a salvo of droplets like slops tossed in your face. Duck for cover, it stops before you get there.

Proceed and get drenched.

This rain, it knows how to push you around. It knows how to bully you while you're busy trying to find a way out of it.

This rain—interrupted by a grim, gray nothing—was what each year passed for spring in Boston. It would go on for days and days with the languid force of a complaint that took on a stunted life of its own whose mind and personality made you simply want to kill it.

It hung on in its feculent decay with absolutely no regard for you—like some rich, ancient, stingy relative hanging around waiting to die only to deny you whatever legacy had once been dangled before you.

That was the essence of Boston.

No other city had a rain like it. No other city deserved it.

The debauched moment in time, however—now that was something exactly the same in Boston as it was in New York or LA.

Even in such a pinched and middling cloister as Boston, the debauched moment in time was always a known yet hidden thing; an abominable tick in the shadows covered up by the soft and wooly lie of the expected. Acceptably finessed and, therefore, neatly ignored.

It was a moment that came lightning fast in bedrooms and offices, dormitories and backrooms--bang! It was over. Sly like quicksilver in the alleys between the cracks in the cobblestones of the cramped downtown, shunted by brickwork and silicate pavement where only specialized eyes could see.

Opportunistic eyes, viral, microscopic.

Those attuned to sickness boiled in depravity knew it for what it was immediately: The moment that writhes up from under consciousness as if a crawler from below a flagstone, but comes down hard, nevertheless. Hard and final. It comes on strong, heavy, relentless, only to at last peter out to weakness, like the misdirected sloppy punch of a drunk thrown at no one in particular in a dive bar—

Or like a woman screaming her lungs out in an alley in the rain.

And it was a woman, wasn't it?

It had to be—that screaming.

Could anyone else shriek and plead and scream in such a way?

Sure. That was it.

A normal urban tragedy: Heel broken, smoke-stemmed legs in dark stockings splayed down to the pavement, the heaving weeping with shock and discomfort; the abrupt heart-breakup.

The drama.

A young thing, beautiful and frail in mascara ruined by the rain, pretty in hot pink chemically tortured hair, alabaster cheeks, lips pouted out and perennially tumescent for sex. But chaste, always chaste unless in trade for those moments of glamour that come even to a prim city like Boston.

Wet breasts in a scoop-necked PVC, shoulder less bodysuit, shining too fully round to be ignored in oblique streetlight.

Certain eyes cannot help but see. Viral eyes.

Off Sleeper Street past six where the avaricious dreamers trundle down Congress, gloating, plotting, but as always worrying, so that the debauched moment in time slips by almost unnoticed. Braving the annoying rain locked in the rhythm of the plan.

Then comes some normal guy, blissfully late from the office cubicle, relieved by time and deadline of the screaming kids, the hectoring wife, the computer up and running and waiting at home with Quicken's household accounting spreadsheet—the nightly fiscal video game of "black hole."

Business types seeing her, adjusting their collars, their hats and their vision *not* to see her. Noses in the air with grasping complacency, Boston style (—forever a town like an arrogant French waiter, either licking someone's coveted boots or kicking someone perceived to be a bit beneath in the ass with a borrowed pair of the same).

Comes the normal guy, bruised ass and all—what could he do but be buffeted along by these currents while acting as if it were his chosen destiny?

When in Boston, you behave as if you don't really *have* to be there, like a Kennedy, Cabot, Lowell, Tufts even a Bush (hell, if you can't have Harvard, take a New England coastline fiefdom instead), even though you were just stuck. Your best hope was to either steer clear of these dynastic family machines or in some way scrape up the chance to grovel at their feet and service them.

A city of toadies and toads refreshed by an influx of over-privileged children of national and international grandees—the fallow of the typical malefactors of greed, celebrity, and influence who dot the four-color landscape and fire the hearts of the mob competing only with "reality" TV.

Kiddieland.

Boston was in many ways a two-sided kiddieland. On one side, fresh young faces looking for fast times to kill time while being groomed for happy prefab life-slots, and on the other side, older, more life-battered predators on the make and jones-ing a mile a minute for that special young, fresh face.

Youth was never just wasted on the young in Boston.

So, comes the normal guy, happy for any opportunity at all.

Happy to get anything at all, happy to get lucky.

Anything to forestall the nightly cozy work-a-daddy death/resurrection scenario.

Like some young thing crying in the rain, for example.

What's wrong, honey? What's wrong?

Rain beat down and stuck, like it was rolling off a body.

He knelt, gave her his coat, lifted her up from under sleek, fleshy arms bared by the bodysuit beneath an inadequate red pleather jacket, so very smooth-shaven and fragrant. Warm and yearning; sticky to the touch.

She was chewing gum amid her bawling, snapping it and smacking her lips, chewing thickly. A little lost lamb lolling its cud.

He held her close to him and she yielded gratefully as he inhaled the sweat-enhanced pheromone scent of youth's perfume.

She wept hard now into his shoulder almost joyously, clinging to him, clutching him, arms and legs still pudgy with child-flesh seeking his warmth and—so it seemed—his rising manhood.

He drew her into the shadows, as in this embrace they were no longer erased within the vision of the Boston passersby but examined lewdly and then hurried past. His clumsy hands explored her as she clung more tightly to him, settling into the warmth and comfort of his closeness, burying her head by his shoulder and neck. His hands probed beneath the body suit as his wrecked umbrella and battered attaché case fell away like a dull husk in the slapping rain and now he was as soaked to the skin as she.

The young thing chewed gum sloppily against the flesh of his neck, sobbing piteously.

It didn't really matter.

Instead of going home, he found he *was* home.

And it had been far too long since he had been here.

He wondered why he ever had left at all.

They waltzed together in a tender embrace further back into the shadows at an angle away from the street corner.

He would do her right there, right then, like he was eighteen again and life was a mysterious gamble he could win with luck and cunning. Fuck the rain. Fuck the work-a-drone drudges trundling by, bullied by the fucking rain and trying to ignore them.

But first he had to calm the weeping.

In his staid, mid-thirties mindset, you just didn't do a weeping a girl right there in the narrow, flooded alley.

No, you comforted her first; coaxed and then refocused the need upon you.

That's what you did.

Come here, honey. Let me make it better. Get you warm.

Get me hot you mean?

Oh, yeah, honey. That's what I mean.

The rain, with added electrical flashes, was unforgiving, and her candy-flavored embrace was just the opposite. Quick and eager fingers found his groin and clasped it firmly, knowingly, with correct pressure. His fingers probed her with inexpert directness.

The rain was giving them and everyone else a beating.

There was a big push to make time.

Together against warehouse brick and hard by stolid dumpsters, they seemed to be rutting and bucking. They rumbled with the thunder and were crepuscular with lightning. Now they were skewed amorphous shapes hardly seen at all by the hurried prim business walkers lunging toward the commute home that was itself barely more desirable than the storm.

He looked up, transfixed, renewed, defined by rainwater like a dreamy icing.

Her clothes were laid open in the half-light, split and unzipped; her pink, firm belly and gentle curves of chest and thigh were defined by wet, shining flashes of light; her eyes dewy with emotion and the intensity of meaning in the moment.

A special moment in time.

He drew her up to him as they threatened to fall comically into a dark puddle.

She breathed candied fragrance into his face, her arms clasping him to her with fierce need.

His hands were on her ass, cupping each cheek and pushing her up into him.

This was the moment to which he really belonged; he knew then, this nameless normal guy, *this moment and no other.*

He couldn't have been more right.

This was the moment that owned him.

The climax came and went, as did the commuters.

A detail cop shone a flashlight on them and barked something at them in Dorchester-ese, a gargled, guttural sneer. The beating rain was like a shield. The cop waved his arm, drawled something vulgar and indistinct.

A kick in the ass from the unforgiving wind was all he needed to move on.

It was after the climax that the crying came again, and the guy knew, as he affected a standard comforting embrace, that this was now the bad moment that had to follow. He was expert in this from years of marriage bed theatrics and knew just what to do; whispering things, adjusting his drenched clothes and groping for his attaché case. She wept into him, hysterical now, despite the satiation and apparent reaching soulfulness of the moment.

His moment.

The moment he thought that had come for him, which in fact did not come at all—until now.

The weeping became a screaming louder than the thunder, which seemed to stop time.

High-pitched, mindless beyond desperate, keening like a suicidal/homicidal woman.

The cop fought his way back toward the alley off Sleeper and was promptly knocked off his feet into an inky ocean of rain by a pink-haired lithe-limbed club girl squealing half naked in intermittent flashes of light. The remains of her clothes were mostly trailing behind her.

The detail cop could have sworn after she knocked him down that she was skipping happily—*merrily* was a word that came to mind like out of a fairy story—across the bridge just past the Boston

Tea Party boat on Congress over by the restored depression-era Milk Bottle concession stand at the Children's Museum toward the business district. Her pink flesh was made to glow somehow breathtakingly under coarse streetlight in the rain.

She was fucking *skipping!*

When the officer got there, he had to radio in several times as the storm really fucked up communications—the electrical disturbance of ions in the air.

Finally, at dispatch, he put in a request for the pizza wagon out of Boston City and a crime scene detail to come meet him on Sleeper as some poor fucker just got his throat ripped out by a crack-crazed prostitute.

There was no more screaming.

But in the distance, he could have sworn that he heard something that crackled behind the thunder.

Laughter.

Like that of a small child.

ONE

It was another bottle morning for Lieutenant. Kay Boyd of Boston's Special Organized Crime Task Force, or more rightly, it was a morning that would have gone much better than it was going if there had only been a bottle the night before. She was slogging through her fifth month of detox and it wasn't much of an improvement over the first. Sure, the night sweats were gone, the shakes—the sheer physiological disgust at being alive. She could kick the physical addiction in just days of agony and weeks of regret. What she couldn't kick was the sleeplessness, the haunted, inexplicable need, the sense of raw betrayal at being exposed to a brutal, relentless reality without the wooly protective buffer of a soft blur of alcohol blooming up from the hot spot in her chest so it could surround and cushion her throbbing head.

Now it was strictly clarity marked by heartburn, exacerbated by Boyd's new passion for popping chocolates. Sugar for alcohol, cocoa for love.

The minor fix replacing the major.

The trivial eating the grandiose.

Every day since the removal of that haggard spirit of misery from her life, career mook Joey X, informant from hell, she had been teetering between coping well and spiraling down. Joey X—Null!—damaged tough-ass punk resurrected from a nightmare of garbage looming over her, evoking guilt and the single best promise he could make. The only promise he could fulfill:

Death.

She was teetering between doing fine and falling flat on her ass now that Null was no longer prosecuting his shadowy stream of homicidal mayhem to fuck up the balance of things. But what landed before her on the desk managed to fuck it up just as well, or perhaps even better. A case file.

She looked up bleary-eyed as if drunk, but instead met the moment sober, weary and knowing.

Byron Wurdalaka, in his cutesy way of playing servile Hegelian second banana, had dropped in on her to press his disadvantage, piss her off and prove his point to ultimate redundancy as to the unsuitability of the new gynocrats who came in under former Commissioner Queen Kathleen. He had dropped in on her to slam her with this new murder file she was now reviewing while making the not unexpected groaning noises. "Byron, you realize that, as per the new commissioner's newest dictum, you only report to me in matters of homicide that overlap onto OC Taskforce territory."

"Oh, but I'm a stickler for that LT. You know that from past experience."

Her expression and demeanor were void yet sweet.

"What I know from past experience, Byron, is that you're an out-and-out prick."

Wurdalaka clicked his tongue. "And we never even dated, did we?"

Kay gave the case file an expert thumb-through then slid it back over to Wurdalaka. "Prostitutes don't qualify, Byron—even if they happen to murder their johns. I don't think she was a contract hitter. There's no overlap here. Thanks for stopping by."

"Read it again, why don't you? Maybe you missed a detail or two?" He smacked his head and winced, typical bad theater of the police. "What am I saying?" he droned with weighty sarcasm. "You're the extra-educated, specially certified MSW what doesn't miss a trick, but for maybe when it comes down to human fucking nature."

"I know *your* fucking nature, Byron. Show or blow. I got meetings and budgetary pleas to make."

"Do a little light reading, LT, would you?" He was smug about something—the hick urbanite high ward redneck grin was slick with spittle. He was drooling at the chance to give her a little grief for having wound up his technical superior in grade and command due to the recent regime change at One Schroeder Place.

She could write him up for insubordination if he didn't comply with her orders and in the current climate of backlash have it actually go through. She knew this made him crazy.

"There's no time and you know it. I've got about a hundred forty of these piled up so I can redo the Ork family tree and see who's doing whom within the new order—"

"Since when is a clusterfuck a tree?"

"Since the power vacuum sucked one into growing."

"You mean now that your buddy the corpse offed the entire Family down to the last soldier who didn't manage to run clear. That's what *you're* talkin' about?"

"I'll bet even you can hear in your head just how fucking obtuse that sounds, Byron."

"Maybe, but we never got a good clear ID on who the scarecrow was you capped Andromeda for in order to protect." It wasn't "for" and "order" but "*faw*" and *"awduh."* Wurdalaka was afflicted by the guttural, repellant Boston honk. Kay had flattened hers with education and mixing through education with the more moneyed and mobile classes.

"You know who it was."

"Stop fucking telling me it was Null. Fucker died for the all the little white slave kiddies after we decoyed him out to cover for a Family informant that they already sent to the grave in bite-sized chunks."

Boyd flushed with emotion. It was in her head, the torture, death, heroism and pain.

Null eviscerated in a chair under the straight razor of crime lord Giorgio "Gomez" Gomelsky.

Emaciated pale bodies, even when black and Asian, of the lost children earmarked to be sold for sex, writhing like worms in container tanks.

Theron "Thing" LeCoeur, capping Grove Hall street kids, his suckerfish lips on her as he tried to rape her on George's Island.

A near thing. A very near thing.

Post-resurrection Null coming down, flack-jacketed, semi-automatic rifles in each hand, dealing death, calm as some dark god, unprepossessing as a stone gargoyle.

"Null was a hero. City should have done something for him, but he didn't fit the profile. They didn't even get around to dumping his outstanding parking tickets."

"You want a drug addicted low-life mook to be a role model?"

"Who else ya got? George Dub-ya Bush? Same difference in my book."

Wurdalaka chuckled, getting off on the exchange now that he was sure the power had shifted in his favor. "Why not? Better the failure and fuckup that made it than the one that didn't."

"Get out, Byron. Come back when you have something more than your inch-dick in your hand."

"Uh-uh, LT. Privilege begets privilege."

"Filth breeds filth, you mean."

Wurdalaka chuckled and plopped himself down in an uncomfortable interview seat in Boyd's office, kicking back as he sat, seeming to bask in the silvery sheen of the Boston murk of alleged spring.

"Chew or screw, Byron."

He folded his fingers behind his head, stretched his legs, let his soiled suit flop open.

"Chew on my dick."

Boyd stood up, incensed.

"Tell me the fuck what you want or get the fuck out of my office!"

Deputy Chief Inspector Phil LaCuna, old, obscenely tall, lantern-jawed and rutabaga-faced, loomed at the door, his ill-cut gray Brooks Brothers causing odd shadows as the gloom outside the windows darkened further. "What is this little interplay about here we're having—a lover's spat?"

"The LT just needs to calm down—she's sensitive."

"Fuck the both of you."

"Need a drink, do we, now?"

"Yeah, Phil. Brompton's cocktail, maybe."

LaCuna's distorted shadow merged with the murk of the hopeless early spring Boston skyline to subsume Boyd's office and eclipse the pasty, craggy face of Byron Wurdalaka. It was as if shadows conspired with LaCuna to blot out all light from the room. Wurdalaka flicked on a light, which was anything but bright. "Well, I could get all avuncular and wise right now and give you some illustrative anecdote me da told me, but instead, why don't I write the pair of yez up? That might stimulate some solidarity between yez, bein' docked pay, sanctioned and all."

"I don't want that, Phil," Wurdalaka said with genuine meaning, covered by sarcastic innocence.

"Phil, you can shove—"

LaCuna stepped forward, loomed over her desk, mirthful intent steeled in his eyes. "Kay, you can think it, but you don't want to say it. Friends and supporters at the top take their nod from the ones below. Get the drift?"

"Fuck—"

"Think it *through,* Kay." A low growl. Teeth gritted.

Head bowed, he added, "—This."

"Youse two can't play nice, I'll have to take your toys away." Cop authority of the old school swaggering, trousers hitched. He left that way, walking like he was back in the 60s, swinging his baton on the beat, squaring up his turf. "You would not like that," he had said, winking.

"No fucking joke, LT, this case has you all over it, whether I want it or not."

She had busied herself by fast-typing e-mails.

"I don't see how, Byron—your perp's a club kid—kind of a reach to tie that to OC, considering the nature of Boston's remaining gangs, crews and clusterfucks. You're bustin' my balls here, Byron, and no mistake."

Wurdalaka reached for the file, paged through and clipped a single report page to the outside of the folder.

"Just read the fine print, LT, and then give me your take."

She took the file and obliged. "Anything to get you to leave."

"Oh, you're gonna want me around, to be sure, you see what's there."

Boyd placed the file neatly atop her in-box case pile and had to react fast to keep it from toppling over. She hugged it with both arms and blushed, knowing she looked slightly foolish in front of the smug Wurdalaka. She sat down and paged through it, looking unmoved.

"You got it, right?"

The pile held firm. Boyd herself did not, knew it, and fixed her hair by reflex to help conceal that fact. "Yes. I got it Byron, like a cramp. Pull up a chair and let's get to it."

"It doesn't look like a coincidence, does it?"

Boyd looked grave. "No. Not this one."

"Ain't no innocent, plain-Jane murder."

"Not when you're talking about the throat-slashing of a chief accountant—"

"Yeah, especially when it's the chief accountant for Malek "The Mallet" Turbot, supreme psychopath, what runs Boston's worst murder crew to date."

She met his smirk with cold eyes and added: "How *could* it be?"

TWO

The housepainters came, and this time there were four of them.

There was Damien "Dimmy" Greco, pocked and swarthy, with darting copper eyes, arms and hands that itched at his sides, stubby fingers flexed and tensed, standing a lopsided six nothing. Then there was Pynchon "Punch" Slothropian, middle-height, middle-weight, middle-aged, middle everything, sandy hair blanching in the bits of frustrated Boston sunlight that came too late and went too quickly.

Some new guy fell in with them for a sixteenth share instead of a quarter, an ace hitter from New York named Coleridge. He wasn't official with the Ork, but enough whisperings from the right wrong corners, social clubs and crack houses gave him the nod. When you've got trouble with muscle, the more muscle you bring on, the better your odds of coming out without a scratch.

Nelson "Nimrod" Stassen brought up the rear, short, squat, rat-faced and squinty, looking like he belonged detailing SUVs on North Washington Street in Allston, where the mark was, the fucking mutts who absconded with a hot million worth of Malek the Mallet's best crystal meth. They were dressed in the type of uniform all housepainters wore; casual looking, but in fact all business. Dark colored, pull-over slip on khaki affairs strapped on with Velcro that could take a good blood spattering and be torn off and dispensed with in one quick hurry.

They looked phony and nondescript, which had been intended.

They were there to deal with the mark.

The mark was a short-haul crew made up of Robicheaux, Kinsella and Millhone. Millhone was trunk music as of last night in the back of Slothropian's Nova, lured out for some private stock of Dallas Dhu on a drunk down at the Kinvara Pub on Harvard Ave., the way drinking pals often go. A few pulls on a long-necked bottle of ketamine cocktail and Millhone practically dove into the trunk of the Nova all by himself. Kinsella took a hot shot in the stall in the little boys room at Avalon and was spirited away by some hunky dance boys in Yankees uniforms, each one duked a hundred cash to drop the mutt in a dumpster down in New Market Square, Boston's unsavory meat district. Junkie-death carcass down in meat-packing land, barely significant enough to make the police blotter, let alone the back page of the Herald. Robicheaux, the muscle of the crew, was left to sit on the stash at a safehouse on North Washington, stupidly waiting for a factotum from the Chicago clan to make the pick-up, pay Robicheaux off pennies on the dollar and get him a berth on the underground express to Canada before they punched his ticket for good.

They stood half a block away, smoking and looking relaxed, like neighborhood guys, sizing up the safe house. The new guy, Coleridge, looked like death; old, tired, gray-skinned and scarred with violence on every bit of visible skin. He must have stood, what, five nine weighing a buck fifty at most? Slothropian hoped he could pull his weight, which wasn't much, but more than most mopes could handle.

He had better.

Being that Robicheaux was muscle and likely sampling the meth he was supposed to sit on, Slothropian had the housepainters split up so as to take four different tacks for entry, each one of them toting Walther PPKs with suppressors, flat black and unobtrusive in proper shoulder holsters, rounds all Teflon-filled for a one-to-two stop shot. For extra measure, Slothropian had a sawed-off shotgun dangling down his back from a thick lanyard under his XXXL warm-up jacket. One close blast and no questions asked.

Muscle on meth was a bad deal and not to be trifled with.

Like deliberate insects, they broke apart and then converged upon the safehouse—an ancient, failed HUD rehab deeded out to Robicheaux's brother-in-law, a not-so-smart entrepreneurial Newton Jew living off crew scores he shared with his sister.

Slothropian carded himself in through the front door of the clapboard three-family of peeling gun metal gray and faded navy trim. In the foyer, he heard Whitesnake playing cranked and distorted off a boom box, steeped in echo from some mostly empty room somewhere upstairs. Must have run on dying batteries, he thought to himself, with all that distortion. That meant no electricity. No, the hall light worked. It meant something else: Robicheaux was ready to travel.

There was no point in pretending he was Chicago personnel—Robicheaux was clued in enough to insist on knowing who would be doing the meet down to advance pictures and penitentiary pedigree. Wouldn't even buy him time to change the clip. He was hoping for distraction, triangulation, then killshot, pure and simple. But that was not going to happen. No, this would have to be a straight-up gun battle, no finesse.

He flattened and froze at the soft sound beneath Whitesnake, then blinked.

The piece was up and cocked in a half heartbeat, then slacked down at the end of the now relaxed arm.

The new guy, Coleridge, standing before him.

Slothropian gestured wildly for the new guy to get back to his agreed-upon approach from the parlor, get ready to take Robicheaux out on the floor above with shots coming up in a cluster from under the floorboards. He made a mental note to rip this guy a new one after it was all over.

What was funny was that instead, the new guy clipped him a good one to the left temple, then grabbed the Walther from his limp right hand.

"Are you fucked? Now numbnuts *knows* we're here!"

"That's the point."

"You're in the shit now, my friend, and make no mistake. When we get out of this—"

"Who said anything about we?" He placed a shot from the

Walther straight into Slothropian's stomach. The housepainter sank to the warped floor by the rotted banister of the staircase, grunting and squealing.

"Motherfucker!" He went off on a coughing jag. "Mother-*fucker*. Your ass—is gonna be served up—on a—*platter*!" Slothropian cupped his hands where the blood pooled, gagged hard with a discordant growling whine.

"Maybe," said the new guy, "but you won't be doing the serving."

Slothropian rocked back and forth in a vain effort to contain the pain.

"You're—*dead!*"

"Is it that obvious? Oh well. Tell me, by the way, do you know anything about Jimmy The Broom?"

"What the fuck?"

"Jimmy The Broom. You heard of him?"

"Hey, rube!" Slothropian screamed, crying for help before the new guy casually put another one in his gut. *"Ruuuuuuuuube!"* he screamed again, his voice flirting with white noise.

"Jimmy the Broom," he said again. "Just tell me you knew him."

"Fucking dead bum from twenty-five years ago, I don't know! Christ almighty, I'm *dyin'* here!"

"That's the right answer," the new guy said, knelt down as if to be helpful, then coolly blew the housepainter's brains out. The back of his head was like a ripe tomato smashed against the wall, and then the rest of him went over on its side like a crash test dummy.

He barely had time to grope Slothropian for the sawed-off and sling it under his coat before cocking the Walther again.

A guy came screaming towards him from the back end of the hallway, thick-set, stubbled with a gut and squeezing off wild shots from a semi-automatic in a lazy spray. Coleridge spun about and shot off both his kneecaps without breathing hard. He walked over to the assailant who was now too agonized a writhing heap on the floor to even think about his relinquished gun, which the new guy kicked away.

"You're Robicheaux, right?"

"Fuck off and kill me already, shitbag!"

"Not today. You get a pass. I don't want you—not that I really want anything, anyway."

"Just fucking do it and stop trying to jerk me off to death. Kill me fucking clean!"

"No, you're not on the list. And I don't think you'll be getting up and putting yourself on the list any time soon." He seemed queerly distracted and at ease, not that this was apparent to Robicheaux, whose mind had been fully commandeered by agony. "They got warrants out on you, Robicheaux?"

"No, goddamnit, I'm fucking dying!"

"Oh no you're not. Not this time. You may even walk again someday. You're a lucky boy, Robicheaux. No death, no jail. But we can still turn that around if you don't answer the next question correctly."

"Fuck you!" Robicheaux whined, squirming and heaving in agony, holding both knees up to his chest and curling into the fetal position on the filthy splintered floor.

The new guy knelt down to him and put the gun straight into his eye-socket, pressing the cornea under the lid. "Let's try anyway, okay?"

"Just kill me!"

"You don't mean that. You've got everything to live for. Not like me. So, tell me where it is."

"Where what is?"

The new guy pistol-whipped him in the side of the head with the butt of the gun, then replaced it in its former position. "Next stupid answer costs you the eye." He cocked the Walther and pressed it to the socket of his left eye.

Robicheaux whispered the answer and the new guy, Coleridge —the housepainter who was emphatically *not* there to paint houses for Malek the Mallet—nodded, got up and left him there, taking the trouble to pick up the discarded clip from his gun on his way.

The new guy made it to the crash room where Robicheaux had been waiting and shut off the boom box. He heard a groan from the far corner of the room. He went over and kicked Dimmy Greco in the side of the head.

"Fuck—*Coleridge!*—why'd you freakin' conk me and let the shitbird get away? Are you fucking crazy?"

"Clinically."

"Your life is gonna mean less than a pap smear when Malek figures this out, pussy boy."

"Tell me, Dimmy, just how smart is it to insult the guy with a gun to your head?"

"Like it fucking makes a difference when we both know you're here to kill me."

"Well, not you per se, but why not you in the bargain?"

"Fuckin' *A,* why not? After that, we both know you're dead, anyways."

"Yeah, but I'm the kind of dead that kills."

"I can pay."

"Can't we all?"

He stood with a bit of a flinch, expecting to be hit, but no blow came. "So do it already and don't talk my ear off. Stop barking like a bitch in heat and bite like a dog, for Christ's sake."

His answer was to shoot Greco in the groin, which brought him down hard in shock and tears amid a deep chasm between a scream and a sob.

"Now," said Coleridge. "Tell me about Jimmy the Broom. Tell it all and tell it right."

"He was just a bum," Greco squalled. "Just a bum! We did him for fun. It wasn't like he was really alive! He was barely even human, for god's sake! Don't tell me this is about Jimmy-the-Fucking-Broom!"

The new guy shot him in the crotch again, right through the metacarpals of the protective hand. "But it is," the new guy said.

"Fuck you, Coleridge! Your life is done, do you fucking get that? Kiss your ass good-bye, cocksucker, because your life is *over!*"

"I know," he said. "We have that in common."

Writing in pain, dirt, blood and tears, Greco tried to make a play. His throat knotted with strain. "Coleridge, come on, be reasonable—"

"It's Null," he said. "Call me Null, and I am nothing if not reasonable."

"Null then, whatever the fuck you call yourself. You can walk out of this—"

"Very true," Null said, lowered the Walther gently, seemingly lost in thought, then shot Greco straight in the heart, almost as an afterthought, which caused him to make a little burping sound right when he laid back flat on the floor and stopped breathing. "But you can't."

Null went back down to the basement where Nimrod was waiting with a black expression on a face tanned from one trip to Florida too many, lined with the short creases of an habitual impatience. "What the fuck took you so long?"

"I'm not very spontaneous," Null said, turning on the light. "I have to think things out before I do them."

"Well, think this one out, you fucking mutt. The Ork is gonna splatter bits of your ass all across Boston Harbor, you keep doin' what you're doin'."

"If I keep doing what I'm doing, there won't be enough of them left to make the effort."

"Turn on the fucking light already so I can gaze at your pitiful mug."

Null obliged, and an icy tube of clinical fluorescent light fluttered on, making moth-like shadows about the space, revealing Nimrod trussed up by a rusted-out washer dryer like a pupating caterpillar. He struggled vainly, folding up and out, the blood crusting off his face and hands, cursing in a series of grunts. It was no go. Null had done too studied and conscientious a job of tying Nimrod's restraints. "You're still fucking ugly, cocksucker."

"No reason not to be," said Null.

"You're the guy—the one that took out the whole freakin' Family minus a crew. Fuck me runnin'. I thought you'd be bigger."

"I'm big as I need to be for what I've got to do."

"What do *I* got to do to get out of these ropes and leave here in one piece?"

"Tell me a story."

"That's it?"

"That's it."

"You're lying."

"I don't lie. I don't have any reason to. I want you dead, you're dead."

"Sure. Why not? Buys me time, anyway, I guess."

"Just a little. More if you make it good."

"So what story you want?"

"The one about Jimmy the Broom."

Nimrod's face crumpled and contracted as if beset by a wave of pain. But for knuckle scrapes, some few bruises and one new bump that rose like an old wen at the crest of his forehead, he was uninjured. His face mugged and contorted as if in a struggle with a tricky concept overtaking him out of nowhere, yet he couldn't apprehend what it was. It betrayed that whatever he was struggling with was just too ephemeral to be fully grasped. He couldn't get it. "This is a gag, just to fuck with me before we get to the point."

"No. It *is* the point."

"This—*all this shit*—four other fucking deaths—for one combustible bum?"

"Three. Robicheaux gets a walk."

"That mook takes off Malek for a mill and change of street-ready crystal and you give him a walk? He's a rat bastard what turns his back on his own. He gets the pass."

"Points in his favor, in my world. If it makes you feel any better, though, I shot off both his knees. He'll be a long time in rehab if he ever walks again."

Nimrod's dry lips went slack for a moment. He blinked both eyes fast, as if to reset his brain. "Okay, Pally, you want the four-one-one on Jimmy The Broom, you got it." When someone's not playing with a full deck, there's always a chance you can deal yourself out of the game, and therefore from losing, entirely. Meanwhile, talking gave him time to try to work himself free from the ropes.

"Tell it slow and tell it right," said Null, training the Glock he had in his pocket on the creased forehead and single eyebrow of Nimrod's compressed, rodentine head. "Tell it right, or I'll keep shooting pieces off of you until you do."

"No need to get nasty."

"Every need with those like you—nothing personal. Just nasty business."

Nimrod chuckled. "Okay, okay. You know Park Street Station on the T?"

"Get to the point."

"Different place 30 years ago—older, colder, hadn't been rehabbed since the 30s. Broom? He was the joke of the place; a bum so dirty, so trashed and wrecked that you couldn't tell where the piss-soaked newspaper and rags he wore began and the fuckin' guy himself ended. Staked out his own little corner on the Lechmere side of the Green Line and no one bugged him but maybe to toss him a butt or a few bits. Fucker smelled like a compost heap in the back of a slaughterhouse."

"That's the guy."

"Fuckin' A."

Null took a pack of Pall Mall straights he lifted off Slothropian from his pocket, lit one and positioned it between the whitened, drying lips of Nimrod Stassen, a bundle of thwarted muscle on the floor. He sucked the smoke in deeply and let it puff out in a disordered gout as he spoke. "Now ya see? That was the human thing to do."

"Tell me more about the human thing to do."

"There's nothing to tell. It was one of those nights when the cold is like an evil God crushing the whole town. You know, when your skin is on fire with the cold and any exposed part of you feels like it's being chewed off in a dark vacuum. We were three young punks up off Dot Ave, pullin' cheapie scores the way kids do, enjoying the power of being immortal and unstoppable, out on the prowl, all of us ejected for the usual attitude and mostly because it was what was done—when you're seventeen, bingo, you're out. You think you're fucking immortal at that age. Invincible. Like bein' drunk and high when you ain't even had nothin'. That's how it happened, you know. It was too cold to hang on the corner or hit the Saxon Diner where the johns congregate, perfect pickin's for a little float and roll, you know? So, anyways there we was at Park Street Station."

"Bored."

"Like the way you get that age. Okay, lemme snap it up. The place was just about dead empty, trains had stopped runnin'. We're killin' time, rankin' on each other and shit, and it occurs to me that

Broom is really stinking the place up—really outrageous. He's like a freakin' pile of living, human feces, for god's sake. Looked just like the Swamp Thing when he shifted his position or tried to wave his arms and get a drink from another fuckin' bum. You know, just connect with another human for a little change, a smoke? So I think to myself, when a pile of feces stinks this bad, whaddaya do with it?"

"You burn it."

"Exactamundo, chief! So we touch off all his trailing newspaper, and he goes up like a Christmas Tree, dancin' frantic across all of Park Street Station like Swamp Thing meets Fred Astaire across an old-time ballroom. Waltz of doom! Funny as shit, too. A homeless bro' goin' out in a true blaze of glory. It went beyond the beyond!"

"And then you did what kids like you do."

"Right on, brother. We got righteous stoned right then and there and watched that freakin' thing die, amazed. It was one of the most beautiful things I ever seen. We hung out, sucked on the pipe and watched till the cops and firemen finally got in there and hustled us out. They didn't think it was us. Punk kids, what did *we* know from anything especially when some bum finally lights himself onto his last suicide fire? What did we know from anything? We was too busy being immortal and invincible and laughing our asses off."

"Wears off fast, don't it?"

"Like you have to ask?"

"And that's it?"

"That's it."

"So what the fuck does all this got to do with Jimmy The Broom?"

"What this has to do with Jimmy the Broom, is *Mrs.* Jimmy The Broom."

"Jimmy the Broom had a wife? Well fuck all. Guess we did her a favor then."

"It's a point, but I don't think she sees it that way."

Nimrod spat the smoldering filter-less end of the Pall Mall out of his mouth so it bounced across the floor cascading sparks. "She's probably dead too, been so fucking long. What I don't get is your involvement. What is a class A housepainter like you doin' wastin' your very marketable talents on a dead bum?"

"Good question."

Nimrod laughed, relieved. He was beginning to get it. This guy was angling for a gig with Malek. It was a smart play. If the Mallet respected anything at all, he respected brutality; he would rather have the mutt who took out two of his best crew working for him than whack him out as street PR. If he was good enough to get through his own, then he should own him. And if that inspired fear and distrust, all the better. Malek lived for fear and distrust.

"Okay, Pally, you made your point. Let's get these ropes offa me and go have a sit-down with the man you want to see. But first we gotta pick up the meth and squash the bug rolling around downstairs."

"I already have the meth." He placed a bundle on top of the rusted out washing machine to emphasize this. "And I'm having that sit-down with the man I want to see right now."

"I don't get it."

"Sure, you do, Nimrod. I'm here on a job. Just like you."

"A job? For who for Christ's sake?"

"I thought I made that clear." Null took a flat can of starter fluid from the pocket of his windbreaker, removed the red cap, squirted it all over Nimrod, then lit him ablaze.

"Fuck no! *No!*" Nimrod screamed, struggling with the ropes, plastic ties and nylon fasteners, rolling about frantically. He shrieked, "You said I'd get out of these ropes, you'd let me outta here in one piece!" The flames spread and he rolled about in a panicked caroming like a grub dropped on the roof of a car on a hot summer afternoon.

"No, those ropes will burn off soon enough, and when you're done burning, you'll be all in one piece, at least until your corpse is disturbed. They tend to retain their integrity, after charring, you know, corpses."

"*You—inhuman—mother—fucker!*"

"On the money. I'm inhuman. I get no sadness or joy out of it. Nothing, not even disgust. No, not very human of me at all. You learn to work with what you have, or don't have. I lack humanity, so I go with it."

"Not—*fair!*" His screams were worse than those of an un-anesthetized woman in full labor. "It's—not—*fair!*"

"But it *is* fair—down to the bone. It's exactly what Mrs. Broom paid me for: Fairness. I see that you get just as much chance as Jimmy the Broom got, though his bondage was drunkenness, TB and old-age. Yours just happens to be ropes and nylon sliding ties. You should be able to move better than Jimmy could as soon as the ropes burn off and the nylon ties melt into your skin. No, it's almost exactly fair. Like handicapping the ponies."

Nimrod continued wailing and shrieking as Null went up the steps carrying the bundle of meth. He turned to face the dying grub in flames on the floor, blinked once, possibly due to the gathering smoke, and emptied the rest of the charcoal starter fluid onto the steps and basement floor, tossing the tin down into the flames. He left, closing the door behind him.

On his way out, Null kicked Robicheaux pointedly in the spleen to get his attention. He had apparently blacked out from the pain. Null recalled dimly that there was no more painful spot to get shot in than in the knees; it was old time wise guy legend that rang true. He kicked him again and Robicheaux curled up, whining.

"Listen, Robicheaux, you're not going to die yet, but it won't be easy. There's a fire in the basement. You've got maybe a good half hour before it spreads up here and consumes the house, the house-painters, you, everything in it. The only thing you can do about it is crawl out of here on your hands and what's left of your knees just as fast as you fucking can. You can try dragging yourself by your arms on your belly if you want, but that might take too long. This time, the most painful way is probably going to be the only way. Got that?"

Robicheaux was slow in responding so he kicked him again. "Got that?" he repeated.

"Fuck, why aren't I dead?"

"Because nobody wants you dead right now, at least nobody who counts. But that's all going to change soon enough. Next thing you've got to do after you get out of here is find a way to get out of the northeast period before they get a fix on you. Got that? Otherwise I should just put one in the back of your head right. For efficiency's sake."

"Fuck no," Robicheaux grunted, struggling hard to get up on all fours, and falling hard like a foal.

"Good," said Null, and went out the door.

Null waited, breathing calmly the dank spring air in front of the house, watching smoke pour out the door and flames licking up through the foundation. No one called it in yet; this was Boston, and Boston being Boston, a 911 call was always made a shade too late, just to make certain the caller wouldn't be thought a narc or a fool.

When at last he saw Robicheaux's agony-distorted face and bloodied arms appear in the smoke-blurred doorway, he took off as if he were some uninvolved party passing yet another dilapidated three-family clapboard house that held no interest for him. Just another one of those old-time white-bread neighborhood guys so emaciated he seemed swallowed up by his clothes carrying a bundle of some worthless junk tight under his arm — as if it mattered.

THREE

The unquiet poetry of the early dinner clatter at the Busy Bee diner in St Mary's, yet another last stand of old-time Boston, marked by the bilious cartoon of a plump bumble bee on a bubble-molded styrene sign and its smug antiquity of mid-century stoicism. The Bee was where the working-class holdovers of two generations ago splurged on specials within their fixed incomes and passed the afternoon with coffee and cigarettes till closing. It was a warm, cheap, dim coffee place with all the gray, starchy food you could eat for money short enough to take you back to the depression, if that was the time when you thought you were truly alive. Steel, plastic, Formica, painted plaster—no clever touches, no soft strategic lights, just a simulacrum of the harsh institutional glare of fluorescence the average patron was used to.

The welfare office, the unemployment office, the VA. The mixed, conflicted smells of the full spectrum of failure boiled up big in the air just like steam from the pots that produced the fare on which the Bee's elder frumpy patrons desultorily dined before having landed there and no doubt grew up with.

Pies and cakes like cardboard imitations were displayed on pedestals under glass on the main running service counter, as if from a museum of pop culture or post-modern fake. But they were dead real.

Patrons smoked in booths marked by "Thank you for smoking

here" signs and honked a gambler's tough bravura in the face of unshakable losses, talking sports, politics, pop culture, but with names like Ted Williams, James Curley and Bette Davis dropped, instead of Nomar Garciaperra, John Kerry or Gina Davis. Laughter was a cigarette cackle, phlegmatic with coughing.

There was an odor lurking beneath as collective as human sweat: the bruised, exhaled hopelessness of oxidizing alcohol. The predictable human mist at the low end.

There was one grim looking younger man sitting there who barely stood out, almost shapeless in his coat and hat, hunched slope-shouldered over the counter as if drunk himself.

He was anything but.

"Careful young fella, you don't burn ya self with coffee. It's scaldin' hot."

He gulped it, heedless of the waitress, another ancient part-time pensioner.

The waitress pouted her slack, heavily lipsticked mouth into an oval, which twisted up jowls dyed pink with rouge under wiry fire-orange hair that might have been a cancer-sufferer's wig, if gray roots weren't readily visible under her paper hat. Her expression was tortured.

"I told ya, it'll *scald* ya!"

The man drained his cup and gestured for more. "I won't feel it, much less taste it."

She left the overheated pot on the counter in front of him with a sigh and gesture of weary disgust. Even in such a small matter, she was simply unable to carry the weight of any authority, be the one who was finally right because situations always nullified her. Even in telling a customer what to do for his own good, this happened. It was always going to happen. It made her sick.

A washed out, shapeless gray woman in a yellow nylon wind-breaker wearing thick, rimless glasses whose stems were wide and a ghostly pale blue plopped down next to Null. She smoked a long white cigarette—100 millimeters at least—freshly lit.

"I didn't know they still made Virginia Slims," said Null.

"They do if you know where to get them."

"I never knew it made a difference."

"Everything makes a difference, Mr. Null."

"I'm still working that one out, but for the sake of argument, okay?"

She stood up and reached beneath the counter for a cup and saucer like an old hand, poured herself a cup of coffee from the pot the waitress left, and took a swallow. The cup and saucer smashed down on the Formica top as several nearby patrons flinched aside while Null sat, unmoved. She brought her fuscia-nailed fingers to her lips and rocked her head from side to side, choking.

The waitress raced over, tossing her cigarette aside to sparks on the floor, slopping a brownish wet rag over the pool of coffee and bone-white cup shards. She did the cleanup in a nervous fury. "I warned ya! I told ya! But ya wouldn't listen! Oh, no, don't know good advice when you hear it!" She grumbled self-righteous vindication as she wiped the counter, then slammed a mop to the floor, cursing gravely. Trivia, for her, had long ago achieved the scale of epic drama in the ever-narrowing bottleneck of a mostly un-decanted life.

"I near choked to death!"

"It's just coffee."

"I burned the tongue out of my mouth."

"You're talking fine now."

Her answer was an exaggerated, wet cough into a cluster of counter napkins.

Null shot a look at the waitress that told her clearly it would be best for her to leave. Something told her not to ignore this. Something told her to go.

The eyes.

There was an unfeeling fixity in the eyes.

It was the look that telegraphed blows to follow—a target lock of expedient intent. She saw this in the eyes of a score of husbands and boyfriends in the past. The instant of dead focus.

She moved fast.

"I'm used to the pain. I've had it all my life. Why—"

"Be grateful for it. It's a good reminder."

"Oh?" She arched white eyebrows wryly. "A reminder of what, then?"

"Your humanity," he said with a hint of a wheeze.

"I can worry about that when I'm dead."

"Yes. It's more of a concern then. Less of a worry."

"Talk sense."

"The punks you wanted pushed got pushed."

The puffy, wrinkled, gray-tinged face hardened and lost the faintest trace of old-age feigned bewilderment. "How hard they get pushed?"

Null slurped boiling coffee with blistered lips. "Under the earth, is how hard."

"Thank Jesus! Thank the lord and God love you, Mr. Null." Her voice was a steady soft hum, void of drama.

"I'm not so sure being loved by God is a good idea."

"You have a better one?"

"Yes. Pay me."

"You want the money now." She was emotional now, a little shocked.

"Is there a better time?"

"Maybe you could wait until my next month's check comes?"

"That wasn't the agreement."

"No, but we didn't really talk nitty gritty, did we?"

"But it was to be paid upon completion."

"How do I know they're dead?"

"Do you want me to describe how each one died? I can go into detail here."

"No, that's alright, you don't have to."

"We didn't discuss an amount, you know."

Her eyes took on a shrewd cast. "We settled on what's fair, didn't we?"

"Yes." Null met shrewd eyes with dead eyes. "We did, in fact. So I'll leave it to you."

She leered for a moment, then relaxed. "Good. Well, then." She settled comfortably on her stool. "Maybe I can settle up today after all."

"You have no choice. One way or another, this transaction has to be completed. Today. There's a zero balance to reach that I won't delay."

It was as if she had fallen back with the full weight of her age right then, making a show of reaching for her purse, fumbling through her wallet for cash.

"You restarted the unfinished cycle begun back in Park Street Station 26 years ago. So, it's only fair that I let you figure out what's fair. After all, Jimmy the Broom's killers have finally gotten what was fair. So now it's your turn. But if it's wrong, Mrs. Durgin. If you do it wrong, and be sure I'll know if you do, I can promise you right now that *you'll* be getting what's fair."

"You can't threaten me."

"I'm not. But you brought death back into play, Mrs. Durgin. Cheat death and death will recover what's owed. Every time. Without exception. Often immediately."

He sipped loudly from his cup, eyes frozen open.

"In this case, immediately."

"What are you saying, Mr. Null?"

"I'm stating, Mrs. Durgin, in no uncertain terms, that if you get the amount for this job wrong, I'm going to have to push you under the earth so that you can join Punch Slothropian, Dimmy Greco and Nimrod Stassen as part of the balance owed to zero out the account. Jimmy too. We don't want to forget him. Do we?"

"So, you'll what then? Kill me?"

"Easiest and quietest would be to break your neck then leave expeditiously as you collapse. They won't be worrying about me. You'll be presumed a stroke victim. More tricky would be a quick pop from the Glock and a non-hasty goodbye. The pooling blood would rule out stroke and things would have to move much faster. There'd be less of a window to slip through. Still, worked right, it could turn the trick just as smooth, I think. The pop isn't very loud, it might take you a second or two to slump over and, once again, I'll blend right in if I don't get excited. And I never get excited. These are the best options I could come up with so far, based on setting and equipment." He looked up at her and said in the exact same tone: "Coffee? I think it's cooled down some now."

He offered her the pot, and she looked away.

"I can show you more than one gun, if you want. I seem to pick them up easily. You could say I was a collector. What do you think?"

She responded with a fan of hundreds held like a stud poker hand in nacreous-veined, spindly fingers. The fan wavered with the trembling of her withered arm.

Null took the hundreds, counted attentively. "You were supposed to laugh, you know."

Her face was stony, ashen.

He drew the Glock, let it hang by his leg by a flap of his coat so she was just able to see it. Mrs. Durgin stopped breathing.

Null touched her shoulder, uncocked the Glock and holstered it. Her once powder-dry face now glistened with a light sweat. "I think that's close, give or take,' he said, fingering a plastic covered menu and considering it as one considers a technical manual. "It's just about a fair price."

"Just about?" Mrs. Durgin had gone pale with fear.

"Close enough, Mrs. Durgin. Close enough."

"You're telling me I was wrong?"

"Yes, you had to be, but if you were too wrong then it would have been too bad."

"I don't understand."

"You were always wrong, Mrs. Durgin. You were led to be wrong and could only cope by doing further wrong—"

"And two wrongs don't make a right, right? I heard that. Oh, you got it all worked out alright."

"It isn't that they make a right. It's that, when met head on, they make nothing at all. And that was the purpose of this—to make nothing of two wrongs. Do you see?"

"I see," she mumbled, backing away.

Null ignored her, finished off the coffee, kept his eyes forward.

Mrs. Durgin slipped awkwardly out the door backwards, nearly falling over another customer as he tried to enter and she was pushing herself out.

Null gestured for the authoritative fiery-haired grand waitress and when she dragged herself before him, he presented the empty coffee pot and bored into her forehead with lifeless eyes. He said: "I'll take one of the specials. Any one of them will do. Any one at all."

———

"Let go of it, you say? Just give it up?"

"Your pain is not some perfect masterpiece. Don't treasure it."

The office was spare, as if the interim quarters for a civil servant, not a psychologist specializing in post trauma therapy.

"Aren't you being a bit pop cultural, Doctor Funambule?"

"Should I quote Heinz Kohut to make the point? You're an MSW, Kay. That would be superfluous. I'm not playing subtextual games with you. What's plain is you're harboring old misery. You need to distance yourself from it."

"Look, Doctor, it isn't that I won't let go of it—it won't let go of me."

"That's you being poetic. The truth is the only life your pain has is the one you give it."

"No, you don't understand. My pain has a life independent from mine because it's the pain of my husband and children—actual, living people!"

"Kay. I can call you that, yes? Okay. Kay, listen, your husband and children died twelve years ago. Presumably, all their pain died with them."

"No, their pain has a life, and the life is in me."

"Guilt, and loss, Kay. Things you should let diminish over time, not nurture."

"Loss is increased over time, not diminished. Guilt just means I care."

"Caring about the dead is ineffectual, Kay. Care about the living. Dumping all your emotional effort into a crypt is hardly what we could call life-affirming."

"I've had it up to here with your pseudo-zen, snobby pop Buddhism   peace-and-contentment-find-your-center-Tao-of-Pooh horse-puckey! Not everything ends for the best, not everyone has a god-given right to well-being and sometimes, Doctor, the very best answer one can come up with for the good of all is to blow some dumb fuck's brains out and that's all there is to it. Sometimes, it just happens to *be* the goddamn will of heaven when you have to push the cluck off the roof instead of bringing him in."

"Angry and violent, Kay."

"You oughtta know why."

"You're drinking again, aren't you?"

"Takes the edge off."

"Try meditation rather than medication."

"Touché, Doctor. What's the point? I'm not an alcoholic."

"But of course you are, Kay, and if you don't do something about it I'll have to write you up for detox."

"No, I'll take another meeting or something. I don't need another write up."

"You've used alcohol so often and so long that you've developed the physical dependency, but you didn't have it at the start, did you? Your drinking was about need, a driven choice. That you lack the history or genetic predisposition is neither here nor there. I think if we could get rid of your emotional need to drink, the physiologic consequences would be rendered nil. You're drinking as an analgesic, yes?"

"No. I drink to lose myself and let the pain and sorrow overtake me. When I drink, I can meet my guilt head on."

"That's honest. Why can't you meet it without alcohol? Inhibitions?"

"Yes. I can't get at it directly. It's with me all the time, but hiding, lurking—"

"Making you do things you don't want to, perverting action into punishment?"

"Exactly. But when I'm drunk it can't touch me—"

"But you *can* touch it."

"Right again."

"Tell me how it happened. The break in, the slayings."

Boyd's cheeks flushed and she jerked up from her chair, thrusting her index finger at Funambule. "You're a fucker, you know that? A real piece of work!"

"Sit down, Lieutenant, and try to relax."

"The fuck I will."

Funambule leaned forward, shaggy faced, sodden eyed, salt and pepper hair a mass of balding cowlicks and beard unevenly shorn and dotted with healing razor injuries. He was short, chubby, wearing an ill-laundered Brooks Brothers sky-blue shirt and khakis way too tight in the waist for his burgeoning paunch. His pant cuffs rode up, exposing mismatched navy and black socks. "Kay, let's calm down and be honest with ourselves here. You relive this every day in every empty moment. It replays like bad streaming video in your head when you sleep, hangs over you every morning like an iron weight of penance when you drag yourself out of bed. What possible difference could it make if someone like me heard the story just once out your thousands of replays?"

"You know the story, Doctor, which is why it pisses me off."

"If I hear it from you it might help me find something not in the file. I don't think these people get all the nuances, do you?"

"No," she choked back.

"They say the devil is in the details, Kay. Let's see if we can grab the son of a bitch by the tail."

She slumped back down in the chair and exhaled: "Fine."

"This was about a client from the Ruggles Projects."

"Yes. Drug addict in a methadone program, standard stuff. Anselm something."

"You know his name."

She spoke it and coughed. "He was bright, funny—

had a spark. I used to think that mattered. I used to think a lot of things I don't anymore. Anyway, I tried to get him into City Year, the urban Peace Corps deal we also used to launder the more promising youth offenders for college. It started out as middle-class awareness building and wound up as a class conduit for successfully rehabbed youth offenders."

"You took a special interest."

"I bought him books, lunch sometimes. He was a charming boy straight out of the razored womb of Tartarus, the Alma Lewis Projects on Ruggles, Boston's Cabrini Green. Crackwhore mother, OG gang-banger father—pride of Roxbury. All standard stuff. I helped him get his GED. Tutored him, in fact."

"And he repaid you how?"

She turned aside her head and brushed away a tear. Quietly, she said, "Don't make me."

"You want to tell me—it's a way of shining a light on the shadows. Some things die in the light, so try it."

"Bullshit . You just want me to re-experience it!"

"No, Kay, I want you to *de*-experience it. Make it a story, make it no longer real and immediate. It's not about becoming closer to the incident, it's about distance, limitation. Modify it as a story and you make it smaller, not larger. You control it, despite your feelings."

"Okay." Boyd lost her hard edge for a moment, her face now somehow vulnerable. "You're right. I'll be in total control when I cry."

"That's true," said Funambule without irony.

Then came the stolid silence wherein the doctor waited patiently.

It was a hoarse whisper. "Long, rain, day."

"Just a bit louder, Kay?"

"It was a long, rainy day. Too long, busy. I took a pill before bed —Vicodin—to relax."

"Similar to heroin, yes."

"Yes," she sighed and Funambule made notes. "I was zonked, listening to the rain. Cutbacks had made the caseloads insane, and Bush One was continuing the same cuts started by Reagan and made worse later by Bush Two. I was making less money and my husband was pulling an all-night on-call at Boston City. The kids were asleep. My four-year-old, Ariel, and the baby, Morty -

"You didn't get much time off with him."

Her eyes welled. "No, thanks to the Republican power lock. We were in debt hiring a nurse/nanny to take care of him during the day, which was still better than four people making it on a resident's income. Anyway, it was late—we lived in a townhouse on Park Drive then, not much then, worth a fortune now—and I was dead, dreaming, hallucinating."

"But you really weren't."

"No, it was real. There was a hand on my mouth, buck knife to my throat. Anselm was standing over the bed, laughing, obviously stoned. 'Now bitch you gonna really help out papa Anse, yo,' is what he said. I looked next to me and Ted was there petrified, sitting up straight, his mouth open, not making a sound. One of them had him by the balls through his pajamas. He was still—trying not—to wake me." She paused and breathed unsteadily. "The three of them took us out into the den. Anselm forced Ted on his knees and demanded he give him oral sex. Ted refused, and he punched his face bloody. I was paralyzed, knife to my ribs. They were laughing as my daughter watched this, trying hard not to cry and failing, Ariel. She wasn't thinking of the huge K-bar military knife at her throat anymore. She was busy watching her father humiliated and murdered. After Ted gave them everything, the money, my few jewels, his heirloom pocket watch and diamond fob, Anselm gutted him like a pig in four moves, prison cuts. I thought stupidly, *How weird, when this kid had only been in juvie Bootcamp, not Walpole or even MCI Concord, for God's sake. Where the hell did he pick that up?*"

She coughed to mask flowing tears, which failed entirely. Funambule scribbled, taking no apparent notice.

"They raped me. I let them. I did it to save my daughter. I did it for her, and for Morty the baby. And I failed." She let room silence vie with her frustrated sobbing. She screamed it then: *"I failed!"*

Dr. Funambule scribbled on.

"It was in slow motion, how he moved that lean, muscular arm with the K-Bar knife right across my beautiful daughter's neck. And I watched him without moving. Watched him do it."

"Tell me what he did."

"Cut, my, off."

"Take your time, Kay."

She broke down, carried by the force of her tears, loud and strong. She stood and riveted angry eyes on Funambule. "He cut my daughter's head off!"

"It's in the file, Kay. I know. What happened then?"

"The room spun and I was going out, losing consciousness, I was sure of it." Funambule offered tissues and she refused them. "But he was laughing, goofing around with his crew, that fucking monster. Playing with my daughter's head. I don't know what I felt or could feel, but I elbowed the one holding me in the crotch and dove for Anselm. To kill him, anyway I could. That's all I knew. He had to die and somehow, weak little mommy me was going to do it. I had to. I was all that was left. I was the only one. I lunged at him, took a punch in the face and still kept on going—managed to grab him by the throat with one hand while he tried to break my other arm. I bit him. He responded by stabbing me with the full length of the blade of the K-bar knife in the side, but I didn't feel it. He tried to pull it out, but I saw how he gutted my husband with it when he yanked it clean and eviscerated him. I broke his fingers before he could yank it out. He fought me off with everything he had, smashed my nose, ruptured my trachea, dislocated my shoulder, but I held on and took him through the window with me, both hands around his neck, squeezing, clawing."

Funambule waited for her to break the silence.

"We landed hard together, like in a falling dream when your heart skips a beat. I tore his throat out before we landed. I killed him before we both died. How about that? The little liberal social worker, the do-gooder!"

"What about the baby?"

"That's in the file too."

"But you need to say it."

"Yeah. I need to say it." Now she took a tissue and wiped her eyes. "That's what just what I fucking I need—to tell you out loud that they took my four-month-old baby and crushed him to death in my goddamn trash-masher! That's what I need!"

"That's right," said Funambule, putting his clipboard on the desk and interlacing his fingers. "And by doing it, what happened? Here we are, talking. Your eyes are wet and your nose is running and your heart is racing, but you're here in the moment with me. Nothing else is really happening. You aren't seeing any of what you were talking about, but you remember disconnected images. What you see is me here in this room, and yourself, and the present."

And it dawned on her that he was annoyingly, irritatingly right. Telling the story was beginning to make her callous to it, like it was some grisly anecdote involving someone else. Some of its power was gone. Guilt flooded her at the thought that she might become hardened to her own experience—to what she owed the love of the dead. She began to speak but found herself weeping instead. Funambule stood up, gave her the box of tissues and let her fall into him, into a sweaty, therapeutic bearhug.

"Kay, getting over what happened to you doesn't mean you don't honor those who died any less. It just means a commitment to your own life coming before your commitment to the dead. It's possible to blend the two, make them exist harmoniously."

He embraced her firmly, and she cried with grateful abandon into the blue rumpled material of his Brooks Brothers suit. Her shoulders rose and fell in the passion of her tears and Funambule swayed back and forth, comforting her.

"You've done better than you know, Kay," he soothed.

"I know," she replied hoarsely, reached around Funambule's ample backside and deftly cuffed both his chubby wrists in her Smith and Wesson high security cuffs. "I do fine no matter what."

He backed off, nearly falling over his desk, struggling reflexively against the cuffs. "What do you think you're doing?"

"I'm placing you under arrest, Doctor. What do you think *you're* doing—molesting another traumatized woman?"

"Kay, this is just an anger response to your grief—"

"No, Doctor, this is an anger response to your crimes." She pressed a beeper clipped to her belt and immediately the door to Funambule's office was kicked in by a gun-toting Detective Bim Hundertwasser followed by officer Grant Monad.

"You rang, Ma-*dame?*" honked Bim.

"I'm alright you two so holster the weapons. This boy's only dangerous for traumatized women on too much Zoloft."

"Geeze, Kay, why'd you even bother bringing us along at all?" Monad said with mock innocence. "Want we should give him a game of pinball on the way down to the unit?"

"Whatever works, Grant," she said, pushing the confused and off-balance Dr. Funambule forward so that he was clumsily bent over his own desk. She kicked his legs apart and mirandized him briskly.

"But you're OC!" he whined.

"True. But sometimes I do favors for major crimes."

"I'm not a major criminal."

"Don't underestimate yourself, Doctor."

"This really sucks!" Funambule whined in a near falsetto when she was done. She pulled him up from the desk hard, then pushed him toward Detective Hundertwasser so that he nearly fell over. Hundertwasser pushed him into Monad who pushed him back. His glasses flew off and his face was the color of aged steak tartar set in a popover so puffed up it was ready to explode. He wheezed as Hundertwasser grabbed him to keep him from caroming about. "This—just—*sucks!*"

Boyd approached him and patted his sweat-dotted face. "No, Doctor. What sucks is that, while being a serial rapist, you're really a terrific shrink. What a fucking waste."

"Fuck you!" he seethed.

Boyd gave him a sympathetic kiss on the cheek and mussed his hair. She whispered, "Still, all-in-all, you wanna know something?"

"What?" he barked in a spasm of rage.

"I think you actually helped me."

FOUR

The sour human smell hit him before anything else.

The stink of fear and surrender, the feculence of pain long past restraint.

Then the sequence of screams.

The screams were piercing, keening, worse than fingernails on a chalkboard piped through reverb. It was a surprise, considering the long reedy frame of the source of the screams, the long, slim dancing body, that they were deafening. Yet, the muscle of the Ork let him scream on, coaxed out shrieks, shrill and desperate calls for help, insensate bellowing and then the chugging grunts of uncomprehending response. It was okay, though. Under control.

As the muscle guy crushing the metacarpals in the long man's grip observed with a half-lisp, "It's *all* good, dawg."

They wanted him to scream.

It was important, Malek the Mallet had always said, for the penitent always to hear his own screaming.

It would bring the guy back to reality when the other senses were blurred.

Nick Andromeda brazened into the main garage of Gary Lee Obidowski's Body Shop, Service and Tow like he was walking into a brothel full of welcoming whores. He seemed at ease, despite a hitch to his shoulder as he walked, his manner and expression proclaiming cocky stud looking coolly back into the face of a doomed man's agony. This wasn't pathology or hubris.

This was survival.

One misstep, one wrong turn of the trick and he would be the bound screamer dancing with an electric drill sunk into his thigh, crying, begging and shitting his pants.

He smiled and acknowledged the muscle of the Ork, like what they were doing was flat out nothing, whittling on wood maybe.

The wounded, human scent all but wiped out the usual pungency of acetone, Valvoline and axle grease. Nick fought the desire to shove a handkerchief over his nose and the involuntary gagging at the back of his throat.

He knew what it was. Not the smell of fear, but the smell of desperate loss, the last letting go of a hopeless life-brawl. Nick swallowed back hard to damp the gagging.

Malek sucked sausage between his teeth, not bothering to get up and shake the detective's hand, and why should he? This pissant hack, detective or not, was just another payroll zombie, a droid thought he was a comer, thought he was some kind of high-flyer going places. Malek sighed, his frown implacable. Youth always mistook exploitation for success, grudging tolerance for freedom. It had to be that way. That was how youth sometimes got lucky enough to make it to old age.

Malek didn't crack a smile at the thought of his having reached old age prematurely, which was plain from his patchy hair, sallow features, desiccated skin, one wall eye. He looked at Nick and suppressed hostility with a savage bite into his sausage and peppers submarine sandwich.

(In New Orleans, they have po' boys, in Philadelphia, hoagies, and always heroes in New York. In Boston, it was submarines.)

Andromeda was sweating bullets, his color was bad and Malek's eyes caught this like two red lobster claws.

Malek guffawed with a mouth full of submarine sandwich cud, articulated in muted deformity: "Franchot! Hey Franchot, already, get Nicky something out the deli bag so he shouldn't starve! Looks hungry to me." He brushed crumbs off the stained Zegna suit jacket.

Andromeda flashed—this was yet another test and he'd better

not miss. It was the constant heart-check straight off the prison yard. The rule was simple: show your humanity and out yourself as a pussy.

And everyone knows what pussies are for.

"Pastrami," boomed Nick. "If you got it." Sweat pattered down from his cheek to the floor and Malek chewed on mirthfully, amid the shrieking, screaming, groaning and whimpering of the long man, watching Franchot place a rolled sandwich bag in front of Nick and Malek with bloody fingers.

Nick treated the blood like so much surplus sauce, tore open the white puckered butt end of the rolled sandwich and glommed onto it with his teeth in one quick hurry. Malek eyed him, frozen in thought. Nick kept on biting.

The long man in his soiled, once-white shirt and tan slacks wailed on miserably as the muscle of the Ork went through the paces of their gruesome, passionless routine. Grim punches punctuated perfunctory jabs with the knife while the shrill keening of the electric drill kept pace with the inarticulate pleading of the man on the table.

Blood spattered, nameless clear liquid flew, tears streamed.

The long body thumped violently against the table where it lay helpless, prone and, even at this extreme moment, innocent.

Nick swallowed hard, slices of pastrami hanging down from his greasy fingers.

He was just getting used to the wild cries and screaming until they began to ooze down to a demodulating moan.

"Tell me it's disgusting, Nicky. Don't be a shy boy."

"It is what it is," Andromeda said, putting the submarine sandwich delicately down on the desk in front of Malek, helping himself to a tissue from the box on the desk and dabbing away the blood and grease from his hands.

"Makes you sick, don't it, Nicky boy?"

The moan choked off to abrupt silence.

Andromeda's shoulders slumped, Franchot, the huge goon and one other shadowy lump of a short, squat man in the back washed up and cracked beers kept cold in a long white meat freezer in back.

He knew what the meat freezer was for—the long man who was now no longer dancing.

"Hey, Padrone," said Franchot. "This mutt's gonzo for now. Want we should use the spirits of ammonia?"

Patiently irritated with the interruption, Malek dismissed the suggestion. "No, take a break, have your beers, but get ready to put in some hours so we can get a little closure here."

"I like that," chuckled Franchot. "We open him up so you can get closure."

"I don't want you to like it, just fucking *do* it!"

Franchot mumbled assent. Nick cleared his throat.

Malek continued eating his sandwich methodically, unashamed of talking with his mouth full or of producing an uneven cascade of crumbs and an infrequent salvo of bits of sausage meat. "I agree it's sick, disgusting, inhuman."

"I never said anything about it."

"But you were thinking it."

"How would you know?"

Malek slammed down his sandwich with a fist and bolted up, spitting bits of sandwich in Nick's face. "I know because this is about men, dipshit, not little cunts running around pretending to be men."

He sized Malek up for a moment and decided he couldn't take him. Though older, maybe not in as good shape, Malek was nevertheless a fearless, psychotic Gila monster of a fighter. Once he bit, you'd have to kill him, and he was very hard to kill, as a graveyard full of former partners, adversaries and bosses from Malek's past silently attested. Plus, punching his lights out now and then dancing a quick tarantella on his face would queer their deal. And Nick was about nothing if he wasn't about the deal.

"Fine, Mal, it's whatever it has to be, I guess. I'm not here to make judgments, I'm just here to make a pickup."

"Don't be a cunt, Nicky! You know what I'm saying." He beamed at Nick brilliantly for a half-second, then let his jowled and tanning-bed wizened face slacken back down to dour.

"I know what you're saying." He lit a cigarette, half-proud of the smoothness with which he did it.

Malek tossed a fat manila business envelope at Nick's chest and he folded his arms over it to keep it from falling. "This is what men do, Nicky, not little cunts disguising themselves as men, not privileged little faggots never had to sweat anything, affecting manhood like a new cologne to impress their swishy friends. Manhood to them is a fucking suit, a car, some bitch wife they only wind-up renting who ultimately fleeces them bare. The true men, like us Nicky, we do what has to be done, the thing that must be done."

"The hard work."

"The hard things, Nicky. The worst things—like calmly sitting by eating a submarine sandwich while some barbaric freaks break, mutilate and torture your best under-assistant accountant to death. This was a man you trusted, who you had over to the house for dinner, knew your kids. You sit by and eat and do your business and keep one eye on these hellish proceedings to make sure they get fucking done, because this is what men do. This is what men are— willing to do the hard things to make a life for children and to protect their family and the ones they love.

"You loved the under-assistant accountant, right?"

Cold fish eyes, no anger. "But this is business. And the business we know knows no love, does it, Nicky?"

"In reality, I guess not." He dragged deep on his cigarette. "You know, he was innocent—"

Malek guffawed at that, slapped himself, then gobbled the last of his sandwich. Nick blushed as Malek shook his head, smoothed back greasy, matted remnant strands of dirty white and axle grease-black hair against his scalp.

"Okay, okay, poor choice of words. But you know he had nothing to do with it."

"Only God and the poor schmuck know for sure. You know how it's done, you been in the world long enough."

"Your boss gets waxed, you go down next, or up if you're lucky."

"He wasn't too lucky."

Moans oozed up to the foreground as the three stalwart torturers of the Muscle of the Ork began plying their trade, literally shoving cracked ampules of spirits of ammonia up the long man's nostrils.

"Do they have to—?"

"They have to. If he was in on it, we'll soon know. They always break, always."

"There have been exceptions, I've heard."

Malek grunted between ambient moans, "Covers all bases, after the death. Like cauterizing a wound. Conspirators scatter, whether he led them or not. We find out what there is to find out, or nothing, and the mutt dies for the greater good."

"Bentham."

Malek's weak eye fluttered. "You're a deep guy, Nicky. That mummified shit lawyer knew what was up for sure, lemme tell ya."

"I didn't know they put Bentham in comic book form."

He patted Nick's clammy cheek. "Brave, brave Nicky. Be careful about judging when to kick my ass and when to kiss it. This business isn't very failure tolerant, my friend."

"I'm not here because of any failure, just business. I'm here for the pick-up and that's it."

"We both know different about that, Nicky. The big blue wall ain't what it used to be. You're here because I have a job for you and for no other reason, and yes, there's a few extra yards in the envelope to remind you just who you're working for, and who you're *working for* is working for."

Nick sighed and sat in the chair, shoved his heels up on the desk to make a gesture of token defiance.

"There was an exception to the torture rule, you know, you sadistic fuck." Nick announced above a sudden ramp-up of shrieking.

The stocky humpback figure in the shadows was busily breaking the long man's feet with a large vise-grip just as zestily as if he were tucking into a boiled lobster dinner, savoring each succinct crack of the claws. All Nicky could see of this lump's face was the blinding white of his teeth flashed in a split grimace, and his thick, low build exaggerated in shadow.

"Joseph Xavier Null!" he shouted to drive home the point.

Malek made an expert grab across the desk for Andromeda's throat and connected. He seethed and spoke low, yet piercingly: "Don't give me your fucking urban myth, you punked-out rent-a-detective!"

47

Nick breathed steadily and did nothing—let Malek take the lead in going for calm. He touched Malek's fingers and one by one, in response, they tentatively released.

The Muscle of The Ork ignored them both, preferring to work the long man instead. They sized it up, knew what it was all about. Malek could handle one guy all by himself no sweat—even a police feeb—and if he couldn't, well then, everyone could just move up a notch, couldn't they? You want to run a tough crew, be tough enough to do it, no matter how old or burned out you are.

Everybody knows there are no easy retirements on the street.

"Don't give me your fucking fairy stories."

Nick was stolid. "They say he survived the torture and then came back to clean house. Wiped out Gomez and the Family leaving nary a trace."

"But Uncle Fester, you mean, down at Lemuel Shattuck—the fruit loop ward. He's alive."

"If you want to call it that. Tell me, did he break, Malek? Did Joey X go down like the rest? Or did he break the Family?"

"He's dead like all them mooks. I wasn't there, but I know that if that mope lasted at all, it was because Cousin It wanted to draw it out, sick fuck that he was."

"But that's how old Cousin It died, isn't it? Tortured to death in his own favorite dentist's chair?"

"But it wasn't Joey X what did it, but some new pro likes to do things Hollyweird style. The whole fucking thing was staged. But, really, I don't care who smoked the Family. I just want whoever it is smoked for good and all and you're the guy who's going to do it."

"I don't do hits."

"You do now."

"Fuck—"

"No discussion, Nicky," Malek snapped. "This is about what men do, remember? And I expect you to be a man about it, not a cunt. Disappointing me is a very bad idea. Just ask anyone senior down at One Schroeder.

The long man wailed piteously as he jittered on the table under three pairs of filthy, ape-thick hands, as if to underscore the point. A Skil Rear Handle Circular saw whined in echo raised in shadow against the back wall, and then the shrieks were parsed by a deep, sonorous heaving that built to an inevitable break.

"You're sure this is the same guy, same one who took out the Family?"

"I don't know what I did to piss this guy off, but I don't give a two shits. He's killing off my crew and he's not going to stop until the Ork goes the way of Family."

"You're that sure?"

"Who else could it be? Some dead mook come back from the grave? A bag man in redemption? I got 'em crawling up my asshole! Like my problems come from dead, buried and resurrected guys other than Jesus fucking Christ himself."

"Funny."

"Hysterical. In all your police training, you don't think maybe it was the one skinny guy seen leaving that house in Allston with my fucking hot million bucks of uncut crystal meth under his arm? Guy what left behind three dead housepainters and one dead ex-muscle?"

"I heard about that at the station," said Nick, lighting up again, speaking above desperate, lunatic animal noises of the long man. "Big fire, three bodies. I thought your rip-off artist got away clean, they told me."

"More dirty than clean, Nicky. I had some friends pick him up a few blocks away, crawling like a baby, both knees shot out from under him. We had a little chat, came to a clear understanding. Then I painted the walls of the van with his brains. Should of made a bigger mess than it did."

"So you do know."

Malek blinked in assent, sat back behind his desk and put on his Ray Bans, perhaps feeling self-conscious about his untreated amblyopia.

"You enjoyed it, you fuck, didn't you?"

"No time for fun and games, Nicky. This is serious business. This is money."

"And that guy over there, that's serious business? *That's* money? You know he had nothing to do with it. You knew before you even took him."

"You got to cover all the bets to win the game, Nicky. There's no doubt about him now, and that's for sure."

Silence came down hard and fast like a falling weight so that everybody looked. Malek quickly brought things back to order. "Fucking stuff his goddamn nose with spirits of ammonia ampules already!" he shouted in a blast of sudden fury.

The hump in the shadows snickered in echo.

"Point's moot now, Padrone. I think his heart stopped." This from Franchot.

"Fine then. Make bite-sized pieces out of him and feed him to the animals down at the Franklin Park Zoo. No traces, no murmurs but from the rats on the waterfront and the ones on the South Shore. Let them do the squeaking."

Nick was sweat-soaked, emptied of resolve, unsteady on his feet. He compensated fast. "After this mutt takes out your murder crew and shoots the knees out from under your muscle boy and then is smart enough to disappear with your hot million dollars' worth of meth, you think a single guy is gonna grease him easy and score you back your drugs? You think that?"

"I think that exactly."

"Where the fuck do you get that idea? You snorting your own product or what?"

"Same principle as dealing with the zookeeper's friend over there. Covering all bets, leaving no loose ends."

"I don't get it."

"Sure you do, Nicky, you're the bright boy down at One Schroeder Place, aren't you?"

Nick blanched, seeing where all this was going. He should have doped it out in the first place, but his own inflated sense of self-importance eclipsed subtle reality. "Boyd," he sighed.

"That's right, Nicky. Very good. It seems our little friend has a big-time jones for your fucking *boss!*"

FIVE

Screaming wasn't unusual on a Friday Night at Club Sang Freud in Cambridge, it was required. Sang Freud was, after all, Boston's most edgy alternative club operating within the two am liquor licensing purview. Gays, Lesbians, Transgenders, Bisexuals, Goth, Ecstasy Ravers—even the cult of secret online S&M roleplay addicts all had at least a night to themselves and sometimes two at Sang Freud. Lumping it all under the rubric of "Alternative" gave the club an excuse to go after any niche crowd in a haphazard, desperately adver-tised trial-and-error fashion. Making Sang Freud New England's only legal above-board and above-ground kinky sex club had worked. Everybody had a night.

The S&M crowd, known as stand and model at the Freud, had their Fetish Friday, a mix of Goth kids, trannies, suburban swinger burnouts, over-the-hill online chat-sexers, and curious tourists longing for kinky sex, or at least the satisfying illusion of it. They all crowded in at ten bucks a pop. This Friday was no different.

They all sought the elusive debauched moment in time.

The trick of that moment, though, is that sometimes it finds you first.

The moment came, and by the time someone noticed, it was too late.

It was a hot night, lots of bodies in vinyl, leather, latex, pleather, black muslin, hot pink taffeta, mock stage sex in chains and fetish inexpertly mimed, a busty somewhat chubby ex-gamine using two floggers in each hand—"Florentine" style—applied to the back of a shirtless be-capped tourist boy as his on-looking friends howled, Gothic industrial cranked so high the ceiling beams and floor joists vibrated, and all three bar stations of the main room squirmed with impatient patrons like a brood of restless fallow seeking the teat of a sow. And there was screaming at a volume even above that of the pounding music.

More screaming came out of the front room by the gate, where old spray-painted, sparkle-pasted furniture looked comfortable but wasn't—all show and no go—and a tall black queen in a cheesy tiara and glowing golden sequin camisole hosted yet another bar speed station mixing Kamikazes and Impalers with supreme abandon. The queen stopped dead for a second as the screaming reached him. It wasn't right. This screaming was different. Somehow it broke up into a distortion that only distorted further the more you tried to make out its meaning.

It was when the wave of screaming crested high in the front room and crashed through into the next that its meaning became clear. The queen was already tossed about unconscious above it, blood streaked and serene.

Saturday morning came particularly early with EMS Ambulances, patrol cars, the chump wagon, a gang of uniforms and a handful of plainclothes, displaced patrons gaping dumbly in an unwanted, illegal congregation of dejected revelers on Brookline Street. Kay Boyd was there, and she deeply didn't want to be, pulled as she was out of a sound sleep by the beeper, the call, the impatient command of a pissed off Deputy Superintendent Phil LaCuna.

Dawn hadn't yet broken and wouldn't for an hour or so, but already the news trucks were there at the minimum distance and with maximum focus. She had a good idea of what she was in for, braced herself and covered her face with a handkerchief when the uniforms who switched off with the black jump-suited bouncers at the gate let her pass through.

She expected a charnal house and was relieved to be wrong, at first. It was after passing the register at the gate and getting to the other side of the death's head belly dancing mural on the plywood drywall divider, that the weight of why she had come descended.

It was a bad scene, and not just in the sense of the aftermath of cheap rock club sweat, vomit and cigarette burned dance-sex detritus.

It was a bad crime scene.

The dim, dire, mysteriously shadowed club looked sad and tacky under the full glow of every lighting fixture powered on, revealing the spotty paint job, exposed wires, half-covered building antiquity of damage and seepage. The whole place looked like a vast stage set about to be struck, replete with prop bodies strewn about waiting to be collected up. Boyd knew the problem right away even before Homicide detective Byron Wurdalaka put his hand on her shoulder.

They weren't props.

"Jesus Christ," said Boyd into her handkerchief and coughed. "How many?"

"Six," said Wurdalaka.

"I meant dead."

"So did I."

Boyd hit tilt for a few seconds.

For a small city like Cambridge, let alone Boston, this was a watershed crime—a full-scale massacre bound to swallow both the headlines and the attention of the politicos for at least the next year. No wonder Boston personnel were already on the scene. Cambridge PD knew they couldn't handle it. Worst of all, there was no real available suspect. She could read this in Wurdalaka's face even before he gave her the rundown.

He started in, clear and decisive, and Boyd's brain went skipping off on holiday, frantically asserting its right to be elsewhere. She had a moment of REM fantasy, running naked on a warm, sunny beach in Barbados, before Wurdalaka gave her a shove.

"You got all that?"

She shoved him back.

"Fuck you, Byron. Why the hell am I even here?"

"Everybody's gonna be here when it gets light, LT, you can bank on that. I caught the first round, but you can be sure I'm not gonna stay primary on this for very long."

"This is a clusterfuck beyond my comprehension," Boyd said, and lit a crumpled Pall Mall 100. "But I don't do homicides, even big ones—I'm an administrator of a task force, not a major crimes investigator. "

"You're whatever you have to be, LT, and that's the truth. And right now you're OC liaison on a sextuple homicide in some kind of crowd control incident run amok."

"From what I see, it's not really a homicide, it's certainly not OC—I mean this is more a licensing, public safety thing, negligence and code conditions resulting in a tragedy, not directed criminal conduct. This has to be manslaughter, probably involuntary."

Yonah Shimmel gave Kay a wave from where he was kneeling over a young, skinny male corpse made up to look like a corpse in grisly redundancy. Caked rusty blood got lost in red rouge, fire-engine red Karo syrup rivulets, bruises mixed with charcoal duplicated ersatz cyanosis. The boy's neck had been broken and one side of his face had been dented in, his cheekbones crushed. Shimmel ran point on a group of criminalists combing through the debris, refuse, lost items, fallen bodies, straggling witnesses and other detainees, scooping up and bagging anything at all that might point to reason for the riot that trampled and killed six ecstasy revelers. "They'll prosecute it as murder, anyway, politics must be served, LT. There are careers here to enhance and advance."

"Where's the owner?"

"Flying in from Miami—he sounded coked up."

"Looks like he'll be our poster child."

"He fits the bill. Greedy party-boy sex club runner indifferent to the safety and protection of his patrons. With this guy's history, he makes a nifty target for the bible thumpers and decency campaigners looking for leverage. He even gave Andrew Kunanin safe harbor before they nailed him on the houseboat. You know: the guy the mob hired to wax Versace and make it look like a serial job?"

"Our boy sent him packing there?"

"So the record says."

"You're telling me he's mobbed up and that's somehow connected to this rioting?"

"Bingo-bango, LT. No flies on you."

"I'll have Andromeda work it. Now, I'm gonna take my leave before I get into something here I shouldn't."

"Way too late for that LT. Before you make your no comment to the haircuts outside, I have a witness needs to share something with you."

"He coherent."

"Not really. But you'll get the gist when he starts babbling."

"You're such a fucking joy, Byron."

Shimmel's criminalists nearly knocked into them as they stepped carefully into the main room of the club where the stage was. It looked more like a battle staging area, a warehouse of medical triage and cheap theater effects exposed in all their tawdriness and cheap construction under the glare of huge brute spotlights in opposite corners of the room. Gangs of EMTs were applying dressings and packing wounds. There was a good deal of moaning and groaning underscoring gruff murmuring and the squawks of walkie-talkies, the chatter and canned music of cell phones.

Candy and silver gum wrappers littered the floor everywhere, glinting gemlike in the strong, uneven light.

"What the fuck happened here, Byron?"

"It was a melee, LT, a real melee." Wurdalaka gestured over to a group of uniforms and two of them swaggered over, carrying between them a tall, weedy, shaven-headed piratical type, his face an abused gathering of blood clots from where piercings had evidently been ripped out of his face. "Whether you know it or not, LT, we are right now standing in the eye of a shitstorm, a hurricane of fucking shit." The man they held sweated profusely, trembling, his eyes glazed and bugging, the edges of his mouth twitching. He looked like he was still rolling on ecstasy.

"You mean a monsoon of shit."

"You might be right. But you're gonna see why when Poindexter here blows. Tell the Lieutenant your little story, Mr. Sejanus. Tell her all about your little girlfriend."

Sejanus struggled dumbly just for show against the grip of the two uniforms and the Peerless standard cuffs around his wrists and looked as if he was about to start hollering and babbling, which he didn't. Instead, he spoke conversationally and reasonably at a rapid clip and interrupted by his own bursts of laughter.

"Red. You know, it was *red*. Really, how it started—it was with the wave, the cresting, crashing wave of red. You couldn't get away from it, man, you just couldn't. Beautiful and terrible and you just had to surf it. You just had to!"

"Is there a point to this, Byron?" Boyd glared.

Wurdalaka knocked him hard with his elbow. "Get to the point, Poindexter."

"There is no point, there was never any point, there was just what the wave brought when it came thundering through my brain —this was some awesome shit! The red wave. It came when we all got maxed on snappers. We were maxin' on snappers and the wave came hard, washed over us all, sucked us under and bobbed us all over, spat us up above again. I drowned and died in the wave, man, when it got onto me, all of them—the wave, running over me."

"This has nothing to do with OC."

"You don't think so, but Poindexter here didn't get to the climax. Go to it, Sejanus."

"What, you're talking about the slut in pink, the flamingo?"

"That's what we want to know."

"She swam the wave, owned it—had some fucking moves." Now he shouted: "Serious-serious-serious *moves!*"

"What fucking moves?!" screamed Wurdalaka.

Sejanus paused, collected himself. Looking composed for a moment, he craned his bald head forward with a leering smile as if to whisper to Wurdalaka and instead bit a small chunk out of his clean-shaven cheek. The detective made a sort of breathless, awkward yawping like a seagull, spun on his heel and instantly crammed his fist straight into the raver's already bloodied mouth.

"Book that fuck on assault and resisting!"

Boyd stepped in front of him.

"This is a gruesome, grisly, fucked up episode, Byron, and you're welcome to it. If the OC task force can spare any people, you'll be sure to get them. But as far as I can see, this case has got zip to do with me."

Wurdalaka cracked a smile, watching Sejanus struggle and kick up helplessly with his skinny, stove-pipe jean bedizened legs and gladiator boots.

"You're gonna be a guest of the Commonwealth for a while, shit wit. Wanna improve your stay, tell us all about the pink lady."

Sejanus went slack, lolled his bald, bloodied head, laughing. "You piece of pig shit, you don't get it. The wave is fucking coming. You're gonna ride it hard, pigfucker. She's gonna do to you what she did to boyfriend over there. That's *right,* detective fuckstick!" He jerked his head toward a cluster of criminalists hovering over a body by the center bar speed station. Boyd left them and went over to it, pulled Yonah's senior assistant toward her and asked: "What happened to that one? Or do I have to ask your boss?"

The short, somewhat chubby forensics assistant with the youthfully cherubic face removed his wire-rimmed glasses and wiped his brow, pouting. "No, need, Lieutenant. You can tell with just a glance."

The criminalists parted and then she saw it.

It made her knees buckle so she had to fight to stand for a moment.

Some things you never get used to. Some things.

Wurdalaka went up next to her to steady her—he could see she was going over.

Boyd gave him a violent push back.

"It's the same girl, isn't it?"

"'Fraid so, LT. From Poindexter's description, from corroborating descriptions of a few coherency-challenged patrons—"

"This is the same girl who tore hell out of the throat of Malek the Mallet's chief accountant?"

"In the pink."

"So, it's mine, isn't it?"

"Politics included."

She snapped open her cell phone, barked at Andromeda on the other end to assemble the crew and get them down to Sang Freud, that they'd just inherited a huge and glorious mess. Then she roused Community Relations Officer Newt Imbroglio out of his suburban slumber in Andover and told him that if he didn't get a PR spokesperson sanctified to comment by Queen Kathleen herself, that she'd start shooting from the hip to the newsies in the street. Newt screamed bloody murder on the other end in a voice audible to all. Boyd snapped the cell phone closed.

She scanned the room, her stomach plummeting like an elevator with a severed cable.

"What the fuck were they on?" she asked half-anguished, the injury, death, blood, and scent of human fluid-soaked despair crashing through the fog of weariness.

"I think I know," said a small, reedy remarkably self-assured voice from the entrance to the front room. Yonah Shimmel. "It's everywhere, if you look."

They stared at him, the thrumming of transformers for the lights and all the ancillary noises of triage and evidence gathering flooding into the void

"It's gum."

"You're a weird little fucking guy, Shimmel, and no question. But this is a weird situation."

"Fuckin' A it is, detective," Shimmel shot back at him tremulously. "Everybody here—100% of the ones on the ground—they were all doing it."

"Doing *what,* for Christ's sake?"

The senior forensic criminalist held up a gleaming silver stick between his thumb and forefinger so they could see it. "Chewing gum," he replied.

SIX

The silver stick gleamed between his fingers as his wire-rimmed glasses gleamed in the half light on his face. "This one's the charm— this one's where the money is."

Franchot lit a smoke, illuming his puffy, jowly, pockmarked face with its large, incongruously pretty agate eyes and pancake nose. "You think so, huh? But you been in a news blackout right, because you don't look like you know." There were ghosts of reverent innocence in his face, which was that of a ruined cherub. There were burns and cracks, folds and fissures in the skin, all made there before the final light went out.

The muscle of the Ork shambled and settled in each corner of the large basement storeroom of Armenian Specialties on South Street, a favorite haven for Malek's meets. They sat down heavily, all four of them, and waited. One goon sucking on the blade of a stiletto with a soulful expression only days before had crushed the metacarpals and metatarsals of Malek the Mallet's under-assistant accountant with his bare hands. He had a soulful look to him then, too.

Franchot knocked the stick of gum out of the rangy, cowlicked, bespectacled man's hand.

"What's the big idea?" he gulped, justifiably afraid to deal head-on with the muscle of the Ork. His eyes were as weak and fearful as a lab rat's.

"The big idea, champ, is that your shit's worse than useless."

"It's gold, you freak. You heard what Malek said. We have a deal on a hundred thousand units to ship."

"We ain't shipping nothing to nowhere."

The stiletto sucker croaked a laugh.

"Suit yourself. I've got my money. If we have no more business together, then we have no more business. I'm cool with that."

"But the Padrone, ain't."

Nerves poorly concealed; a quavering. "Well, so what does he want?" The man was already suppressing the shakes, pinpricks of sweat gathering on his smooth, wide brow. He was sizing up the place for an escape. It looked thin and unlikely: a dingy too-small window raised up at sidewalk level, and the one doorway leading to a dark, cramped, dust-moldering stairwell up to the shop's storefront at street-level. There was no way he could fight through the muscle toward any possible egress. He reasoned quickly and rightly that they would have to carry him out, and that, for whatever reason, they no doubt likely would.

I'm well and truly fucked, he thought, his hands going clammy.

"He wants you and a big explanation as to why six kiddies pegged out during a riot at Sang Freud in Cambridge Frid'y night. That's what he wants. And no more distribution."

"I just make the stuff," he lied weakly.

"Well, sonny boy, I don't think we made any deliveries to *that* club."

Feigning relief and feeling none: "Oh, that! That was just a test market, that's all."

"Yeah, fucko? Lemme tell ya, your test failed."

"Not at all. I think it was a huge success."

Franchot blew out rum blossomed, depraved choirboy cheeks and slammed a fresh copy of the Herald down on Malek's desk so the 80-point headline was plain above the fold: "Freaky Friday Night Massacre." The subhead told the story in a quarter of the point size: "Six youths killed in kinky club riot."

"Excellent," he said, trembling. "Really, it's an indication of addictive need and titration."

"You think this is good?"

The goon with the stiletto laughed at that.

"I do. It means once it cycles through the nervous system and metabolizes, their brains can't do without the special electric charge of the effect—the neurons have to go rapid fire to reproduce a similar state, or they have to get another dose. Either way, it's a win/win."

"I don't get it, but you can tell Malek all about it down at the garage."

Garage. Hot flash: that meant interrogation and discipline or, in a word, torture. "It simply means they have to bang their heads against the wall so that it will feel good to stop. Roughly, if they get violent enough and express it with correct intensity, the cessation of adrenaline and serotonin fluctuation will essentially mimic the benefit of the drug. Don't you see the possibilities?"

"I see it's possible they may hang us all, and the Padrone sees it the same way. So let's get going, shall we, Mr. Fucking Wizard?"

A thin voice from the dark stairwell said, "Why don't you guys stay put for a while?"

Four guns were pulled from the four corners of the room.

Franchot threw the stunned nerd against the wall beneath the grimy window. "Get the fuck down on the floor, Hortense! We got us a rogue."

He obeyed and cowered on the ground.

"So, sweetheart, you come back to bring us our meth, or did you just come here to suck us all off?"

Null, at the doorway, grim, haggard.

"The meth isn't on the table, but we can discuss your accountant. I didn't do him."

"You're lying."

"I have no need to lie. It's just a fact. Contrary to appearances, I don't care about Malek. Or anything, really."

"Ya—sure. We'll get some due diligence on it and let ya know, Pally, alright?"

"I don't do humor. Gave it up with cigarettes, gambling and heroin."

"You do death though, don't ya, fuckstick?"

"Yeah. I do that."

Franchot cackled. "This I wanna see." He nodded to the muscle. They had slowly risen, weapons slyly positioned, eager to outgun this feeble-looking wizened putz.

"Okay," said Null, calmly exploding a copper stopper round right in Franchot's throat. Just under the response spray, he dropped and rolled hard into the room, knocking one of the Ork down to the floor, straightening up fast then kneeing him into unconsciousness by jolting his brain up from under the chin.

He was rewarded by a bullet nick to the shoulder whose deliverer he instantly and thoughtlessly shot through the heart with a nine-millimeter exploding round that made a large, sloppy crater out of what once was his back. The huge goon's cohort grabbed the stiletto out of his hand and stuck Null hard in the chest with it. Null, not even breathing hard, yanked it out and calmly slashed him into pieces right through his Versace leather jacket. The huge goon bore down on him while he was slashing, gave him punishing smashes to the head and ribs no such small man could weather. But he seemed to ignore them.

Null was unaffected, save but to bust out hard and fast with his arm to deliver a hammer smash directly to the eyes, which sent the huge goon flailing backward into the wall and flat on his ass, there absolutely being nothing and no one in the way to impede his falling.

That meant that Mr. Wizard, the nerd, had slipped out the door when the fun began.

The huge goon was not to be daunted. As Null finished cooling his cohort by making him eat the long blade of the knife, the goon put him in a choke hold with twenty-two inches of well worked biceps squeezing down hard on carotid and trachea. He had moved quickly and the hold was solid, the leverage right.

Null calculated the odds, still killing the cohort, knew that this was it, but kept feeding the cohort the knife blade down his throat nevertheless, just as if he were still winning. And to his mind, he was.

The goon kept squeezing, no let-up.

Null's vision went red, then black, then he dropped the knife and the world itself as well.

That was it for him—

Or should have been.

The goon let go.

Null lay in a heap on the floor amongst the corpses, panting. As his vision came back, he realized that he was watching the goon being ridden by a boy with a slight frame, like a moose with a jockey on its back. The goon was hysterical, crashing himself from wall to wall, caroming about desperately to get the boy off his back.

It wasn't happening.

Null struggled by rote to get up off the dust-caked, lead-painted concrete floor, but he had to wait for his lungs to coordinate with his throat, and for the crease in his trachea to snap back a bit. It made no sense. There was very little reason for him not to be dead, but he wasn't. And what saved him was the boy on the back of the thug, riding that goon like a seasoned circus performer.

How did the boy do it?

Null had to wait there on the floor for his vision to focus to enough clarity to find out.

And what about the dweeb, the nerd in the glasses who had cowered in the shadows before slipping out?

Why was he at the center of this?

Null hefted himself up to a seated position, watching the dance of the goon and his furious jockey as, darkened with blood, he spun down to the ground in a weak effort to dislodge his attacker. Jockey boy was railing, it suddenly came to Null, screaming "Eat that shit, motherfucker!" over and over again at the same shrill pitch as laughter. It had looked like the jockey was prodding the goon on either side with something like spurs to keep him going.

He couldn't have been more wrong.

On either side of the goon going in—plain in returning light—Null saw that they were buck knives sunk into the goon repeatedly to stop him in his tracks.

No sooner did he grasp this than the goon let go and went down hard like a horse shot out from under its rider. But in this case, the rider rode him down screaming in triumph.

By the time Null could stand up straight, the boy was at his feet on his knees.

Null had already filled his hands with both guns well in advance of any move.

"Don't kill me, Lord!" said the boy, looking up with cracked and damaged eyes and a sallow complected face. "Please don't kill me."

"Tell me what's most efficient, and I won't."

"Let me serve you, Lord."

"I don't need a blowjob."

"God has humor."

"Get up off your knees and back away three paces, please."

Before the boy could obey, the goon moaned and tried to heft himself up, but Null put two nine-millimeter rounds in his head, which made a mess where he now quietly lay. Then the boy stepped back, quaveringly.

"Neat," said the boy.

"Not especially, but I don't do the cleanup, so it's not my problem."

"Lord, I want to help you in what you're doing, because I know you came to help me."

"Wrong. I'm not here to help you. I'm deciding about killing you."

"You have the power of life and death. So do it."

"No. I only have the power of death."

The boy looked at Null's topcoat, spreading aggressively with dark blood.

"You're hurt."

"He missed the arteries and heart. I'll be okay." He flicked a dollop of blood from the site of the wound against the wall so it made an audible splat.

"God cannot be killed."

"I should kill you."

"Then do it." He squinted those cracked eyes shut.

"No, it would be out of balance and inefficient. Don't I owe you for freeing me from the neckbreaker?"

"God owes no one nothing."

"I am not God."

"He sent you then."

"Possibly."

"Just tell me what you want, what to do, and I'll do it, Lord."

"Get the hell out, don't call me Lord, and don't follow me."

"But I have to follow you."

"We can assume a few more employees of Armenian specialties will be headed down here. I don't think another skirmish would have much of a point."

"Lord, the point is wiping them all out because of what they are, what they do—they offend you and they have destroyed me. Malek, his crew—all of them—they killed my life and soul and left me to walk around knowing it with this hole in me sucking on my insides till I die, which won't be long."

"Dramatic and familiar. I can't be moved to tears."

"They killed my love."

"Love is overrated. And once I overrated it too. Not anymore."

"You're too far above it to be able to see."

"Other direction," said Null, beginning to wheeze. He opened a Ziplock baggie with tannish powder like brown sugar, put some in his palm and sucked it down in one long snort. "Now I'm going. Stay here with the corpses if you like, wait to take out a few more droids if you can, or go save yourself. It's all irrelevant. You're irrelevant too. What's relevant is that I need medical attention." Then Null saw it -- the sweat and trembling, the wan nacreous skin, the wasted look and the cracked jaundiced eyes. "You need medical attention too, by the way."

"No, I had medical attention. Not much they can do. Nothing they can do."

Null spun about and headed up the dust-clotted steps. "Nothing I can do either."

The boy followed himself out into the raw Boston day, wind whipping in its usual cruelty off the harbor and kicking up gangs of silicate and debris off the street, scourging the skin, tormenting the eyes. They both tasted dust coming up into the air and to both of them it meant more of the same. He turned and grabbed the boy's shoulders. He wheezed, giving up on the idea of sounding fierce.

"I'll hold court in the street and blow you away right now if I have to."

"No need," he said. "You say it's irrelevant to you whether I stay or go, live or die. So if it's irrelevant, if I'm irrelevant, then why does it matter if I follow you or not?"

"It doesn't."

"So killing me would be inefficient. A waste of effort. And I could come in handy, just like I did in the basement."

"Where you saved my ass."

"You let me see it that way, and for a reason. You need to see that I'm with you. So, here I am, following you as ordained."

"It would appear so."

"Then I'll be with you until it's done, until I'm dead."

"Which won't be too long, if Malek has his way."

"Probably, but it won't be too long for him and his friends either, as long I'm with you."

"Come along then. It's late and my blood-loss is getting out of hand. I need to go while I have enough buzz in me to work like energy."

The boy unfolded a clean, blue bandana from the inside pocket of his soiled down parka and stuffed it into the wound on Null's upper chest and lower shoulder to stanch the blood.

"Pain doesn't bother you."

"I'm past it," he said, meandering into the immaculately modernized and strip mall re-hab'ed South Station and let the escalator carry him down to the Red Line.

"One day I'll be past it too."

"Yes," said Null. "We'll have something in common then."

"Life everlasting?"

"No, we'll both be dead as the blues."

SEVEN

Kay Boyd caught hell before noon on Monday.

At 10am, Malek "The Mallet" Turbot and fifteen rotating members of his indeterminate crew were rounded up. They were arraigned consecutively, gathered en masse at Suffolk County District Court, sequestered behind the shops and offices of Center Plaza by the flat, arid field of brick that fronted the colossally twisted, seemingly unfinished behemoth of City Hall. An I.M. Pei design, one wag described City Hall as looking like an obsolete industrial machine. A dingus, a framis, a widget that just didn't work. One by one the crew shuffled in place, swayed and slumped as the wan-faced swarthy judge honked, drawled and sneered, dispatching them all with quickie arraignments and expensive bail settings without remand. One by one they were bound over to Superior Court for pre-trial hearings and one by one the bondsmen averted their collective stay at the Charles Street Jail.

By the time Kay was taking the full journalistic flack for Queen Kathleen broadcast from the soot-stained steps of the McCormick Building in Post Office Square which housed Suffolk Superior on the fifteenth floor, Malek and Company were celebrating their release at the Red Fez in the South End, having a banquet brunch and dancing hard to Ouds and Bouzoukis. Kay was beginning to feel Malek's attorneys would make this charge go away, which would make the next, better-founded charge less credible. But a target was needed for the public outcry over Sang Freud right away, and few were equipped with a better bull's eye than the chief thug of the Ork. Lame as it was, they would prosecute it to the hilt and when the furor died down, fizzle at the end, let it all plea down. Detective Nick Andromeda backed Kay up at the press briefing but said nothing. He was feeling squeezed, heading down for patsy mode, and he didn't like it. He was a bagman/button man working both sides masquerading as a cop, but then again, how many of the higher-flying cops were doing or had done the same?

LaCuna didn't have to anymore, yet he kept his hand in, trafficking with the worst of the crews to make sure he was covered for the next power struggle and for his ultimate retirement. And LaCuna was a good portion of the squeeze.

Now they were trying to make him a hitman, force him to pervert an in-the-line shooting into a criminal kill for convenience. Worse, Nick felt that his qualms over it amounted to not much more than a kind of moral hairsplitting.

It wasn't as if the already declared dead Joseph Xavier Null didn't deserve to die. He, or whoever was using the urban myth to cloak himself, was a killing machine, a death-dealing golem, stupid yet infallible. And the truth was, it wasn't an easy matter to kill someone, not like pressing a button or making a leisurely killshot as was the commonplace on TV and in the movies, even in the ridiculous, over-amped "hard-boiled" or "noir" mysteries. People just didn't die easily. They lingered on messily or survived horrible trauma. Things went wrong—jams, misfires, jitters, interruptions, neurotic moral habits. These malfunctions and nervous hesitancies and the damned human connection when the eyes met always slowed things up, allowing for things to go wrong. In fact, it was the desperate connection of a lingering and reluctant humanity that *made* things go wrong. No question, it was desperately difficult and painstaking work at the level of neurosurgery, house painting. This was why there were less hit-men in the US than there were lawyers.

It took a special talent and the kind of training you couldn't get from Harvard Law, despite the fact that the risks and recompenses were often largely the same.

This Null, however, this gypsy contractor lugging around

Malek's hot million in meth made it look easy the way a circus acrobat made the flying trapeze look easy.

It took muscle and sweat and determination that went beyond will into obsessed monomania to take someone out slowly and carefully, that was a given, but to do it rapid fire like that, no let up, no hesitancy, with smooth extemporaneous purpose? Well, it wasn't human. It wasn't being a man, as Malek had said. No, it was something else altogether.

Regardless though, whether he wanted it or not, he had the mark, this Null fuck who had a talent for killing, and for surviving the kill.

The allegedly dead man who killed like it was nothing.

There was no getting out of it.

All of this made him nervous and queasy.

Still, Malek had a point. Boyd was somehow the key.

Boyd would be the one to open him up for the killshot. And for what he had in mind, she wouldn't even know he was doing it.

His palms dripped sweat as he squinted against the hot camera lights on the podium. He grinned an empty grin, listening to Boyd field the usual round of stupid questions meant to emulate the public's level of interest that would never be directly answered.

Wurdalaka laughed himself silly, knowing that Boyd herself was being made part of a dog and pony show in a case going nowhere, like the Torso nanny slaying back in '95, a glitzy sleight of hand misdirect for under-funded, overextended and less than qualified police work. Front page fodder and little else. He was still laughing when Boyd took refuge in his office at One Schroeder.

"Let's don't get into a pissing match here, Detective. You're working *for* me, not *with* me. So can the back talk and let's figure out how we can make this hum job of a case go away."

"You always did have the bigger dick, LT, and no question."

"We're gonna have hell connecting this to Malek's crew, aren't we?"

"You got the lady in pink."

"Nobody's got her."

Boyd sat down in Wurdalaka's chair and lit a cigarette.

"This is a no smoking office, LT."

"Write me up, why don't you?"

"I'll leave that to Captain Parseeman—he's gunning for your ass."

"Because I'm task force and he's just a precinct administrator."

"He hates having authority over you that he can't really use, LT. It's a potency thing."

"You think the lady in pink is the doer?"

"What else we got? Malek's got a thing for kiddie-flesh, he sells 'em wholesale to Boston's underground suburban chain of pervert cults. You know, the ones you never read about in the Globe, the ones that don't exist?"

"Now there's a task force for *you* to run. I like my job."

"I think the country club crowd would have me reassigned to Mattapan Square first."

"So you think Pinky is out on a revenge kick on Malek for selling her sister to the Concord Carlyle Order of Grand Chingon, or what? Maybe some lover? And what about the club kid with his throat torn out? Your witness said this guy and Pinky were getting busy in a dark corner before all hell broke loose at Sang Freud. The kid's got no connection to Malek, just a relief bartender down at the Lynwood Ale House. Fronted a band with the attractive name Urticaria."

"Yeah, but Joy-Boy's all mobbed up. The owner, Brad Swole's, a *definite* connection to Malek."

"Sure, but indirectly. He's mobbed up at a higher level than the Mallet. Joy Boy Swole's livin' large and stylin' down in South Beach half the time. The Freud is nothing more than an absentee cash cow to him. From this I get nothing. I don't see motive. I don't even see involvement."

"You're going to indict him, though."

"Damn straight! Not much choice about that. He's the poster boy. Besides, he'll do a few tricks for us, give up a few choice tidbits on Malek and his brethren before his lawyer beats it all back down to Cambridge City Licensing Board level.

"They'll demand a month's closure as penance, of course. Possibly two. That's a killer."

"Sure," Boyd drawled wearily. "62 Mondays, closed consecutively. That oughtta teach Joy-Boy a lesson."

"You just want to slap him around a little, don't you, LT?"

"Every job has its perks, Byron, although we can all take comfort in the upcoming wrongful death suits against the Freud. You coordinating the canvas?"

"Heading out to do so, as the Queen hath authorized manpower and extra shifts, at least for the week."

"I'm adding to the mix. Monad, Hundertwasser, Andromeda and a few other droids will be pitching in on the canvas and interviewing. But I'm beginning to get a sense the OC element here is coincidental. A teenaged pink-haired babe in pink and black spandex, latex, PVC whatever who loves 'em and leaves 'em with their larynxes ripped out doesn't really ring like OC in any way."

"What about the gum?"

"Shimmel's lab doesn't have anything yet. So far, the gum just looks to be a harmless club freebie for promotional purposes. But what I don't get is that if it's promotional, why no labeling? Why no web address, phone number or club date stamped or printed anywhere on the gum or the wrappers?"

"I'm as baffled as you are, LT. But you're running the show. Mine is but to do and duck and cover when it all blows up around you."

Monad appeared at the door with an angry impatience, rapped hard at the jamb to register the pain on his knuckles as if that might clear his brain.

"We got more, Kay."

"More what, for god's sake, and don't tell me it's bodies."

"Four of 'em, floaters all, down by the channel."

Boyd hit the intercom on Wurdalaka's desk console. "Sally, find me Yonah Shimmel and get him down to my office immediately, if not sooner." She turned her eyes to Monad and asked softly, "Kiddies, Grant?"

"Not this time. Hardcore players all the way." Monad's face was red, his expression taut with evaporating control. "These were some bad dudes."

Boyd rose wearily, and Wurdalaka stuck his foot up on his desk and shoved a nine-millimeter mini into his ankle holster. "How bad, Sarge?"

Monad kicked the door and turned to leave, mumbling, "Muscle of the Ork."

———

Andromeda canvassed hard, but only in the communities where Null once could have been found: Shabby, pub-flecked Andrew Square, the abandoned warehouse shooting galleries of Sullivan Square in Somerville, the sleazy betting rooms of Beachmont in Revere, the track at Suffolk Downs. Nothing. The barest echoes of Null remained in the paid-off bum stories of what a loser he was—it just didn't jibe with the creature that took out the sum total of Gomelsky's Family and left Fester the Confessor a raving basket case down at McClean's Hospital.

Were there *two* Nulls?

Or was there no Null at all?

There might as well be no Null at all, since he must have gone to ground after the mysterious disappearance of mob boss Gomelsky. The newsies played it up like Gomez got away with the gelt and skipped the charges, but the dive bars and tap rooms along the Southeast Expressway had a different story, that he was earmarked for donor transplant while still alive and some contracted pathologist harvested his organs without the merest modicum of anesthesia.

He remembered Null having finished the last of the Family's gunsels and torqued-up torpedoes in the open-air prison museum of George's Island. The fucker just stood there looking like a disheveled scarecrow, not even breathing hard, the gory evidence of his art everywhere to be seen: Thing LeCoeur beaten to death over stones, Wednesday and Pugsley maimed and mutilated, soldiers sprawled over ledges of masonry and flung on the ground, shot halfway to hamburger. There was a connection he didn't spot at the time, running toward them, this Null fuck square in the site of his Ruger 45 semi. He could see even at a distance that their eyes met and locked together, which is what gave him the moment for the clear shot.

Then Boyd rifled-up like a practiced sharpshooter and took a hunk out of his left shoulder without even taking a breath just before he could make Null's face explode.

Boyd wouldn't talk about it with him, encouraged him to press charges, when she knew he wouldn't—more a loyalty double check than a gesture toward martyrdom. He still ached to know, as much as his shoulder ached in recovery, just why she'd shoot a fellow officer in order to let some multiple-murdering vigilante punk get away clean.

It wasn't even clear that he did get away, but for the incident at the safe house in Allston.

They all saw him drop like a sack of laundry into Boston Harbor's inky, freezing cold water; no boat, no life-vest, no nothing. Sank like a stone, by all accounts, from the officers who pursued him till he took the big dunk, to the MDC tug personnel who watched it all on the deck offshore.

Then he comes back out of the blue to rip off a rip off for a hot million of meth? Just like that? Takes out three experienced house-painters in the bargain, maybe just to underscore the point that pursuing him wouldn't be the best idea? Finally, he leaves the rip-off artist alive, albeit with no knees, to tell the tale just so that Malek could finish him?

Nothing about this added up straight at all.

And no surge of meth ended up on the street as yet either. Null, or whoever it was, was sitting on it. This made no sense. He should have turned it over and skipped off to Cap D'Antibes or Tahiti already.

The whole thing was so atypically Boston, there was no logic either of stuporous sentimentality or of avarice.

Why would Boyd want to save this jamoke when she was the one in the first place who was most concerned about burning him down for good and all in a righteous shoot? When does wanting to blow the head off a lowlife mook translate into blowing apart the shoulder of your right-hand man and chief subordinate simply to give the scum a chance to run?

The obviousness of it stopped him in his tracks.

Wait a minute.

"Could this be love?"

Then he got the radio call and his head spun like coming off a fatalistic weekend bourbon binge. As Hundertwasser put it: "We got us four floaters, baby. Button man Parvum and company out of the Ork, just took themselves a permanent dip in the channel."

Andromeda said one word to himself aloud that changed everything, that resolved all doubt and opened more questions than he could mentally formulate as he gunned the Lexis down Mass. Ave. heading for ninety-three.

He said one word and it made his skull vibrate.

"Null."

EIGHT

They called him "Heap" or "Lumpy" but his given name was Filmore Lakeworry. They had been calling him Heap or Lumpy since the second grade, and there were just too many of them to beat into a quiet respect for an abandoned Mic-Mac Indian boy named Filmore dressed in the hand-me-downs and shabby overalls of foster care. What was worse was that these names were actually apt and not without solid descriptive basis. Filmore was in fact low and squat, always the shortest boy in his class. Being that he was almost as wide as he was tall with the apish posture of a near dwarf, it was just about impossible to combat all commentary.

But it wasn't for lack of trying.

After having been sent home one time too many to face more cracks of the strap on his naked ass, Filmore knew in his child's mind that a different solution was in order.

He did the only sensible thing: he embraced it, beating down only those comers who wanted to take the derision any further than that apparent acquiescence. So the quiet deal was struck, the acceptable level of ridicule adopted and confirmed. He chose his battles by the code of the crowd and no one blew the whistle.

Being that he never lost a fight, a certain level of fear was passed off as respectful distance, and it suited him from that young age on, or so he thought.

Filmore was far from stupid, but by rights he should have been closer to stupidity, if not a permanent resident of it.

His face betrayed the morphology of fetal alcohol syndrome with his wide thick head, flattened exaggerated nose and squeezed almond eyes, and if his cortex had been smoothed out somewhat by this defect, it was minimal enough to leave him cunning and shrewd and able to complete many higher functions which he often deliberately chose not to do. He liked to think there was so much ability to begin with that the grotesque defect barely made a dent in it. It set him apart for special treatment while at the same time giving him cover to do necessary things. One of his best tricks was to act confused, then come up behind a detractor, an opponent, a disciplining teacher and pointedly dispense with him, either with a quick, forceful beating or a handy disappearance.

In the hands of the Commonwealth, he had learned the quiet ease of the long homemade shiv, the exacting leverage of the garotte.

Filmore was clever in making unwanted individuals disappear handily.

His third and last foster family had three older and considerably larger Jewish sons—the parents liberal accountants from Shrewsbury who took him in out of social guilt, status for tonier Newton and Wellesley friends and charitable committees, in addition to making homeownership and REIT investment numbers work during the heyday of the 80s trickle down recession. The compassionate spirit was not among the Steingross boys, who made Lumpy their punching bag and the butt of every humiliation that could be inflicted on a new adolescent, exposing his precociously adult genitals in front of the girls volleyball team and beating him bloody in the JFK Junior Highschool Lunch commons, dumping him with food. They behaved like New England white-bread preppie jocks, picking on the smaller, weaker, confused and hesitant creatures who were Jewish enough in their aspect to distract from the grudgingly known taint of their own Jewishness. Feebs like lumpy were perfect foils for the deflection game.

Lumpy played stupid. Lumpy played along.

Lumpy took it in stride.

Eddy Steingross died drunk in his wrecked Trans-Am.

Lenny Steingross ran away from home and was never seen again.

Sammy Steingross stopped talking and had to be hospitalized for "nervous exhaustion."

The truth was, Lumpy was feeling his oats, testing his abilities by playing "retard" and suckering the Steingross boys one at a time with the sort of ruthless desperation that allowed for no mistakes. He would have been a suspect, but for his disability, the mild mental illness that kept him in the special classes where he could dream away the time without any effort. And Lumpy learned long ago the world was in denial about murder, from the first boy he had drowned as an experiment in a toilet at the New England Home for Little Wanderers.

Tragic accident. Poor confused, weepy little FAS Mic-Mac boy having to watch it all. Sad.

The wounds of class.

The rape of Sammy Steingross couldn't be brought up or talked about and was something Lumpy picked up in the hands of Youth Services from the older boys. It was simple: if you marked a boy like that, then you owned him and he caused you no further trouble. You established an intimate connection, or he killed you. And Sammy wasn't even a killer with his two bigger brothers to back him, never mind alone.

Lumpy had been marked and owned lots of times, in Juvie lockup, on the grounds of Leverett Saltonstall Youth Correctional in Dracut, but the ownership never stuck.

Since that very first accident at Assault 'n' Stall—the death of a clumsy, bucktoothed Canuck kid with his cervical spine shattered—Lumpy knew that he possessed the facility to kill. Everyone back then knew the fish-eyed, mildly retarded boy was far too slow and docile to have done it. He could hardly tie his shoes. And the few inmates who knew said nothing and bartered silence for use of Filmore as muscle.

He didn't mind—it kept him busy and it gave him a place in the world.

He had even bawled convincingly like an infant when they picked up that first suspicious corpse on the grounds of Assault 'n'

Stall, just as he did at the latter-day disappearances of his foster brothers.

It was hard work getting Eddy to drink all his dad's Chivas, then daring him to take the Trans-am up to Breakheart with the brake lines cut. Harder still drowning Lenny in the quarry and then keeping him sunk nice and deep with dumbbells from his own home weights set. But having achieved his adult height of four feet eleven inches at an early age, he was nevertheless precociously strong, a horribly tortuous knot of hard muscle, compressed and compacted into his small frame by either a mirthful or angry god, depending on what looking at him did to your gut at that moment.

When Lumpy was of legal age, he dropped out of high school, burned down the Steingross house without so much as a thank you and headed off to join the rest of the young men of his disaffected and grudgingly atomized tribe. This meant working construction, and not just at the most menial hod carrying level. No, Lumpy joined the elite of the highest paid workers dancing effortlessly along the narrow girders and slender scaffolding of the buildings in Boston. Whether genetics, training, or some hybrid amalgam of nature and nurture, the Mic-Mac Indian men had zero fear of heights and an ability to move fast at the most perilous level as if each of them had for years been a practiced balance beam gymnast. The biggest state construction contractors recruited them, sending spotters up the Conne River in Newfoundland, known to some as the Miapukek First Nation of Mi'kmaq, and down through Aroostook Maine, hotbeds of the Human Being or L'nu, the new politically correct nomenclature for the Mic-Mac who nevertheless still worked construction, got soused and brawled in the pubs with the rest of the hard, defeated men of the city.

Lumpy was an edgewalker.

He could hang his balance on the edge of a steel beam 500 feet up and never tremble a twitch.

The stereotype applied, and at the age of 17, he was welding and riveting hundreds of feet up with the other Mic-Macs and the occasional Boston Irish supervisor who would sweat and count the minutes until a few of the solemnly mirthful human beings lowered him down to the temporary elevator on a plywood landing. He was a natural hireling for the mob crews that came and went over the years of power-struggle and consolidation to take their cut of the construction boondoggle, from unions, low-bid kickbacks and inspectional assurances. One day, a muscle guy decided to bully Lumpy. He was quickly found beaten to the knees at the feet of his confreres. They dumped the guy and signed Lumpy on. One day, mob work outweighed skyscraper girder dancing when the Ork took him on as added muscle—with bonuses for the occasional disappearance.

Lumpy now did a different kind of edgewalking.

He was there at Gary Lee Obidowski's Garage, watching Andromeda mix it up a little with the Padrone, and he helped work on the under-assistant accountant at crucial points, though without enjoyment. It was always humorless work grinding weaker flesh down to agony and then death, with some slight degree of satisfaction if that flesh was in the person of an enemy, but little else. Especially when it was all for show, especially when the outcome was already assured.

The money was good, that and the inclusion within a group that didn't hector him so much as it ignored him even while he executed informal-seeming commands with mechanistic precision. It was something. Being left alone entirely—never having to give an accounting beyond the requisite violent act—and then being recompensed impressive chunks of clean, bankable paper were greater satisfactions still. There was also a fleeting perverse pride in his work —in doing it well and not with sloppy abandon.

But alone was alone, and at best, but for the occasional prostitute or retribution rape of the loved one of whomsoever had flaunted Malek's wounded dignity, a cold comfort of hard-won sanctity.

But for the gum.

He was given a few sticks of it by the geeky dweeb and it changed him.

Lumpy was flooded with feeling, yearnings and a sense of connection to all living things after he was handed the first few trial sticks. He wanted to love, to not only take, but be taken by a woman with passion; to exchange deep and detailed compassionate understanding with others like himself, and even those not like himself he could somehow strike a chord with. Chewing the gum, he felt a profound sense of being a link that helped keep the entirety of the great reality of life together. He was integral to it, a crucial part of what made the world and the universe work and run as it did.

The gum gave him a sense of destiny, an assured knowledge that humanity was actually the greatest value, and not just the cheap, monkey-like thing used, run over and dispatched to achieve your ends while groveling for survival before yet more lordly and fortunate primates. The preciousness of life flooded him like rising tide in a cramped, crabbed estuary; he wanted to celebrate it, preserve it, protect it, touch it and feel it touch him back.

Then the gum subsided and he ran mad into the street with nerves on fire to crack heads, beat faces, break every imbecile he saw in two until the sorrow would take him that might bring back the joy. It came like a wave and he needed to ride it, let the world understand and experience his justifiable rage, his passionate wrath, smashing them all to clue them in to the clear and basic fundamental point of life—

That and another stick of gum.

It was what he was after tonight, walking effortlessly along the gutters of the dilapidated three-story Edwardian in Arlington in the dead of night. It was what he wanted deep within his 59-inch chest when he crashed through the shuttered window of the gambrel roof into the attic to make his presence known. He let his footfalls sound loud on the old floorboards of the chill and musty attic and nimbly negotiated the trap door folding ladder down to the third story hallway without a thought of suppressing any noise. It was surprisingly bright when he came down and let the spring-loaded trapdoor creak back up. The lights were burning everywhere revealing how truly rundown the house had become, with cavernous fissures in the plaster walls, loosened baseboards and the wood floor bearing the damage of carelessly installed wall-to-wall carpeting even more carelessly removed.

Lumpy barely had time to recognize just who it was approaching him in long, tentative strides down the hallway, being that he had to get over the two empty black and sightless ends of a double barrel sawed-off shotgun that met him square in the eyes.

There was the sound of a wheezy, stertorous breathing.

The holder of the gun trembled and squinted behind it. Lumpy smiled, knocking the stunted double barrel off to the side as an afterthought.

"Dr. Benway, I presume?" he said.

NINE

It was an opera of anguish sung in screams that went unheard.

It was a music like the blues coming from far beyond a distant past that could not be connected with.

So Null's face constricted to a grin as he breathed out a gout of air like taking a punch.

"Tell me it hurts, Null," said Missy, compressing a dressing on the wound. "Tell me you feel it."

"Waste—of—breath," he replied, lying there on the gurney, his scarred and sinuous chest exposed. He failed to quell a coughing jag, which took him. Missy pushed him back to the gurney, tolerating nothing from Null but his injuries. She cleaned and dressed a succession of wounds, stripping Null completely with the expertise of an experienced triage nurse, barely jostling him. The boy with the knives averted his eyes and turned his back to Null averting shame.

"What's with the kid? He have to be here?"

"He thinks he does."

"Kid, you should wait outside."

"I'm not going anywhere."

"I can have security make you."

"Let him stay, Missy. He thinks I'm God."

"From the looks of him, I should book him a room here. Kid, you know you need the cocktail, right? You're full blown and no joke." She grabbed his face and revealed the white patches of candida on his gums, the Kaposi's sarcomas on his forearms. He pushed her back with surprising force.

"I'm no fucking kid. I'm twenty-two."

"Relax kid, physiologically you're eighty."

"I keep forgetting e-room types are only nice to the rich."

"Missy's nice to exactly no one."

"It's too late for me. You ask him why I'm here and what I have to do."

"It's all about lost love," Null croaked, experiencing stress as Missy scrubbed down gashes and splits in his skin, irrigated the gaping wound that just skirted the carotid directly below the collarbone. "Revenge. Avenge. Something you do when hate is all you have left. Or a memory of hatred."

"Don't remind me," she sighed, working Null's wracked body like a cut man working a boxer between rounds.

"Can I remind you about the autopsy you did on the fuck that lost your love for you, then?"

"You don't have to. I know I owe you, Null, which is why you survive all these wounds that should have put you out long ago." She glared at the boy with a sidelong glance, then went back to suturing up the splits in Null's ashen toned skin. "I just don't owe Blueboy here ice in January."

"Nobody owes me but Malek The Mallet. And it ain't ice he owes."

"The kid wants blood."

And to punctuate that, a small jet of Null's blood splattered Missy on the cheek and she stanched the site hard with pressure from both hands. "Somebody get this fucking kid out of here!"

"I'm not a kid. I'm nineteen!"

No orderly or resident or even security officer came, despite this breach in the general quietude, order and dull intensity of the Mount Auburn Hospital emergency room.

"You don't plan on seeing twenty, do you, Jack?"

"He plans on suicide by killing," said Null with an airy calm.

"It's hit-'n'-run. That's what I go by. Not Jack."

"Kid wants to be a comic book character. Why not call yourself Deadboy, or something? True-to-life, comics. Dyingboy, maybe."

"Call yourself your mother, why don't you? My name's Ken. Ken Embers. Don't ever fucking call me Kenny."

"If you watch the cartoons like I do, you'd know they killed Kenny."

"Yeah, but he comes back every time."

Missy screamed it: "Will somebody get this kid out of here so I can treat this man!"

Security constables came and dragged the kid off to a waiting area—two of them—then they rooted themselves standing over him until it was apparent he had no intention of moving and perhaps even a compromised ability to move. His fever was back and his hands trembled. They left, the kid being obviously sick enough to be left alone.

Null lay there on the gurney, breathing evenly. Missy wiped her sweating brow with her bare arm, blood coating the latex glove on her hand.

"What's with the kid?"

"A hanger-on I can't shake at the moment."

"What are you, a pedophile?"

"I'm a nothing-phile. Literally."

"I don't believe you don't feel nothing."

"Me too."

"Kid should be in a hospice somewhere. He's got less long than you."

"How long I got?"

"Not long, you keep showing up like this. Keep it up, Null, you'll get necrotic tissue, gangrene. One day, someone will stab or shoot you beyond repair. Then that'll be it."

"Something to hope for then, if I had hope."

"You're as pointless as my husband was."

"Was it pointless when you autopsied Gomez, as he squealed and cried all the while through the duct tape over his mouth?"

"No. It was restitution."

"Restitution? Did it bring Nat back? Did it restore him?"

"No. It restored me."

"Good, and now that you've restored *me*, you can suture up the wounds and let me get the hell out of here so I can do what I have to do."

She dug in ferociously, pulling lengths of suture material tight in Null's skin as she emitted little grunts. "And what would that be, pray tell?"

"Playing your scenario straight out to the end."

———

Death tenement squalor in Grove Hall, Mattapan, smack in Police Area B—ancient projects like red brick bunkers hunkered down from the days of the Great Society and the War on Poverty both lost long ago. Street-lamps pricking up from garbage-strewn wide concrete and broken hilly weeded tarmac streets like hypos, the tips of which appeared sharp and threatening but which had turned blunt and useless against the skin of the low sunset sky. Huddled figures over-dressed in good weather and bad. Bashed-in, busted, rotted out, weather-beaten clapboard three- four- and five family houses littered with filthy laundry, rent garbage bags like piñatas from purgatory, mangled plastic toys obsolete from Holiday charity toy drives from days of yore, all shaded the gray streets with hopeless populace and gave the smooth new thoroughfares and the ancient pot-holed cow paths slathered with cheap tar, a sense of being central to a village of a kind.

A primitive village of the remnant welfare food-stamp issued crack-pipe doomed.

This was where Null lived.

It was in the basement of the Fidelis projects, a bombed-out post war experiment in enlightened New England social integration run amok. Decades ago, corrupt maintenance men and superintendents lived there, trading inattention and exploitation for rent and making heating and basic decency of accommodation a side business. Null and the kid went through the cabbage, feces and urine acrid smelling lobby by the elevator-turned-fireplace and the graffiti paeans to Tupac Shakur, Snoop Dogg, 50 Cent. Li'l' Wayne and the rest of the pop cultural droppings of anger and impotency masked as swagger.

Neither Null nor the boy gagged at the thick scent.

When they negotiated the black, dust caked, cobweb-mossed dingy gray once white oil-based pint sheathed steel spiral staircase down to the dark fetid basement foyer whose elevator bank had long ago become a crack hole and unisex bathroom, it gave the boy an incongruous jolt. After Null spun down through several locks, including one old style New York police buttress and swung back the seamy brown painted steel-faced security door back, it revealed a space that was bright white, immaculate and nearly empty.

There was a cot, pulled neat and tight with hospital corners on the blankets and sheets, halogen lighting bolted in from the ceiling smoothly plastered white, stereo speakers hooked up to a turntable, CD changer and amplifier perched on a low glass coffee table spotlessly clean, a refrigerator, sink, television, all of it not more than five years old. All of it on the winning side of the battle against a persistent collection of urban dust. It looked like the quarters of a military prisoner quarantined for debriefing. It looked like the place had been burnished clean with toothbrushes, painted down to the finest crevasse between molding and wall with Popsicle sticks and fine attention, scrubbed, mopped, wiped down, dusted and purged for thousands of hours.

That was because it had.

"Better than I thought," said the kid.

"It's ethical," said Null. "An approximation, like most of what I do."

"You can't take the cot this time. I need to lie flat and recover."

"The floor is fine."

"It's clean," said Null. "No rats."

He pointed a remote and too-loud blues abruptly filled the room, moaning, old, lonesome, crackling with antiquity, channeled rage and hopelessness. Real blues, delta blues, Charley Patton's original guttural conviction in the solidity of strife.

"What the fuck is that?" the kid, Ken Embers, asked.

"God's music," said Null, lowering the sound to a level less able to give the sense of penetrating the stony tomb chambers of his new self to permit some depth of raw human feeling to at least have a presence there. Like always, it was a splendid imitation that climaxed in failure.

"It's a wailing death chant! It's fucking painful!"

"Exactly."

He shut out the lights.

————

Null didn't sleep the way other men slept, but then Null did very little that was like other men.

The kid slept, though, soundly through a delirium of sometimes violent reenactment.

Null, blank of mind and heart, empty and serene in an oblivion of human will, having forsaken now the sound of the iPod MP3 screaming blues, field hollers, work songs and moans of Leadbelly for the urban bleat of street crime in the air and the old forgotten crimes of another dispatched and ruined adolescent's life. Ken Embers was a talker in his sleep, and he went on and on in the flat and half-swallowed tones of the somnolent confessional like he was struggling to get it all in at once.

He was just another mechanical pipe-fitter's son from Billerica, not a garden spot to begin with, a post industrialized rural sink hole of urban sleaze with a long criminal tradition of cozened New England secrecy. There was no unburied truth in Billerica, just a sanctimonious outward shell of half-garbled fact. But Kenny spoke of his past with barely any garble at all in febrile sleep.

His father, a distant disciplinarian whose only closeness to him was his hands on him, started visiting him at night after his thirteenth birthday in order to further put his hands on him. The kid was his by rights after all, as chattels, to do with as he pleased when he pleased until he could make a man out of him. It was the safest way to keep the family together, without the outside risk of pursuing the blasphemy of his need more directly in the taboo open Boston gay scene. And for it to be with his own blood, kept it feeling natural and not at all as sick as it had felt when he was in the army.

To make a man out a boy, you first have to make a punk out of him so he understands just what a man is from what he is not.

This was taught to Daddy Embers in the communal tile shower stall of the bivouac on Parris Island.

Domestic tranquility was assured, but for a dog.

The dog in question was no mutt, but a pure-bred, a boxer named Goldie, who bonded close with Kenny. When the dog grew big enough, it tried to protect him. Daddy Embers was on him one night, making him scream and cry, to which his mother turned a deaf ear sunk deep into her pillows. Goldie, in turn, sunk her teeth deep into Daddy Embers right thigh and stopped him cold while raping Kenny, making him run madly after her, pants around his ankles, drunk and falling over. That was the first time.

The next time, Daddy was ready for the dog, when he pounced on Kenny, kept him pinned under the blankets and this time didn't enter him with bloody abandon. He waited there, making mock noises just as if he were at his son in the usual day.

Goldie came fiercely bounding.

She landed hard on Daddy, receiving for her trouble the flat bottom of a metal pot swung full in the face.

Daddy beat her with it, full in the face, as she went at him, still trying to save the unsalvageable Kenny. It ended after her skull was fractured and her left eye was gone.

The noise was so bad the police visited, found the boy cradling his lolling dog in a puddle of blood, Daddy and mother screaming, caught in a volley of a hollering frenzy. The police didn't guess—they knew, told Daddy in no uncertain terms, they *knew*, which only made him laugh, so they shrugged him off a warning and did nothing. Goldie recovered and kept watch over Kenny with even more ferocity, right up until the day she disappeared.

According to Daddy, some mean kids in the area—neo-Nazis, he had said—found her, tortured her with a knife and killed her by forcing her to swallow a lit cherry bomb, then tacked up what was left of her to the side of the house as a warning to Kenny, who was already showing signs of being as queer as a three-dollar bill, as Daddy liked to say. Kenny took her down from the side of the house in a fog of adoring love, regret and frustrated tears.

Kenny buried her hide alone.

Then he belonged to Daddy all the way, that is until he was too old, used, drugged up, dragged out and shattered to be cute anymore. *As worthless as his fucking half-blind boxer dog.* Then when Kenny was diagnosed with a prolapsed anus and had to eat up the health insurance deductible with emergency surgery, well, that was the last straw. Sixteen was the age Daddy had to make it when he was a kid, and his own father drove him off in the station wagon and deposited him in downtown Boston with five bucks in his pockets and a warning not to call home. Sixteen would do for Sunny Boy too, who was queer as a three-dollar bill, anyway.

After booting Kenny out, Daddy told everybody in the Taverns on Main Street that he was a runaway, then pulled up stakes with his generally half-in-the-bag wife and went to live in New Smyrna Beach Florida, where the local of the pipe-fitters union had purchased blocks of favorably priced properties for cronies of a particular type. And Daddy had done his time as a sidelines head-breaker, when government contracts were lean, before the sinking of the Central Artery's Big Dig made everybody fat again.

Kenny was the original dispose-a-kid. Trick him out, suck him dry and dump him into an emptiness of helpless consent.

After the usual suburban tour of the chicken hawk circuit that started off in Chinatown and wound up somewhere on Pleasant Street in Belmont, Kenny was rescued by fellow chicken and some-time bagman, lookout and distributor for Malek the Mallet's crystal meth' and Ice line, Jimmy "Blue Eyes" Swain. Though the rest of him was as near to black as it could be, the eyes were cerulean— heartbreak summer's day. It wasn't long before the two boys as lovers pulled a railroad flat together in Quincy, distributing Malek's produce all over the south shore out of Blue Eyes' wounded used Fiat.

They found Jimmy in the crushed-up Fiat in a gully out in Mishawum, fingers, toes, nose, legs and elbows broken. Paranoid Malek had decided that ol' Blue Eyes had gone into business for himself, which although untrue, explained as much absence, irre-sponsibility and missing product as Malek needed to have explained. Blue Eyes had explained that he was HIV positive, but Kenny didn't care. His life in his eyes was over, but for shared moments of inti-macy between them.

Malek paid for the funeral, gave Kenny a spouse's stipend for a few months, albeit grudgingly. He was sentimental about such needless death of the young, even when doomed, gay, drug and disease-ridden as was Blue Eyes. A stone punk, who didn't last more than a few hours down at Gary Lee Obidowski's Garage.

Ken Embers recited all of this in disconnected, free-form fragments which Null pieced together with penetratory focus in the darkness. He had the shakes and night sweats, calling for the dog, the lover, the help of god.

Null said one thing, having analyzed the kid's life for possible value and use and finding none—two words:

"Balance due."

And he restored balance of a kind from out of the intermittent quiet by loudly blasting the blues.

The kid woke up screaming and Null, feeling nothing at all, nevertheless screamed with him.

TEN

They were down by the detritus at the banks of the channel, where the bay separated Southie from Boston proper. The newsies surrounded them off the Congress Street Bridge, perched with panel trucks on the embanked remains of the sunken boondoggle of the Central Artery. News helicopters hovered overhead, blasting herring gulls out of the way and whipping up chill Boston mist over the perma-stench of the harbor channel where in the shallows four well-suited bodies lay.

"Clusterfuck," said Chief Inspector Phil LaCuna to no one in particular. "This is a clusterfuck of major proportions."

Capt. Parseeman grunted assent and kicked at the collar of a corpse as wiry, stylishly coifed Yonah Shimmel, senior forensics specialist, protested.

Wurdalaka and Boyd arrived, pushing through a confusion of thick blue uniforms holding back the curious. Monad was already there, coordinating a hip wader canvassing crew.

"We got us a bum dump," said Wurdalaka.

"Muscle of the Ork," said Shimmel. "Tell me something I don't know."

"Don't get testy with me, Shimmy."

Specialist Shimmel: "You know what happens if you piss me off, right?"

"Woe is me. I'll be last at Suffolk to get good blood work. Why don't you work this, you weird little fuck?"

"I was going to say I'd have to kick your ass, but I think I'll let Lieutenant Boyd do it for me. She always does such a good job kicking your ass, anyways."

Boyd's cheeks reddened, and she laughed for cover.

LaCuna clapped his hands for attention. "Children, children, do you mind distractin' yourselves from your little pissin' fracas there and getting back to the clusterfuck at hand? Kay, why don't you sing us the song while Shimmel provides the bouncing ball? Do the honors, will ya?"

Shimmel studiously rolled over each top-coated, be-suited corpse in the shallows until their bloated, ruined faces were visible and his team helped drag them up further onto the smashed concrete, rusted pig-iron and garbage strewn shoreline. His crew, like herring gulls themselves, began picking at the corpses in tugs of curious hunger.

"Good news, everyone. It's not a war."

"So we're over-reacting?" LaCuna delivered with a half-humored leer.

"It's not like you don't know it, Phil."

"Just sing the song, Kay."

"It's a dump, is what it is. This isn't the Dorchester Gangsta Boyz sending a message to the Ork, or the Charlestown Cholos off on some vendetta. No, no, what we have here is housecleaning. Malek the Mallet trying to get some mileage out of a dead loss of manpower. No, these dudes had a run in with someone and they got the bad end of it, but I don't think the doer put them here as any kind of sign."

LaCuna's face took a purple tinge of impatience, making his rum blossoms spider out from his face in relief like vines. "What if I think he did—staged it to piss us all off and pick a fight with the Mallet?"

"Then you'd be wrong, sir," said Wurdalaka with a honk that was as disrespectful as his phrasing was deferential. "That little freak Shimmel has it bagged already, spices—bay leaves, cumin, tumeric, preserved lamb—shit, these guys all bought it in the same place and that place wasn't here."

"You forgot about the lack of water in the throat and lungs."

"No, you're just presuming that, ya weird little fairy."

"Stop trying to date me and get to the point."

"The point," said a husky, self-assured voice from the embankment above them by the shoulder of the nearly demolished Surface Artery, "is Armenian Specialties down on South Street. That's the story the soles of the shoes tell. They all died in one of Malek's chosen playpens, no doubt in the basement where the stock is kept." Andromeda, looking down upon them all with harshly narrowed eyes, his topcoat flapping hard like a tarp in the lacerating harbor wind.

"You get the gold star as usual, Nicky," said Boyd, yawning. "The appearance of these corpses is pure Malek, sending a message of a kind we're not supposed to pick up."

"You sure as shit love to overcomplicate the obvious, don't you, Lieutenant?"

"Indeed I do, Inspector. In fact, I'd go so far as to say it was a gender thing, if we didn't have a female-friendly police commissioner who was already a wee tad sensitive about such old-time department pigeon-holing."

"Don't give up your day job for standup comedy anytime soon, Kay. Your delivery needs work."

"True enough. But Malek's doesn't. This is strictly a face-saving move."

"I don't get it," said LaCuna, feigning ignorance to goad her.

"Simple, Phil: What these bodies of the muscle of the Ork say loud and clear is 'So what—you offed some of my guys. Big whoop. I have an inexhaustible supply of them, soldiers up the ass. In fact, I have so many goddamn soldiers that I can give these punks to you no problem, show Boston and God I have no shame about putting my soldiers anywhere, even in the mud of the fucking Channel. It doesn't matter. And why doesn't it matter? Why, I have so many more soldiers up the ass that eventually I am going to shove a good number of them right up *your* ass. And there's nowhere in Boston that I won't do it. Wherever you think you can hide, you won't be safe. Gloat all you want, but if I have dead soldiers in the Channel today, you can bet your mother's pearls I'll be having some live ones in your house tomorrow.' You better believe that this is the message he's sending to the crew that did this, in clear terms."

"You nailed it, Kay," Andromeda said with admiration that lacked any trace of irony. "Pure Malek."

"Neither of you quite nailed it," drawled LaCuna, with that high ward, South Shore nearly British yet almost Australian sneer. "The point really is the crew what ripped off the crew what ripped off one hot million bucks worth of crystal meth from the machinations of the Ork, and how many Malek has to kill either to get it back, or make sure such like never can happen again. No, our boy Malek is in a pickle, no two ways about it."

"A weak king," Capt. Parseeman chimed in happily after for so long having gloomily kept his silence, his eyes idly tracking the stilted progress of the gulls. "I think we should pick him up."

"No," said Boyd stiffly. "He's perfect as is. If weak king he be, then the crew will be coming for him and the rest of the Ork to take over their supply chain of street drugs and earn turf quickly with a take-over rather than a build-out. No, we could get ol' Malek on a host of middle-grade misdemeanors and several counts of a class B felony of improper burial of a corpse. We can get him anytime, so why not get him *and* the guys that did this and nip some new crew in the bud at the same time, nuke the cancer before it metastasizes."

"We'll have to have a budget meeting on it," said Parseeman, "but I'm sure we can work up something."

"I think it's a tasty proposition." This from LaCuna.

"I'm down for it if Kay thinks we can nab them all." Andromeda. This might free him of Malek and yet make him more lucratively useful to the swine at the same time. He grinned, broadly creasing new keloid scars across his face.

"Problem is, we don't know who this new crew is," Wurdalaka offered snidely. "We don't got nothin' comin on the street about it. And that's not normal for this kind of thing. Guys that do this, they got a hell of a lot of ego, lotta social wounds to recover from. Why ain't there more noise about it? Why ain't they crowing?"

"What if these guys are slightly smarter, with a bit more self-control?" proffered Parseeman.

"If they could do that, why not play the market and bilk the real criminals in town instead of these gang bozos?" LaCuna adding a gem.

"What if it ain't a crew?" said Wurdalaka, hitting it and knowing that he did.

A fat gull above them let out a cry, then plummeted like a stone into the bay.

Boyd and Shimmel stared at one another, sharing the same single, chilling thought that locked their gazes hard in the silence:

"What if it's just one guy?"

———

The banging was fiercer and more primitive than the blues, the screaming of the kid or the mimicked screaming of Null combined. It was a heavy metallic pounding whose rest stops were filled by drawling Boston ghetto voices cursing. The immaculate, white-lit room, bare but for the expensive, unobtrusive Bose speakers fresh from the warehouse in Framingham, was under attack at the ancient fire-exit door whose alarm mechanism was long ago frozen by plaster and paint. The door itself was clotted by both, thick, steel reinforced, and already threatening to crumble at the hinges under pummeling of the unseen but presumed battering ram behind it.

Kenny Embers, the sick kid, was already up and at it, throwing himself against the door, already sizing up what was happening, straight from his nightmares as if they simply bled over from dreams to reality and swept him along. "Help me, Lord!" he cried, "or they'll get in."

Null blinked and said nothing.

He dug his fingers in the package of meth', careful not to violate the surrounding plastic beneath the paper bundle, pulled up a palm full of powder and shoved it into his face, snorting deeply. He let the remains from his hand sift back into the bag then secured it under his coat.

The pounding worsened, with creaks of give at the hinges added. Laughing curses were interspersed.

Null approached and pulled Kenny off the door without a

thought. The force made the kid stagger backwards. "Why not let them in? Better yet, we'll let ourselves out."

"They'll kill us is why."

"Can't kill the dead, kid. Didn't they teach you that in school?"

"I'm not dead yet and you can't kill God."

"We're both dead, kid. You just don't know it yet." Null grabbed the kid's arm to steady him. "But trust me. They're deader still."

"I trust you."

Null unbolted the door and kicked it open with everything he had, setting the battering rammers on their ass in the dank, rotted tenement plastered squat-flat that abutted his own personally rehabbed illegal space. There was no pirate line of electricity coming in, so a painter's lamp clipped to a broken joist with a cord running out to a utility plug on the side of the building had to do. Two Dorchester Gangsta Boyz were flat on their asses in the urban dust with a heavy steampipe weighing them down on the floor. A third one, short and pockmarked with a do-rag tied as a burnoose watched nervously off to the side. The fourth, a tall, big bellied rust-hued thirtysomething in oversized gang leathers multi-colored with standout reds and golds gleaming in the half-light regaled them and brandished a chrome plated magnum.

"Thanks for opening up, cuz. We heard you had the nicest squat in town and we thought we'd take it for our own selves. Bring it back to the community from a white ass thug pimp, know I'm sayin'. Heard you gots drugs too, some load of gak. You oughts to know down on Dot Ave. that shit be mines."

"Gonna smoke Mr. Fucking Skeleton's ass," muttered one of the rammers pushing himself up from under the pipe.

Null kicked him back down again, seemingly lost in thought.

Ken Embers squeezed the twin knives in his falling-down-to-his ass baggy prison jeans pockets hard at the hilts. He was aching to use them.

"Gimme the gak, chief, you and your boyfriend live. If you don't, I kills ya and I takes it, anyways." He flashed a gold-capped grill smile from his slack and sodden mouth.

"Cap the fucker, Cheese, and just take the shit."

"Who is this guy?" Null asked without interest.

The short, fat pockmarked one with the fancy do-rag had this to say: "That's Heavy Cheese Petomane, bitch, number one drug lord of the South Shore and movin' in on Back Bay. Show some respect."

"You're number two, then?"

"There ain't no motherfuckin' number two."

"Sounds fair to me," Null more parsed than said, and tossed the package of Meth straight at the big-bellied Gangsta Boy called "Cheese." When the dealer jerked forward to catch it, Null spun about almost too fast to see. Cheese went down, clutching the package minus a face and most of his head.

Null stood rail-rigid, the sawed-off held parallel to the pitted, rubbled floor, its lanyard still around his neck. The fat one in the do-rag standing in the shadows looked as if he were having a heart attack when Null hunched over, the sawed-off locked hard into his body, and calmly took out the two on the floor with a close grouping of shots.

"I think this might mean you're number one now."

Kenny Embers made for the do-rag sporting Gangsta Boy, both knives out, but Null stopped him. "Not yet, kid." He looked back at Null, wounded eyes lusting for blood.

Do-Rag trembled, rendered inarticulate by death and survival, while Null gathered up the weapons, tossing the chromium magnum up and down in his hand under the painter's light to test its heft. "The fuck you want with me?"

"You're number one, aren't you?"

"Fuck!" Null swooped down on him like a falling shadow as the painter's light swung. He took his guns, the cheap low carbon steel sling-style switchblade, mace and stun gun, braced him against the wall and leveled a middle-grade punch to the face to get his attention.

"You're going to deal a little Crystal Meth for me, number one. Got that?"

Do-Rag stuttered in terror, in the full knowledge that he was directly in the hands of death that could at this moment do with him whatever they would: "What-what—what it cost?"

"Information, number one. And a good, clear work ethic."

"Say *what?*"

"Well, you work for me now, and since I lack humanity, mistakes just aren't as well tolerated. You'll have to be very careful."

"Careful of what?"

"Inefficiency. You could be fired for that."

"Yeah? So what?"

"So this: When I fire you, you can be sure it will be done with a bullet straight through the brain."

Ken Embers gathered up the array of weapons from Null and took them back to the immaculate, blinding white squat as Null watched Do-Rag silently figure out what was expected of him. Null didn't have to say a word, as it had been made clear in the matchstick pantomime of the street:

First you get rid of the bodies; then you pick up the drugs.

Ken Embers, meanwhile, had no trouble with God suddenly becoming a drug dealer.

After all, hadn't he really always been one?

ELEVEN

Lumpy was working the gum, hunched over an antique sorting/wrapping machine run off pedals with pulleys from the floor in rapt fascination—an artifact of the days of the Lowell Mills when Beacon Hill Brahmins were feudal lords and workers were little more than non-unionized, rightless serfs. A bygone era, they said, which was true. In the new world order, the new underground workforce was as rootless as it was rightless, belonging to nothing, to no shrunken, compromised unions, much less to the land, and Lumpy had been part of it long enough to know the best chance was to head further underground. And so he did, sweating with furrowed brow as he commanded thick, awkward fingers to work the louvers of the antique machine, catching and pinching off bits of his flesh that regardless left him undeterred.

Stacks of unpackaged, shining silver sticks of gum surrounded him with a disorganized spillage like distorted dominoes falling on the floor, strewn across the makeshift sawhorse and plywood worktable in the former parlor of the Arlington Edwardian that was now the gum production room. The weedy, scrawny, fawn-like man known as Dr. Benway paced wildly about the space, despairing of ever getting Lumpy to leave. He wrung his hands and hunched, stooped, then stretched up and paced, skirting Lumpy at his perch.

"Listen, umm Lumpy—"

"Filmore," he grunted, fighting to master the apparatus with sausage fingers that slipped and fumbled at each small lever. Naked sticks of gum flew bent from his fingers. "I am not Lumpy no more." He said it, knowing full well he would always be Lumpy. People would never stop calling him that. It was simply how their nature coped with his.

"Filmore, we can't do this."

Boiling sweat, Filmore Lakeworry growled, "We-will-do-it!"

"But Malek—the Ork—they don't want it. We can't take them on. There's just two of us, for God's sake!"

Lumpy worked the gum without pause, making two mangled sticks for every single one folded, stacked, then dumped in a small bundle into the sliding collector chute to be plastic foil wrapped with the hard stamp of a pedal. "Listen, you and me, we make our own crew, Dr. Benway. You're the brain, I'm the muscle. The rest will work out as we go. It's not so hard to figure."

Benway attacked the table violently, causing naked gum to fall to the floor. Lumpy went on undeterred, mastering the wrapping. "Goddamn it, it's done. Malek gave me a thumbs down. Now I'm a candidate for Gary Lee Obidowski's Garage, and so are you, Heap."

"Don't call me Heap, neither. Call me Filmore, please. It's not much to ask."

"Filmore—whatever—we're over. It's done."

"Not over until I say."

"You're not listening!"

Lumpy looked up and smiled. He nevertheless fumbled the gum. "You know, I hear pretty good—maybe better than you. No need to shout, be rude."

"Look, Filmore, I barely escaped from the basement of Armenian Specialties two days ago. The muscle was taking me down to the garage. You know what that means. Lucky for me, it turned into some kind of major clusterfuck for hitters. If that lone gunman hadn't shown up looking like some half-dead scarecrow and coming on like Clint Eastwood, you'd have broken every bone in my body by now."

Lumpy shrugged. "It could have gone that way."

"It would have."

"God makes funny jokes."

"Yes, and usually I get to write them, but not this time. Now, I'm like a ghost, a shadow, a silverfish at the edges of the filing drawer. No registered ID, no prints on file, three sets of passports, birth certificates, licenses, no credit history, disposable social security numbers. This house isn't even on the tax rolls and the title is historied and pedigreed under the name Freddy Cannon."

"Buzz-Buzz-A-Diddle-It. Tallahassie Lassie. So?"

"So, you found me, anyway."

"I tracked you. I always want to know where everyone does business with the Ork lives. Just in case."

"In case of what?"

"In case of anything."

"That makes no sense."

"You don't get the gang logic, do you, Doc? Now, if you'd a survived a place like Assault 'n' Stall when you was coming up, you'd know by now how to be ten steps ahead of the guy holding that motherfuckin' knife to your throat. But you not that way, not you, no, you the type meant to be a punk, which is why I'm here. Can't have just a punk do this gum alone. No way."

Benway blinked, as he strained to think like Lumpy for a moment. It just didn't work. "The point is, you found me, they'll find me."

"Don't worry. We find them first, then it'll be okay."

"Okay? You call a bunch of fucking hitters coming down here to make grease spots out of both of us, okay?"

"We take it to them, not them take it to us." More gum came out, neat and clean, as lumpy interpolated a greasy rag into the process to mop up the blood from the plentiful little wounds in his fingers. He stepped up production, peddling furiously, his thick arms stubbornly straining and bulging at the material of his denim jacket in an effort to keep up.

Benway wet his finger, adjusted his horn-rimmed glasses and proclaimed as if he had the power to do so. "I'm going away now, Lumpy, and that's it. You can have it all. The house, the gum—take all of it. Hold court here for all I care. Whatever you do, I'm lighting out through Canada and up through Vancouver Isle out onto the west coast of the US."

"Maybe later you will, sure. But for now, you go nowhere, Doctor, or I'll hurt you bad. You know I can do that easy. And not just for calling me Lumpy, either. You know I can stop you way before you ever make it out the door. No trying involved."

Their eyes met and Benway's gaze broke away almost immediately.

"So, you're gonna make us have a last stand against the muscle of the Ork right here—Boston's worst and biggest crew? You just want to call them all down, and have them annihilate you so I can watch, so that later they can drag me back to Gary Lee's garage— make some repairs until I wind up another tortured corpse in the muddy Charles. Good thinking, Filmore. One hundred odd mooks against two. There's a plan."

Lumpy held up a shining stick of wrapped gum, smiling, widened his fish-eyes without blinking, shook his head slowly side to side and said. "No, Dr. Benway. Way I got it figured, it'll be like maybe 100 odd mooks versus about as much of this fucking city as ol' Lumpy wants."

Benway's face went blank after he got Lumpy's thought. It was a small, clear, fleeting thought, and he almost missed it. But when he got it, he knew what it meant instantly and its meaning was crazier than the fear of the half-dead scarecrow that Malek the Mallet no doubt had by now.

"Tell me, what happened to Gary Lee Obidowski."

"He retired to Florida when Malek bought him out."

"Bullshit. Malek doesn't do that."

"Sure he does, Cochese. I swear we sent him to a real nice place near New Smyrna Beach." He pronounced Smyrna as "some-earn-a."

"Where is that?"

"Near Orlando, Daytona."

"Nice," said Benway absently.

"'Course, you know we had to send him there in about forty-seven different suitcases, though."

Benway sighed. "I suppose I did know."

With that, Lumpy gave him a wink, with a broad smile that cracked like a fault-line across his even broader F-A-S Mic-Mac face and went back to working the gum.

———

The fucker Null was nothing.

That was all Andromeda had, working Null as he worked six other just as muddled, just as dead-ended cases. This was what they stuck him with, even at OC. This was the thankless task he had been bribed to do in service to LaCuna, the Ork and by the forces down at One Schroeder close to his eminence, mayor Tommyknockers. The better you were, the worse the work you got turned out to be. He was made early on for a talented baggage-handler, so early on the bad tasks kept falling his way. That was how he made public relations as a patrolman. That was how he made detective, no beat ever having been walked.

All he had really discovered so far on this drudge run was that Null was dead before he ever had lived.

His father died a rank-and-file casualty of the Winter Hill Gang over a small time dope burn. Prostitute Mom died hard in a knife fight with a john, but not before white-haired, portly and florid-faced Eamon "Uncle Jimmy" Cuchulain had moved in to fuck his older sister and then pimp her out on the street. Innocent waif-like Joey started life as look-out, then graduated to runner, then did post doc' street work as the defunct Family's bagman of choice for all the lower order jobs. Blew it all on the ponies, touting a system that could never work, since it relied on an element of chance. Everyone who was anyone knew that in modern times there was no chance allowed in horseracing. Sure, sis was a National Merit Scholar. What did it get her but a berth in an AIDS hospice with Joey X "DQ" Null giving up a scholarship to Harvard, thinking he could extend her life with his nimble advocacy? He might as well have given himself a hotshot of horse right then and there.

As it is in the course of high stakes commerce, so it is in the business of the street. When you're fucked, you're fucked. Period. End of report.

Null had begun fucked. End of the line right from the start.

There's just no way written or theorized or whispered about in the dark alleys, broken bridges and lost cul-de-sacs of Boston to *un*fuck yourself. In Boston, as in most other narrow, cozened places stuck close by an unforgiving sea, fortune favors its own.

Yet wasn't Null in some way chosen, fucked as he was?

Yes, Andromeda had thought, zig-zagging his '99 Saturn through the traffic on 3A heading back from Fields Corner, Uphams Corner, Codman Square and other doomed mostly race-mixed South Shore ghetto enclaves of wolf pack crews that made up much of the bottom end of the nation's secret economy.

Yes, Null was chosen, alright.

Chosen for crime, solitude and death.

His ex-wife murdered by Family hitters, Wednesday and Pugsley Impetigo, smothered to death under 500 puffy pounds of Wednesday's obese feminine charm. Uncle Jimmy taken out likely enough by Thing LeCoeur, a much tidier smother job wherein the old pimp pegged out, choking on his own vomit. Null himself done slowly to a turn, disemboweled in Cousin It Cavilli's dentist's chair. Hospitalized, a hopeless catatonic after three solid months of non-stop torture, wherein a finger was severed, a testicle removed, a hamstring sliced through, fingernails yanked free, a drill sunk into his flesh up to the bit again and again—a host of precise and angry pains delivered against him until his consciousness broke free like a helium balloon relinquished by a child and gone forever.

Like a scene out of Fritz Lang's "M."

In its merciful way, pneumonia carried off what was left of his body as he lay wrecked in a hospital bed in deep psychosis, and that was that.

All well and good.

So, who was Dr. Benway then, the geek-mook who passed himself off as a psych' resident and who worked Null right into an early grave with a bogus new therapy for catatonia?

And who then if not Null was the lone hitter that took out the Family like a hot knife cutting through butter?

No mercy, no hesitation, no mistakes.

And who was it then that Boyd would have shattered his collarbone for with a single distance shot from a scope rifle, in order to prevent him from capping the cerebral cortex of the deadly ace hitter, whoever the fuck he was. Who if not DQ Null, dimwitted, decoy informant in a game far larger than his niggling comprehension of heroin baggies and the Racing Form could ever embrace?

The only person who might know was stone crazy—

Which was the reason why he aimed the Saturn straight for Lemuel Shattuck State Rehab, for what he expected would only be some weirdly cryptic and disconnected answers. All part of a thorough kill, all part of leaving nothing to chance.

All part of wholesale death delivered directly to the retail provider.

Andromeda's badge got him access to the day room with a minimum of fuss. He came to the place of the marginally functional crazies, depressives, mopes and dopes armed with hot cocoa. He came to the last gasp of the once much-feared number one crime power of the streets, the Family, to meet its one remaining ranking soldier. The behemoth in the purple robe and gleaming, thinning grease-black hair sat slack in a chaise-longue baking his well-leathered face in the sun, lolling the stub of a dead cigar up and down with his pouch of a mouth, his thin lips making a tight seal about the butt as it moved. His eyes squinted into the light, his head bobbing slightly with a muffled chuckle stuck in his throat.

Nadio Solecise, better known as Uncle Fester the Confessor, kiddie porn lord, blackmailer, enforcer, loan shark leg-breaker, ace hitter, now the last remaining survivor of Joseph Xavier Null's alleged vendetta against the now defunct Family.

Andromeda handed him the cocoa as he sat down on the ottoman by his swollen, venous calves.

"Drink it slow, Fester. It's hot."

"Thanks, scumbag. Like you think you actually fooled us with your mope act. That'll be the fuckin' day."

"I was doing just fine, Fester, and you know it. But as we both know, I was superseded. You had much bigger problems than me."

"Fuckin' mutt," Fester mumbled, sipping cocoa resonantly through his teeth."

"Yeah, he's a fuckin' mutt alright."

"You got no fuckin; idea about that shitbird. He's got no scruples about killin' anyone for any reason. Mutt don't care, like one those scum-bum Al-Qaeda's and ISIS's. But colder, sneakier, the little prick."

Andromeda leaned in and whispered: "Is that right? Think he can hear you, Fes'? Think he's still watching you and knows? Think he's listening in right now, like he's the goddamn NSA?"

Fester's eyes went wide.

A blur distracted Andromeda, made him jerk left an inch.

It was the cup of cocoa sailing past him only to carom against the elongated, capped head of a recently medicated schizophrenic who was too slow to react. The cocoa cup splattered against solarium glass and male constable attendants in blue security uniforms came, warded off by Andromeda flashing his badge.

"Your story is that DQ fucking Null came back from the dead to wreak revenge on The Family."

"Old news, fuckstick. He already did that. I'm the last one. The only capo left, and when I beat the kiddie porn, murder, attempted murder and RICO charges with the whacked monkey routine I'm doing here, I'll be back running things and that fucking Mutt will be a throw rug in my outer office."

"Unless he kills you first."

Fester chuckled cagily.

"Nah, he's not gonna kill me, not as long as I keep pumpin' intelligence into his Irish white ass. Not as long as he thinks I'm crazy and punked out enough to wet his little ear with all the things he wants to hear." Fester rocked his head like a black bear rending a salmon, sniggering his anticipated triumph over his tormentor.

"You've got some time left to visiting hours, don't you, Fes'?"

"You're here, ain't ya?"

"I'm different. I'm the law."

"There is no law, fuckwad. We both know that."

"No, there are laws Fes'. It's just that the laws we live by you have to know in your ass—like a boot from your old man. Otherwise your ass gets served on a platter to the more successful rats what know that cold."

"Okay, fuckstick, whatever you say. But your bein' here tells me a lot. For instance. It tells me you have a job of work to do for the scuzzball who owns your ass down at One Schroeder."

"I'm here on police business, sonny boy."

Fester belched and stuck out his beefy tongue, rolled it then retracted it back into his slack lipped pouch of a mouth. "Semi-police business, maybe you mean. Pally, there ain't no flies on me and I'll tell yez why: You're here as bag man for that wall-eyed freak Malek just like DQ Fucking Null was a bagman for me back in the day."

With a sigh, Andromeda buried his fist into Fester's pallid yet beefy face, sinking sagging lips in below yellowed teeth and drawing if not spattering blood. The twenty-something constable rushed over with the brio of a bouncer on steroids to deal with this, and Andromeda kicked his legs out from under him without a thought before he could make a sound, watching him go down comically while Fester blubbered bloodily with laughter. When the constable got up looking like he might rush Andromeda, the detective pulled his Ruger 44 semi-automatic from his shoulder holster, aiming the black hole at the end of the barrel straight at the tip of his bulbous nose. The constable flinched and stayed down. Andromeda smiled broadly, then holstered his weapon smoothly.

"Simmer down, kid. Fester-boy here don't need no help here, do ya Fezzy?"

Fester snuffled into a bloodied napkin juicily: "Fuckin' A."

"You don't need no lawyer, do you, shit-heel?"

"Nope," Fester said, muted with a jarring liquid snuffle into the bloody napkin.

The constable shuffled off in his ill-fitting uniform, looking at Andromeda poisonously over his shoulder, then snapping his head to the front as soon as Andromeda caught this.

"I'm gonna visit with you a while more, Fes. You care?"

"Like I got a choice." He stuffed the saturated napkin up one nostril and tilted his head back to stop the bleeding.

"Like you do."

"Fuck, this crazy routine made me fucking stupid. I shoulda seen it. It's righteous obvious. Oh, I gotta get out of here before I lose my edge all together."

"What do you mean?"

Fester fell prey to a coughing jag that hocked up blood, which soon transformed into a chuckle.

"You ain't here as a bag man, Pally. You is here as a button man."

After this fact lay leaden in the air for two minutes, nothing further was said between them. Nearly an hour later, as Andromeda was dozing off, Fester got up from his lounge chair, animated and attentive. He began speaking shakily, almost frantically, falling all over himself as if in the presence of a senior mob boss or a celebrity.

Or some person or being he was terribly afraid of—

Null!

Andromeda bolted up and had the Ruger out and cocked with a round in the chamber ready to fly. But he did nothing. Instead, he stood transfixed in a kind of awe.

Fester was backpedaling, making excuses, apologizing, dickering and speaking in servile tones with trumped up laughter to absolutely no one. There was nobody there! With his gun extended, he stood there trembling with rage and humiliation. That fucker Fester, he was either actually crazy or, *worse,* using him as a prop in his crazy routine. His knuckles went white around the handle of the gun.

Either way, he had been fucking had.

Either way, before leaving, he threw Fester the worst beating of his entire career, which none of the constables, by the time they were called, had the courage to stop in the face of his wildly waving Ruger and his repeated, "I'm-a-fucking-cop-god-damn-you!" status.

Either way, he left the huge former enforcer of what was once Boston's worst criminal crew a bloody, pulpy mess on the solarium floor as he strode off, hardly having worked up a sweat, looking for Null.

And when he found him, he would put two careful rounds right in Null's brain, neat as you please, and that was a steadfast promise he made to Jesus and Mary both as he lumbered into the front seat of the 99 Saturn and gunned her up hard.

TWELVE

The steaming, thick coffee splashed right in Malek's face and thirty-year-old arraignment pit-bull wunderkind Wat Tyler Schulman called it quits right then and there. "Interview over, peeps!" he shouted affably, his short, wide, impossibly shouldered powerlifter's frame dancing to and fro nervously from classic wing tip to classic wing tip in his wide-lapelled post-hipster's zoot suit. His flaming red hair was slicked back with pomade tighter than a Parris Island marine's bunk tucked sharp with hospital corners.

"It's over when we say it's over, Watty." Boyd said this with glum resignation, replacing her now empty "Drink-up-you-have-a-better-chance-of-being-kidnapped-than-getting-married" coffee mug.

Wat smiled, shrugged, and pounded hard enough on the door to make the entire interview room shudder. Boyd was sure she felt the vibration in her knees. The door opened in a flash from the outside and Byron Wurdalaka leaned into the room with a hangdog look asking, deadpan, "Trouble, girls?"

"No trouble, detective," Wat said with blustery ease. "Nothing we ain't seen here before. Kindly charge Lieutenant Boyd over there with assault and battery on my client, release Mr. Turbot or fucking charge him please, and do it pronto so I can beat the shit out of the next case Major Crimes tries to make at arraignment in about twenty minutes." He looked at his watch and his face went slack. "Guys, we had better hurry. I could be wrong about the time."

Malek sat there at the long interview table, not even bothering to look at Boyd's smoke-stockinged legs as she swung them from the edge of the table where she sat. His knuckles went white, and he wept rivulets of murky coffee tears running down the dark-tan, exaggeratedly porous skin of his taut, angular face. An amber wraparound visor to protect his amblyopic left eye from all light cast a tinted shadow on already grim features.

"No charges," Malek seethed. "Not for me, not for them. Do your job and get me out of here."

"Oh, we'll charge you, Malek," Boyd said, sliding off the desk. "Don't you worry about *that*. What have you got on him, Byron?"

"Four floaters in the Channel, six corpses at Sang Froid, maybe more if this little fight for supremacy continues LT."

"Am I here at your little fucking tea party to listen to your bad jokes and your tawdry little fucking fantasies?" sneered Malek, dabbing a handkerchief at his face thoughtfully provided by Schulman. "Charge me or let me the fuck go. I didn't come here to be mocked and insulted."

Boyd smacked the wraparounds off his smug and mottled face with a wide stroke. Their eyes locked for a nanosecond, then they both simultaneously laughed as Wurdalaka eased in and sat in an aluminum polyethylene chair that was straight out of the seventies, his back set against the wall. Malek sighed, shook his head and buried it in both hands like an exasperated great uncle in the hands of the family misfits.

Detective Sergeant Bim Hundertwasser watched bemused, suspicious and uncertain as whether to laugh himself or to start knocking heads, his thick forearms crossed bullyboy style at his mastiff chest. He would never give up straight thug street cred' for PR, even for now abdicating Police Commissioner Queen Kathleen herself. Oh no. He knew who he was and anyone on the street who didn't, would.

"Malek, you came here for me to annihilate you like the seamy little water beetle you are. That's the only reason you're not in lockup now. How this happens is just a matter of time. Strictly speaking though, up to me, you don't leave here in one piece. Today."

Schulman grabbed Boyd's arm and wrenched her around to look him in the eye, except he was so short he wound up looking her in the neck. He ground his teeth and whispered loud. "You're getting in deeper than you want to go, Boyd. I'll subpoena room tapes and show this little farce to all. I'll bring IAD down on that nice coiffure like a Tsunami spillage of shit. You had better—"

Boyd pushed him off balance, Wurdalaka tripped him, never having had to get up to do it, and Hundertwasser caught him hard, slamming him against the wall. "Assaulting an officer is a legal taboo, counselor," he said, wrist-cuffing Schulman hard enough to leave marks.

Schulman was perplexed yet professionally conciliatory: "Guys, this is stupid. You know better than this. It's baseless crap that won't stand."

Hundertwasser pushed him back amiably and gave him a hard, measured shot to the thorax. "Ya? Maybe so, but you won't stand either, bub." And he caught him before he fell.

Schulman heaved.

"Get him the fuck out of here, Bim, book him, process him, then lose the ticket."

Hundertwasser herded the doubled over attorney out the door and down the hall, dragging him out as if he were a wounded calf.

Boyd got up from the edge of the table, wandered over to where Malek's visor had fallen, and replaced it on his stoic, dripping face. "You know, you started a goddamn war in my territory, you stupid cowardly little fuck," she said with a sort of clipped cheer. "You went and fucked everything with your territorial trafficking squabbles and now your ass is mine. Now and forever."

"But I don't know—"

Boyd was up and waving her arms at this as if the room cameras really were working, which they never did.

"You don't know, you don't know—blah-fucking-blah. Everyone knows you know."

Malek stood up. "Make it stick, then, you bitch. But for now, with no attorney and no charge, I'm out."

"I'll make what's left of you stick to a far wall at Concord Reformatory, don't worry."

Malek went to the door to the hall and jiggled the locked knob angrily. "Come on, you no good hacks, open the fucking door. Time to book me or let me *book!*" Malek spun back around expecting a rabbit punch and with a crafty turn at the corners of his impassive mouth bragged, "No matter what you do, whatever bullshit hummer charge you stick me with, I'll be out by dark. It don't matter if you make Schulman a human Jacuzzi for every jocker boyo down at Concord Reformatory that wants to jump in. Lawyers are like laptops—pricey at the beginning, useful until you throw the damn thing out the window and get yourself something faster, better and cheaper. I got another Lawboy booting up in the lobby even as we speak. He'll be here if I ain't out in an hour, stupid clowns." He sat back down at the table as if he were ready to negotiate. He smiled. "So what do you wanna do until? Game of pinochle? See who's got the biggest dick? So far, I think it's between me and the Lieutenant."

Boyd punched Malek right in the face so blood splashed out from the sides. His eyes went as dead wide as a shark's and he gulped air hard.

Wurdalaka sat back flat against the wall and snickered in that grating gutter Boston style. "You ain't figured it out yet, Chief, have ya? No matter what the fuck you do, no matter how good the fucking lawyer you got is, no matter if he's from goddamn Hale and Dorr or Dewey, Cheatham and Howe. Simple fact is motherfucker: You ain't got nothing coming!"

Hundertwasser dangled a clean handkerchief before Malek who swiped at it like a truculent kitten. Boyd shook one hand limply in the other and whined a few soft curses.

"What's the matter LT?" Wurdalaka asked, his heels now up on the edge of the table. "You break a nail?"

"You're psychic, Byron. That's it exactly. I broke a nail on that fucking mutt's face, and I just hate that."

Malek was laughing with his face mashed into the wadded handkerchief. "You broke more than that, Boyd. Say goodbye to your career. You broke it all just to take a swipe at a piece of shit like me. You took yourself down a peg and raised me up about fifty. Fuck all, I should put you on the payroll too!" Despite the satisfied mirth in his voice it sounded as if he were talking into a boot.

Wurdalaka, Hundertwasser and Boyd all laughed.

"They don't make 'em like they used to do they," observed Hundertwasser.

"No, they sure don't."

Wurdalaka got up, stretched, paced and offered an explanation. "Listen, fuckstick, you need to stop watching so many cop shows and reading them Harvard boy mysteries. This is the fucking machine shop where fingers and toes get blown off and no one gives a rat's ass. There ain't no room tape, never has been, never gonna be. We either tape your confession, you write it, we write it up, or there's nothing. No record, no impartial oversight. All you got is three decorated stand-up cops grilling a punk local crew badass not long for this world no matter what happens. Your lawyer? Well, he's a tyro—got out of hand and we put him in protective custody. How did we know the fucking ticket would get lost and that he'd get mis-routed to Concord? We're just cops you know, not the brightest bulbs on the tree. We ain't that great with paperwork, just ask the Globe. Meanwhile, while your new Lawboy boots up downstairs, I could slip my new 45 Ruger here out of its holster, shove it neatly up your ass, blow your entrails out through your eye sockets and IAD would clear the shoot in six months without blinking. Not even the Weekly Dig would bat an eye. Just an unfortunate mishap affecting a deserving felon. Hey, shit happens."

"'Tragedy and Inquiry at One Schroeder' I can see the backpage header now," quipped Boyd. "Not even a star-billing death."

Malek sighed. "The old days is over, ain't they?"

"Over like the Family, fuckstick. Over like Gomez Gomelsky and crew."

"Over like your Armenian ass, you don't give us the skinny on this war right quick. Over like your goddamn testicles for calling me a bitch!"

Malek released his death grip on the wadded handkerchief pressed to the center of his face and laughed and laughed and clapped his hands as the bloody thing fell to the tabletop. "Oh, you guys are way too good to be working here. I have *got* to see to it to get you all a better gig. Why I should be shaking in my custom Gucci booties. What choice do I got—I come across, or I become a mishap?"

"Comes the dawn," said Boyd. "Maybe I'll do it myself."

Malek rolled the bloody handkerchief into a ball and hit the gunmetal gray wastepaper basket in a single arc with an offhand toss. "So, you're as bad as me."

"Worse," muttered Boyd.

"Oh good. I wouldn't have to feel so bad then if one or even a few of my guys catches you alone sometimes and decides to fuck you to death then brings me the head so I can fuck out what's left of your eyes. I mean, you might consider something like that as being '"fair is fair'."

Boyd unholstered her Sig-Sauer and slid it across the table toward Malek, primed, loaded, condition zero. She got down to his level, narrowed her eyes, and glared at him. He took her meaning right away. They had reached the crux of the event and there was no backing down or undoing it. This was unadulterated street, informed and educated by the prison yard. There were few moves to be made here, and yet they had to be made quickly. If he just sat there, Hundertwasser and Wurdalaka would throw him a truly professional beating, and even if he won that beating without grabbing for the gun, they would likely shoot him, anyway.

"Well, what's it to be, bitch?" Malek smiled broadly because he knew at that moment that things had come round his way.

Hundertwasser and Wurdalaka's guns rose up.

Malek spoke jovially. "Well, Lieutenant, then I guess I had better tell you a few things."

And so he did.

Malek made it clear that there was no war, and then he proceeded to make it clear exactly why there was no war, and for good measure tied in something about a new drug some whack-job crock doc tried to get him to push out through his channels to the street. Thanks, but no thanks. Who needs the grief?

Malek talked and talked, happily, volubly with bonhomie and charm and left free and easy, albeit bloody and rumpled and dabbing at his face as you please.

When he was gone, alone in that drab institutional room stinking of piss, sweat and fear, Boyd broke down and cried inexplicably on Wurdalaka's shoulder, much to his confusion and chagrin. She couldn't tell him why, but it was all there looming in the air like some cheesy special-effects ghost from a Z-grade direct-to-DVD horror flick.

The nightmare she had started would never end and would always come back to her:

The nightmare of Null.

———

The nightmare awoke from empty dreams and unfulfilling sleep. And why not? He was sleeping the sleep of the unmedicated tweaker —the speed freak brought down by indifference and neglect. Dry and wisplike, Null became active in his Mattapan squat, kicked the floor panel he set up and pirated lights burned the air, humming like restless bugs. Kenny the kid was shivering deep in dreams in a corner of the floor near the bolted entry huddled against a duffle bag of collected weapons and guns from the late drug lord Heavy Cheese LePetomane and the now obeisant replacement called "Do- Rag." Null yanked him up and threw him in the shower, low-riding pants, filthy boxers and all.

The kid made noises of protest drowned out by the gruff and echoing wail of Howlin' Wolf"'s "Evil."

He dried himself with a ratty but surprisingly clean towel and helped himself to Null's threadbare set of Good Will Clothing discards neatly folded in an impromptu and homemade chifforobe painted as lead white as the walls of the squat. He squinted, watching the Lord God Almighty snort lines of meth off the clean dull metal face of a filed down machete.

Why not? If God could be a drug dealer, he could certainly snort crystal meth, whether he needed to or not. God did not object if he took some himself. It was a sacrament of sorts.

They hit Codman square, the harsh frost thick and gray in the dark morning air and Ken Embers asked shakily, "Is this the time?"

"It's always the time," said Null, reluctant God.

They ate at Bardu's Superette on Shawmut Ave, a grimy, seedy quickie mart and coffee shop for day laborers, all-night drunk pensioners, SSI derelicts and their unsupported hangers-on mixed in with the occasional shapeless and defiantly dignified transsexual prostitute. They ate two specials, Egg McNuttin's they were called, scrambled eggs wrapped in flatbread filled with mystery meat and grease and offal downed with coffee. They ate joylessly, mouths bitter and numb with meth, throats constricted and metabolisms pulsing.

Null dragged his persistent charge onto the cramped trolley car of the Ashmont line for the long, drudging ride into Park Street Station to change up shallow, narrow steps for the Green Line Cleveland Circle LRV. The kid was hardly conscious, Null propping him up with an iron-solid shoulder, herding him onto the car. He dragged the boy like a dreamer through the car, yanked some professorial dowd out of his seat and arranged his acolyte across it as he squirmed for purchase, reclining against the Plexiglas window. The kid clutched his hands in threadbare pockets, saying something about theology that was swallowed to a murmur by the groaning of the train.

The trolley dragged on above ground out of the mouth of the underground to the outskirts of Boston, up rills and ridges, following the wavy, tree-congested divergences of Beacon Street past Coolidge Corner and up through Washington Square, the stone Jewish section of town where old banks had been converted to delicatessens. When the trolley jerked to an unsettled stop, Null dragged Kenny Embers up on his feet, who rubbed his eyes and waved away the hands of his deity even as he was herded out the folding accordion door of the train.

It was on University off Beacon, a retrofitted help center—multi-service center it would have been called decades ago, with new MSWs and humanities graduates dealing with social awareness of issues of alternative sexuality, STDs, runaways, drugs, for a pittance or a stipend long ago when youth was far more epidemic. Now, the parcel of prime rental real estate was occupied by the Dapper O'Neil Shelter and Service Group, a final stopgap before the street for dispossessed gay men. This was where Null dragged him, the boy weaving in the street and in his mind still spoiling for a fight when there was no one there and nothing to fight at all.

The building was white-stoned at the façade, a snowy gray ivory with bits of soot-smudge dappling its contours, marred from the latter part of the century before last not quite as old as the building itself. There was a large, dome-ceilinged foyer that opened to a high, curved staircase not quite spiraled, whitewashed with a cheap undertone of blue. The hard wood floors were shellacked to a plastic sheen coating over speckled gouges of damage blackened with time. A cotton pseudo macramé area throw rug covered the center of the floor in crushed and rumpled disarray. A student sat reading Kant's Prolegomena at a gun metal gray institutional desk from 1952. The air had a carbolic, Lysol kind of tinge with motes of dust dancing in the air, defining the light from the high, unshuttered windows and a chicken-wired oriel at the crest of the concave inner dome.

The student, a pudgy dreadlocked hermaphrodite in Wallabys and loose blue shirt tails over olive drab khakis, placed down the Prolegomena and disappeared into a side room, mumbling something in a half decipherable patois. Taking his place just in time to dodge a flailing Kenny Embers was a stocky woman in a knockoff Donna Karan business suit wearing wire trifocals resting heavily on her nose and an incongruously filigreed blouse that bunched up at the stomach right where her skirt tapered in. "Can you get him into my office on your own, or do you need help?"

"He don't need no help," heaved Kenny.

"No he don't," assented Null.

The woman shambled off to high ceilinged, cramp-walled side room sparsely decorated with cracked plaster and paint of a dirty cerulean blue and plumped down behind an ancient mahogany institutional desk blackened with age, opened a manila file and began scribbling, ignoring the heavy tilted screen of an outdated computer monitor glowering down on her.

"This is the candidate?" she asked.

"It is," grunted Null, pushing his unwanted charge down into an aluminum framed green Naugahyde mismatched chair.

"Candidate for what?" croaked Kenny.

"Residency," the woman mumbled, not looking up from the file. "Mr.—uh?" She cleared her throat.

"Null"

"Null. You realize that Kenny is going to be here for quite a while?"

Glazed eyes wide, Kenny shot up from his chair and Null grabbed him hard from behind, immobilizing both his arms. "Don't you have some milieu therapist type guys here to handle this?" he asked.

She recoiled from the melee, more practiced than shaken, and hit the low-tech wireless intercom added onto the side of the obsolete console phone. The male nurses trundled in, grabbed Kenny off Null's hands with a thick economy of motion. Kenny spat, and Null stood unruffled. Kenny kicked up both legs, Null deftly dodged his kiddie-sneakered feet and one nurse caught an elbow to the chin from Kenny's akimbo flailing.

"Watch out for the hands in his pockets," Null stated. "He has knives. Kid liked that character in that old Conan the Barbarian movie. The one that swung the double pig-stickers, one to a fist. Better hold him hard or he'll hug those blades right to your spleen."

They did and Null collected the knives, set them on the administrator's desk.

The Nurses dragged him off, his legs kicking out and back and he squirmed up arched from the torso. The male nurses, moonlighting bouncers or vice versa, barely twitched carrying him off to the Quiet Room.

"Rubber room?"

"Until he settles, then he gets his own room with a bed and some extras. A little comfort, if the dementia lets him feel it."

"It's gonna cost me."

"It doesn't have to, Mr. Null, but we only have resources for so many and a long list."

"Yes, of the well-connected, well-to-do. Sure. I'll play. Set him up good and you'll get our donation."

"This is hospice care, Mr. Null. It's usually not for the long term, certainly not in Kenny Ember's case, and what's left over from what you give goes down the line."

"There's no slowdown in death is there?"

"Not that I have ever seen."

"We have our work cut out for us, don't we, Mrs. Coelacanth?"

Her face darkened and puckered in a little, and she made a soft coughing sound.

"I have no idea what business you're in, Mr. Null. Mine is to hold back a tidal wave of tears with a rusty bathtub."

"Go easy, Mrs. Coelacanth. We're in like rackets together, you and I."

"And that would be what, Mr. Null?"

"I dry up that tidal wave you speak of and keep it from your door. I take care of the ones you never see—the ones you shouldn't see."

"And what about the one you dropped off here, then? What about him?"

Null was unchanged in demeanor—mathematicians, undertakers, and pathologists all had more passion in the throes of equations, embalming and autopsies than he showed in discussing what was presumed to be a torturously dying friend.

"Why, he's a mistake," Mrs. Coelacanth. "Just another mistake in a world where the wrong routinely run roughshod over the right."

"Very virtuously spoken ,Mr. Null, but we've no place for high morals in the house of death."

"Yes. So I'm aware."

"And you leave this mistake with us and flit off—we hope for the sake of a donation."

"Yes, exactly. I'll be donating the bodies of those who made the mistake in the first place straight into the earth."

Mrs. Coelacanth looked pale watching him turn and step out, neither happy nor sad, heavy nor light, just a blur of a soft-spoken man with no really distinguishing features (other than scars) who might as well have been nothing and no one at all.

———

Toad and Badger came along briskly from the shadows on the dark thoroughfare toting a box of tricks meant to produce a diversion on their way to meet up with Ratty and Mole, or so it seemed in the sooty twilight by the jungle-like treescape of the twisted paths that diverged and connected around Park Drive along the Fens. They were, in silhouette, charming anthropomorphic grotesques out of Kenneth Grahame's Wind in the Willows, meant to delight and frighten children in a mildly threatening absurdity building toward a comic climax of unresolved violence. And though they were criminals of the hardest kind, that was exactly what they were intending to do as they trundled a dark, heavy box toward the old 1270, a gay club that abutted the schizoid duplex of two others like it: Ramrod and Machine.

What they were intending to do was to mildly frighten and move the gay sex children and chicken hawks of the clubs into a clot of distracting violence to block the arteries of intrigue.

What they intended to do was to survive a meet with Malek the Mallet and the muscle of the Ork, set in principle to dicker out the drugs but in reality was to be just another whack out session to put an end to the wayward inconvenience of Lumpy's master plan.

Lumpy was settled in his mind to whack them out first.

He was going to ambush the ambush and Benway, seeing this, was cannily going along for the ride until he could find a way to serve Lumpy up to the thugs and use him as cover to make a clean break for it and get out on the fast express to Canada.

Benway had plans for the gum, and they didn't include crime crew retribution and a quest for human connectivity relieved by the freeing impulse of breaking heads. They didn't include making Filmore Lakeworry a loved, accepted and valued member of the social order, and they didn't include both of them being schlumped, dumped and buried by the paranoid Malek the Mallet and the Muscle of the Ork.

They did, however, include a whack out on Lumpy and a Canadian getaway with the gum for a foray at the club scene in Toronto —the Canadian ballet, or lap dancing circuit ruled by the Russian mob in that city. They would be easier to deal with than Malek and his crazy-quilt operational terror /aversion of the authorities, keeping them at bay with discretion and stealth when anyone could tell you that the authorities who counted for anything were for sale to the last man, or woman, anyway. Yes, he even believed OC Taskforce Director Kay Boyd had her price, but Malek would rather appease the opposition by whacking out members of his own crew than risk being at odds with a corrupt city government and its jackbooted, thug-bellied police.

Typical Boston.

You couldn't even trust the nature of its own corruption.

Caught for a moment under the blistering street neon, held in relief against the trees and bushes, Toad and Badger became more Lumpy and Benway, looking at once ridiculous and malevolent in the sharp star whiteness of the light, their hard cargo of gum swaying into the shadows like a thick pendulum. A motion detector froze open the light, harsh and fierce, only for a moment, like lightning in a silent storm, and they both stopped dead. Then Lumpy let out with an inarticulate bark or cry meant to startle some beast or drive motion itself perhaps back into being and the two of them trundled the weighty box across Boylston Street directly into a broken pavement alley by a back lot for illicit parking, garbage and the scurrying of rats, human and otherwise. They dropped the box in sandy, graveled dust, which made weedy Benway cough pathetically as Lumpy reached for a rusted crowbar he didn't have to feel for to grasp hard by the bulkhead, of which he used the hooked-end to yank its metal doors open.

A voice cried out displeasure in the usual Boston honk: "Hey, whatcha doin' thay-uh?"

Lumpy was cool. He exhorted, "Just a delivery, man! Cub Group, they know all about this—something special from your friends down at Symphony." It was right Boston code, invoking both the company whose silent majority owner was the Ork and then again code for the Ork itself. It was a happily recited double threat announcement that invited no retort.

"Don't drop it," warned the honk.

Too late. The box slammed down with bang to the dry, compacted earth floor of the basement. Lumpy jumped down from the bulkhead's opening, bypassing wooden plank steps while Benway crabbed down gingerly. Lumpy had his arm behind his back clutching his gun, an anonymized snub-nosed thirty-eight with fingerprint proof tape around the handle, a quick discard. Benway bent down nervously, securing the box. One of the young hip-hop thugs from Southie or Dorchester in a spotless white tank top over some kind of cloth prison jeans, looking like a dapper pantaloon clown, stepped up and faced them, hair so slicked with mousse it glistened as if studded with rhinestones in the sharp wooden yellow of the basement light.

"Watcha gut thay-uh, chief?"

"Got a big, good night for you, dollface? And I ain't no chief." Lumpy made a smooching sound.

The thugboy, who obviously worked at the club tending bar helping the DJ run cords and cables, gaffing, manning any and every other chore at the pleasure of the managers, possibly unpaid but by suspect barter—backstage passes, drugs, VIP access—had no time to question Lumpy's explanation. He was poised to make a remark, but then was smartly elbowed straight in the face, then punched in the spleen with such speed and sureness that Benway had almost no time at all to avoid being knocked down by his falling body.

Lumpy motioned for Benway to grab his feet and together they dragged the thugboy into the open walk-in refrigerator. Thugboy started to rally but Lumpy bent down and cracked him one hard to the jaw, and he stayed down instead, blood trickling out his nose onto the cool, widely divided wooden planks that kept boxes of wine and snacks and kegs of tap beer above a pool of foul dark water resting beneath.

"What now?" Benway asked, failing not to quaver.

He grinned: "Freebies, baby. We just giving this shit away!"

———

Do-Rag was running down Tremont (pronounced Tree-mont) in the South End. His face was on fire with streaks and forced points of burning that were actually nothing but cold sweat catching the air but which had blossomed all over his body just a few minutes ago.

And why shouldn't it?

After all, he had just met with death face-to-face for the second time in his life and would live to tell about it.

That is, he would live to tell about it if he made no further mistakes. Trouble is, being terrified rendered him prone to making further mistakes. And making mistakes is not something you can survive doing in the meth trade very long. He was more nervous about this than he was about carrying the half pound of crank under his arm that could put him away down at MCI Walpole for about twenty years. He was hustling his way to the no-name crib where Gangsta Boyz piped up and did business. He was going to pitch a room full of street-mean sociopaths as wild as himself, full of grit and fear and cunning, and try to turn them to a meth distribution crew under a new boss they'd never met much less heard of or cared about.

He needn't have worried.

There were blood spatters and bodies by the time he cried "Yo-yo!" through the reinforced door left curiously ajar. Girlish distorted divas in heavy makeup were tending to the two bodies, as if they were still alive. The rest of the young men in the room and their smaller fauns looked shell-shocked, but when Do-Rag started stammering out the new plan they were attentive with a newly serious intent to listen. Some conspicuously had blood on their faces and spattering leathers and boots. Some just had a look on their faces from which only one thing could have been concluded:

Null had been to visit.

THIRTEEN

With executive thoroughness, Toad and Badger, Lumpy and Benway, situated bundles of gum strategically about the club; at the entrances to the upper and lower floors, the VIP entrance up above and the main entrance off the street, doing their best to blend in with the mopes and early gawkers, hip-hop baggy-pantsed and clean tee-shirted thugboys staking out their territory for the night. Then the two separated, parting ways to more effectively bribe the lanky twink boys to spread gum throughout the club. Lumpy hugged them hard, whispered in their ears, stuffing wads of cash in their jeans. Benway palmed them the money, keeping a nervous distance.

Weapons came next, which, of course, was the reason for their basement entrance in the first place. They had to prepare for a meet with the Muscle of the Ork. Both of them knew just what kind of meet this would be, and it wouldn't be a tensely peaceful sit-down.

No, this was going to be a whack-out fest.

Lumpy taped a 30-clip AR-15 pistol under the main table in the cramped and velveteen VIP room, taped curved buck knives under each seat and a Taurus 709 nine-millimeter atop the liquor cabinet that held whatever it was the club treated as private stock.

Benway had a French serrated edge switchblade in each pocket, squeezing the ceramic handles of the knives as he walked the club, pacing out of place and stodgy, reeking of being either a narc or some pervo-creep way out of his depth. Actually Benway was in his element—that buffer zone of prescient sureness just before the chaos storm of violence hit. And he had a core of calm to cling to just as he clung to the handles of his knives, knowing the Ork wanted their renegade soldier/enforcer/garage-torturer Filmore Lakeworry much, much more than they wanted the dweeby, reedy mad chemist, architect of the flawed and useless gum. Benway was a nuisance who failed to make them the money promised and brought down Boston's Finest Slime in Blue upon them—true—but Lumpy, well…

Lumpy was a threat.

And the gum itself was a mystery they had yet to figure out but would soon.

Lumpy danced, bumping twinkboys with his wide hips while Benway paced and fretted, and then the muscle of the Ork petered in.

They had no fear of making it a gun show. The cops were bought down to the one undercover blending in at the Men's room to roust out a twink or two for Ex or coke, amyl nitrate or crack. Roscoe Blank—the biggest of them—brandishing a Ruger forty-five nine mil. Special, nodded to a manager conspicuously using a tablet to track the scene, who waved them over to the VIP room. The muscle of the Ork elbowed and shouldered their way through the awkwardly moving crowd doing their warm-up trance dance and filed into the private room, weapons unholstered and drawn before they shut the door to block out the synth whine sex thump dance noise.

They got the knives and AR 15 under the seats, no problem.

Lumpy grabbed Benway off a panting, sweating twink boy who seemed to be having a panic attack and gave Benway a panic attack all his own. He nevertheless still had it in him enough to stuff the twink's pants pockets and waistband with shiny packets of the gum.

"What the fuck?" keened Benway over the music.

Lumpy spoke slow but loud. "Is it time to be sociable yet?"

Pushing out of Lumpy's grip, and whining: "They're here to whack us out, genius. There's NO good time to be sociable."

Benway dusted himself off as if Lumpy carried a contagion, like anthrax or typhoid.

"No, no, you're the genius, Benway boy. And you know exactly what I mean. When the fuck does it kick in?"

"They get the kick in about ten minutes and I'm armed, by the way, so don't get cute like that again."

Together they coolly ascended steps to the parapet where they hung at knife point with a very nervous geriatric twink boy DJ until Benway gave the sign it was about to break. "We better get in there soon, hombre, or there may not be any way of getting out." Lumpy nodded and they hustled back down to the VIP room, bracing two of the muscle on their way, Lumpy with short a punch to the abdomen and Benway with a curved German Solingen steel blade up the gut, taken back as fast as it was delivered.

Another of the muscle was blustering through the crowd but was stopped by a wave of fists and rubber-soled feet.

The dance crowd was breaking into small riots.

Something was building; the air was electric and copper-tinged as if with blood.

At that exact moment Lumpy chose to kick in the door, weaponless, Benway dragged along and trembled behind.

"Hey, it's party time, chief!"

Roscoe set the terms. "Get the fuck in here and give us the rest of that gum and whatever cash you got from trying to turn it, and maybe Malek won't make you revisit Gary Lee Obidowski's garage to eat a drill-bit sandwich." They each held up a knife like a candle, smiling, and Roscoe drew down at the door with the assault rifle. "We found that you left us these, you fucking mutant dwarf Indian moron. Party favors just for us?"

"Yeah", said Lumpy, grinning. "You'll get what's coming, believe me."

"Give us what's left of the gum, that fuck Benway, who screwed it all up anyway made, and get the fuck outta the district. Hit the Canadian trail."

"Hey, where's that fuckin' party?" Lumpy asked with jacked up faux innocence.

"The party's up your whore mother's fuckin' ass where my dick was last night."

Screaming and banging erupted during the pause, and the door to the room, though locked, sounded as if it might jiggle open at any second.

"This was the sitdown, the meet, and this is how you handle it?" Lumpy lamented. "What's the goal? Money and drugs, but what do you get? A gay club fart. But sometimes, guys, just for playing, there's a consolation prize, you know. Lucky you."

Benway, hiding on his knees at the back end of the table behind his partner, had his own Bushmaster AR 15 set between Lumpy's legs and let loose under the table with a 60-clip, blowing away feet and knees and groins and hanging guts. Then the door burst open and a sea of angry, ranting bloody-faced twinks, rentboys and hip-hop Harrys, pants down at their knees and below, swirled into the room, pushing Lumpy back to where the Taurus assault rifle lay taped at the private stock cabinet. He grabbed the barrel, thrust himself atop the cabinet and gutturally squealed with delight, "Motherfucker, ain't we got fun!"

Then he sprayed the room with nine-millimeter exploding Teflon rounds.

The Muscle of the Ork was quickly reduced to a ghastly sort of human mush, a collage of medical surgical debris.

Benway was flat on the floor, his bird-cage chest heaving, breathing hard, clawing linoleum, and Lumpy grabbed him up by the wrist. "Twinkle-toes, you and me gots to book!"

The club had suddenly twisted into a fleshy tornado of violence, blood, piss and flesh flying this way and that. There was simply no way to get through it without being ground down to a pulp by its sheer weight, volume, and force. So they didn't go through it. They slid under it. They dropped back down to the basement, angling their way out the same way they came in, each hoisting up rungs to the back alley through the still-open bulkhead. Then a gentle tableau: Toad and Badger, stooped over and cautious under the sharp white light of the arched street lamps, scampering across the Fenway toward the dark, rich wood of the Fens, disappearing with barely a rustling of leaves back into the deep, black sheltering shade of the bowing trees.

———

"I am going to give you back your humanity."

Malek the Mallet, sitting alone in his darkened office, jerked forward as if from a dream at the sound of this intruding voice. His amblyopia was bad today, so the dark provided scant comfort, even while he wore his amber wraparound eye visor with the opaque left lens. The sparse Danish modern furnishings seemed a fanciful blur, like a stage setting of a kind, remote and sliced away from the action at their center.

"It's a gift you can't refuse."

Malek lit a smoke, tossed the match at where he guessed the source of the voice was, and missed.

"Take your gift and shove it up your ass. In fact, give me time and I'll do that for you."

"You should be grateful."

Malek spat. "You should be dead."

"I am," Null said dully.

"Don't get poetic with me, Pally. You're breathing. You're still acting like a boil on my ass."

"Is a virus really alive, Malek—a coelenterate or an amoeba, for that matter?

Malek growled with contempt, phony philosophy, doggerel poetry. He growled loudly, with spittle in contempt: "Get the fuck in here and whack this fuckstick, already, would ya!!"

"They're busy, Malek."

There was knocking and thudding, sliding, but no entry, no kicking in of the door, just a short burst of scuffling along the ground, then more thudding.

Malek was astonished: "They should be in here already, giving you a good goddamn rip-ass party!"

"First come first served, Malek," wheezed Null. Would you like to look outside for an accounting?

"What fucking accounting?"

"Two knee-cappings, a sucking chest wound, severed arm and foot, one evisceration. I think there was at least one decapitation."

Malek bolted up, pulled a Sig-Sauer, and squeezed off some rounds that flashed in the shadows until he started losing his breath, choking and making guttural grunts. The Sig-Sauer flopped down noisily to the table.

Null's fingers had met and crossed atop Malek's considerable Adam's apple and then squeezed in unhesitatingly. His struggling knocked the yellow wraparound visor clattering to the floor.

Pounding the table, Malek coughed out: "How is killing me going to restore my humanity?"

He spat blood.

Null released him, stepped back into the shadows.

Malek scrambled for the Sig-Sauer, shot twice behind him.

There was palpable silence, deafening after the explosions of the rounds.

"No, death won't restore your humanity to you—your sensitivity, empathy, vulnerability. Death is the sure cure for all that, even as I am surely cured of all that—the cure and the disease it leads to from which you suffer."

"Me too. So the fuck what?" Malek squeezed off more shots and missed.

"You see?" asked Null, wide eyed. "It's happening already."

"Suck my dick."

"You're afraid, which you should be. Good. It's a start—giving you back your humanity."

"C'mere and let me shove the barrel of this Sig up your goddamn zombie ass! That'll make you human!"

Null clicked his tongue, moved tremulously into the scant light of the room and threw Malek a long, brutal procedural beating, pounding certain parts of him so hard with the butt of the Sig, that a sloshing could be heard. Then he in turn flung it across the office like refuse once his subject was cooled out and down to a twitch and a moan on the floor.

Malek keened, "My fucking meth—the gak and the cash, you… zombie…fuck!"

Null knelt down and whispered into Malek's ear, "The gak and the cash are mine, Malek. It's over, so forget it. In fact, to tell you the truth, this whole town's mine. That's over too. And that you should etch very hard into your bleeding brain." Then he stood.

Malek sputtered some sort of sub-verbal argument. Null lit a cigarette, puffed hard, extracted it from his mouth and held it up as if to examine it.

Then he knelt back down and straight-arm smashed Malek in the mouth.

Still kneeling by him, Null produced an ice pick from his coat and casually stuck it through Malek's ribcage as if a magician skewering his assistant for show, prompting him to jerk up. Malek gaped blood out of his mouth in wide-bubbled foam, prompting him to squeal airily desperate obscenities as he reached clumsily for Null as if in total darkness. Null yanked the ice pick out fast and Malek fell backward, squirming like a grub.

Null then unrolled a bit of thin clear plastic tubing from his inside coat pocket and a companion ruddy-colored rubber bulb about fist-sized bounced on the floor. He slid one end of the tube into the bulb and the other end into Malek, sticking the end into the ice pick wound.

"Squeeze the bulb," said Null.

"Go fuck yourself," Malek gasped.

"Do it. It will re-inflate your lung, which I just collapsed with the icepick. Keep squeezing it and then make the call on your cell to EMS. Should take about a half-hour for them to help you. Unfortunately, there's no other help more immediately available outside your office door."

"What-do-you-mean?" It was an actual series of croaks.

"You know just what I mean."

"Prick!" This was rasping , like a cough.

"Sticks and stones, Malek. I told you, this is my town, and the gak and the cash are mine too. And as much as it matters so are you!"

Malek gurgled low for a response, but abruptly, just like a cheap piece of hastily ignited flash paper whose thin remnant ash drifted slowly, almost invisible to the ground. Null wasn't there anymore.

Another night.

The clawing at the bedding, the hot and cold sweat, the shakes, the broken chocolate bar on the nightstand which failed to stave off the need, the fire in the pit of the stomach no amount of cheap, store brand soda pop could quench.

The revulsion.

How many hours of the clock, how much time did she have left before they could take everything from her again. How much more could they take from her? How much more could she take of that?

Take, take, take and no give unless it was her doing the giving.

How these thoughts fall upon you in semi-sleep; regret itself became a semi-dream.

Her lungs were a bellows breathing cinders.

Her brains were beaten ragged.

Her eyes registered light despite the dark of the room, despite her eyes being squeezed shut hard.

Her ears screamed, and wrapping the pillow around her head did no good.

The screaming was real, undeniable, solid.

She dove for her phone.

Wurdalaka, droning, "LT, we got another one. Big brouhaha down at the 1270 on Boylston—freaking messy."

"You been down?"

"No, I ain't been down, but they called me to call you, the guys that don't wanna deal with this. They said you'd love it."

"There was gum present, wasn't there?"

"Wrappers scattered hither and thither."

"How bad, Byron?"

"I got your numbers right here," he said, fumbling with his new tablet.

He told her as few details as he had heard himself from slave dispatch and she gagged hard at turning on the light: Eight men out, near twenty wounded badly enough to be carried off to Boston City ER, over 100 injured, loss and destruction in the hundred thousands."

"Pizza wagons dispatched?"

"They're already there doing the cleanup with Yonah Shimmel and his part-time student band bagging and tagging."

She laughed a bitter, quiet laugh. Boston freaking CSI. Big time pro's. Comedy clusterfuck.

"Where are the news trucks?"

"We got three already. The night shift got no problem holding them back."

"Let 'em in and have Yonah preside."

"Ya got authority for that, LT?"

"And what did they tell you, Byron? The wonks upstairs."

"They told me they were going to try to tie the whole thing this time to Islamic Jihad, blame it all on the towel heads. Al Qaeda, Sheik Al Ahazared crap."

"I bet they did, them and their "One Boston, Boston Strong" gang. What else they tell you?"

"We're fucking Boston Strong now we used 100 men, all contiguous police, 200 FBI flamers, enough tactical SWAT equipment to capture Switzerland to whack out one kid, corner another one half-dead holed up in a boat trailer so we can break our arms patting ourselves on the backs on such a difficult fucking collar."

"One fucking Boston."

"Just one fucking Boston," replied Wurdalaka grimly. "Thank God. That's all we fucking need. Any more than that and I'll declare a fucking jihad myself!"

"You're talking heresy," Wurdalaka.

"Who doesn't in Boston?"

"So what are we doing, Byron?" Her sweat smelled like gin, which made her stomach collapse in on itself and ache.

"Sure, LT. I'll let 'em in. Let that faggot Yamaha boy play den mother in the carnage and debris to boot, just as you say. Anything you want. Oh, but the wonks upstairs what don't want to get involved? You remember them, don't ya?"

"How could I forget?"

"Well, they told me to tell you NOT to fuck it up. We're fucking heroes these days and we need the drop dead print press, the slick back TV hacks and the dweeby genius web fairies to eat that up with a fucking spoon."

"I'm sure that was verbatim, too, wasn't it, Byron?"

"Fuckin' A, LT."

"Fuckin' A," she droned, and switched off.

But not before she failed to suppress the vomiting.

FOURTEEN

He was dressed in the light patched Khaki and corduroy of a tenured college professor, possibly Tufts or Northeastern. He strode about the grandiose lobby, scanning the art and post expressionist pseudo-Giacometti sculptures of One Schroeder Place, Boston Police Headquarters, waving his laminated pocket slide-in visitor's badge this way and that as if a lost, and helpless tourist. Though it was obvious, he should have known where he was going. He should have known better. It was in his face, with the smug, ironic smirk on it. A purposefully strident Bim Hundertwasser bellied into him from behind and grabbed him, spun him about and pointed him in the direction where he should be going. The officer didn't rough him up in the slightest, was almost gentle, in fact, as he steered him about. The too-well shaven face burst into a thin-lipped grin. His cologne rose in a thick scent like ghostly ectoplasm off his face.

"This way, Perfessor," said Hundertwasser.

It was a light and airy conference room used for politics, internal celebrations, retirements. Good view of the water and the famous Boston wind-puffed sails of community boating. There was a spread on the table; cold cuts and sandwiches on chrome platters, tea and coffee in big, stout urns, a tray of cookies and plenty of cups, saucers, spoons and forks for cake.

"Have a seat," Hundertwasser growled and pushed him down,

but with subdued force, just enough to remind him of his contempt, but no more.

Boyd, Inspector LaCuna, Captain Parseemen and even senior forensics specialist Yonah Shimmel were already seated at the table. Boyd lit a smoke and no one stopped her. LaCuna slid her a lone saucer to use as an ashtray. "So what?" Boyd harrumphed.

Wurdalaka chiming in, beat and surly: Ya. So fucking what?"

"Look at all this nice treatment for a guy what usually gets his nose all broke up when the security cameras aren't working in your cheap shit interview rooms."

"We're all thrilled to have you," LaCuna drawled icily. "Fresh from Boston City Hospital at that."

"Careful ya keep that lung inflated," Wurdalaka japed.

"Where's the law-bot Watty Tyler Schulman?" Boyd, irritable and unnerved, needing that drink.

"He's still touring the catacombs, I think," LaCuna crooned.

"We got an empty interview room downstairs, if that suits ya better, fucktard."

"I don't need no law-bot this time, bitches!" Malek "The Mallet" Turbot chuckled, as if having heard a good joke after smoking a Cuban cigar and killing some Remy Martin cognac. "We all know you want what I have, so why pretend? You want to hear it or not?"

"You need a lawyer," groaned Boyd. "A high-priced shyster Like Wat Tyler Schulman because you're too stupid not to step in the shit by yourself."

"We'll see about that, Lieutenant. I think I'll have one of those little sandwiches. You make me one?" He nodded at Boyd and she played along grudgingly, fingers trembling.

She threw the half-made sandwich at the wall.

"Just fucking spit it out, Malek, before I shove it back down your filthy gullet and out your criminal fucking ass!"

Malek chuckled again. "We both have the same problem. I am not whacking out my own soldiers, not that I ever would whack out anyone, of course you know. But I got two guys gone wrong on me. They're not with me anymore, but they still think they are."

"You're saying they're trying to kill their way back in."

Wurdalaka stood. "Just lock the fucktard up already!"

"No, listen for just a fucking minute and do that One Fucking Boston-Boston Strong Ass dance you do, will you? Listen, Mr. fucking Boston Strong, it's the Indian! This Filmore Lakeworry, Mic-Mac construction worker. He's a wrongo, a fucking rogue. He's not doing it for money, power or even for some trim, but he's taking out my guys, anyway, him and his faggy little sidekick."

Boyd's eyebrows launched. "Faggy?"

"I was being indecorous."

"Don't tell me his name is Benway."

"Claims to be a doctor. Came in with Harvard and MIT creds, clippings from Tech Crunch, Technology Review...."

"Fucking gum!"

"Fucking monster clusterfuck! I paid him good cash money for a designer drug. So, he comes up with the gum delivery system, something the kiddies would all enjoy, tiger-striped Juicy Fruit—"

Boyd bore down on him. "So, you could dump all the gum in the clubs and get the kiddies used to it, dry up the supply and cash in."

"But it's all fucked now! Stuff was supposed to be the new legal Ecstasy, fucking Molly for the sexed-up fag hags, but instead turned everyone who used it into a homicidal maniac. Now we got to clean up that gum or—"

Wurdalaka said, "What's this fucking *we* shit?"

"Or you'll be charged and arraigned on at least six felonies I can think of, from attempted murder to fomenting a riot!" LaCuna chuckling with well-fed complacence.

"But I only found this out now. I'm giving you all the info I got to help you solve the fucking problem." He produced some slim binders from his coat lining. "I'm even giving you the little faggot's chem notes."

Nick Andromeda droned sleepily from his seeming fugue state. "And you're giving up Benway and the Indian for us to take that little problem off your hands for you."

Malek laughed, hands holding in his belly with spread fingers to be dramatic. "Truth always is the funniest when you get down to it, but that's it exactly. Fucking delicious, you ask me."

Boyd, nerves frayed and trying not to think of the winsome scent of gin: "And we get exactly what?"

"I help you with a little problem you can't seem to deal with. For instance, I know you've been having lots of trouble with some badass hitter needs to go as of yesterday. I get it done quick, clean and legal. One fast jerk and into an unmarked grave he goes."

"You're talking about murder, fucktard," Wurdalaka whined. "Whilst sitting atop a stack of holding cells with a bunch of pumped-up cops who'd just as soon arrest your punk ass as shit on it, genius." The truth of the "One Boston" remarks was still bugging him.

Malek really started howling now. "The truth again, I tell you, is nothing short of hysterical."

Even Boyd looked puzzled, until Malek said, "I'm going to get rid of your little problem and you're not even going to have to pay me to do it."

"And what little problem is that?" mocked Boyd.

"Why, a little problem named Joseph Xavier Null, in fact, former decoy CI. A copy of his death certificate's right in one of those binders, if you care to look."

Andromeda looked away from Malek at this point—it was almost a signal.

Blank stares around the table as Malek quickly fashioned a sand-wich, dipped it in mustard and let it drip down the corners of his mouth when he asked, almost without obvious mocking irony: "Oh, you didn't realize he wasn't really dead?"

———

He was squat and pudgy, patch-bearded somehow slovenly in his brilliant blood-orange Suffolk County lockup jumpsuit. Grant Monad shepherded him inside one of the windowless interview rooms. Kay Boyd sat waiting for him, fidgety and in need of a cigarette, though she hated smoking. He was hand and ankle cuffed with a belly chain for ease of control, yet he managed to plop down in his seat defiantly.

He sighed flecks of saliva.

"You know the deal, Doctor, am I right? Are we on the same page?"

"Sure, Lieutenant Boyd. Anything to get out of the catacombs and not be leered at like a cheap whore."

"Are you saying you're not a cheap whore?" Boyd leaned in on him, looking serious. He could see the fine blonde hairs on her chin in the half-light.

"No, Lieutenant. I just don't like being leered at like one."

"I thought that was an appropriate turn of events for you, Dr. Funambule, considering the methods you used handling your female patients."

"Yes, wonderful irony. I feel I'm being speeded on the way to recovery, to finally being cured of my filthy predilections."

"Screw it, Funambule. We both know what you've got doesn't have a cure."

"Shhh, Lieutenant. We want to preserve the illusion that all the torture that's been thrown at me of late has had some rehabilitative value."

"No, it was just torture."

"Yes, that's what it feels like."

"You know what I want, Doctor?"

"No, but I'm sure you'll be telling me. And if I give it to you I get released *or*—"

"With an ankle bracelet and a reduction in charges." She finished for him.

"You swung this?"

"Here you are, Doctor."

"So you're saying it's in the works?"

"I'm saying that this is your best crack at it, so stop picking at the deal and start producing."

"I can't produce until I know what you need. Do I have to guess?'

"There'll be plenty of guessing in a minute. I'll tell you what to guess at."

Funambule wiggled in his seat to rattle his chains, then held them up. "Can we get this bling off me first?" Monad, still standing, stepped forward with a hint of menace.

"We can when you make me happy so let's start making me happy."

He let his wrists clatter back to the table and mumbled something that sounded both drunken and unintelligible.

"I expect you to make me happy," she deadpanned.

"Oh, the pressure!" he sneered.

"So do it!" Her eyes narrowed.

"Hit me," said Funambule, realizing the double entendre and squinting hard like a stressed-out iguana.

Boyd straightened up and laid it out. "What I've got is a guy what likes to impersonate doctors, has funny concoctions that work sideways rather than the way they're supposed to. Manages to fool experts, attendings, on-calls, hospital HR's, you name it. He's always developing some new mind-altering junk in his basement and getting some sort of credibility for it, somewhere, despite its destructive impact."

"You want a profile."

"Work him up for me. From how many times a day he masturbates to how he feels about his mother."

"I thought you had specialists doing these things in your OC taskforce."

"They give you way too much TV down there in the catacombs, don't they?"

"Life is an easy journey of entertaining facility and completion, including state-of-the art in all the arts covered by the central art of spinning specious reality-based simple-minded fantasies."

"Everyone's too overworked for anything else."

"He's in his forties, graying and deeply frustrated about it, not a college dropout, but a life dropout."

"High school dropout?"

"Seems too savvy for that."

"Savvy?"

Funambule shook his shaggy matted hair, motioned for a smoke. Boyd tossed him a pack of American Spirit with matches. He lit up, dragged. "No. Thought he was too smart for high school. Dropped out to prove he was superior to anything they could give him. It masked his inability to fit in enough to actually graduate."

"He obtained his medical education by alternate means?

"It wouldn't make sense for him to even have a GED."

"Then how?"

"The ablative is the entire explanation of his progress and character. The struggle to surmount his defects defines his criminal need."

"Childhood?"

"No father, far too much mother."

"Let's get back to the medical proclivity."

"He's an auditor—every class he could or can get. An autodidact, but a hack. He's also got only a barely above normal IQ and is quite unable to socially integrate thanks to mommy's efforts—the sexualizing of his role in the absence of the father making him the responsible man-child lover."

"He was raped?"

"Not physically, sociologically."

"The medical, please."

Funambule lisped and spit, "He's a monomaniac, an autodidact monomaniac trying to prove what he can never prove, hence a dancing performer in a criminal Grand Guignol he can't really stop. One step forward, two-steps back, caroming on he goes."

"Alone?"

"No. He's too needy and weak. He'll have a platonic lover, a partner, probably an unspoken homosexual master-slave relationship wherein he's bullied, grouses about it, but secretly thrives on it. At best, he's living on borrowed time. His lover protector will probably whack him out long before you get to him."

"You're pulling this one out of your ass, aren't you?" she sneered, getting angry.

"Of course I am. Where else do you expect me to pull it from? I have no data, no real facts to go on except whatever horse flop you wanna toss my way."

Boyd slammed down a thin file. "This is all we got down to the single picture of him—the so-called Dr. Benway." She slipped him the file and image. Funambule gazed at them and blew smoke rings.

"How arch. He named himself for a character in a transgressive surrealist novel."

He pored through it, humming some universal nursery rhyme,

licking his fingers before paging through. He dropped it to the floor with contempt. "Dip shit," he said.

"We thought so."

"So he's a destructive, indifferent, all-powerful nit-wit, privileged by a corrupt society."

"Is that what he is?"

"No, but it's what he wants to be. And that name. It's a clue to his real name. It would have to be or it wouldn't make him feel smart, which no matter what he does, he never really *does*."

"Something to do with Burroughs—"

"Or Grove Press. Put your house geniuses on it. They'll come up with a name."

"How can we get a name without a location?"

"You can't, but if I give you the location, you certainly can."

"You're bluffing."

"Of course I am, but I want your nearest available ADA to make me a deal for probation, community service, time-served, what the fuck. Get him in here, write it up, validate it and notarize it before God and everyone else, and I'll tell you."

"Got an address?"

"Nope, but I have the town. When you figure out the name, which I already have, you can do a cross-grid and get the address and pick the son of a bitch up."

Boyd slid halfway across the table and pressed her face close to the slobbering, piebald, nettled maw of Dr. Lucius Funambule. "If you're lying, I'll make sure you become the fattest, hairiest, most bloated ass human pin cushion in the history of corrections."

"I know you will, but think it through. You got a mamma's boy never really left home. Means the suburbs. Too poor not to fake being a doctor for money, so it doesn't mean Newton or Concord or Belmont or Duxbury. He's a sober boy, never any substance abuse on himself, only on others. So, he likely comes from a dry town, big old houses to make experiments in, lots of quiet neglect, distant neighbors thickly settled—"

"Arlington!" she cried out like a forgotten game show answer.

"And now, out of loyalty and fucking decency, get your ADA to move his butt over to One Schroeder and type me out my fucking deal!"

"I always said you were a very good shrink, Dr. Funambule."

"That's how I managed to get laid looking like this," he sighed sibilantly.

"No, Doctor, that's how you wound up in Central Lockup."

———

"Suck on it!"

Do rag was on his knees, his red bandana dank with sweat, the muzzle of a thirty-eight Chief's Special pressing firmly on the back of his tongue, making him gag slightly, wide eyed.

He was trembling hard.

"Suck on it or reach for it, you little prick. Either way, I blow rounds through the back of your fucking head for kicks I don't hear what I want to hear." Nick Andromeda was icy, stolid, rigid, yet in some way, slack.

He cocked the revolver—condition zero—the firearms state you don't want to see with a two-inch muzzle knocking at the back of your throat.

He slid out the barrel slowly, gave the mook a minute to recover.

Heaving, sweat-drenched, a near gag response: "What you want, dog?"

"I want your boss, homey. Serve him up and off you go."

"You don't want him—he kill your bitch ass!"

"Wrong answer, genius." And with that, Andromeda knocked him down to the slick, greasy pavement with the butt of the Special. Grease and cleaning liquid made sad little rainbow puddles in the black broken tar of the back alley behind Bo Shek's Dim Sum in Chinatown. "Try again, please." This was soft, almost patient.

"Real talk dog—he kill us both and think nothin' of it. You don't want him, he want you, prolly. And if he does want you, you are done. He's serious fuckin' business!"

The reply was the side of the Special to the face, knocking Do-Rag back to the pavement.

"Gimme the gak you're carrying, homey."

"I can't, dog. The gak belong to him, and he kill my ass before he even get to you."

Andromeda drew back.

Hands up, waving. "No, dog. Don't hit me again. That cracker's crazy as a shit house rat and five times scarier than you. You don't want to fuck with him, not ever!"

"You know how easy it is for me to put an end to you right now with a clean piece and a quick call for backup, right?"

Slit-eyed, wiping blood from his lower lip. "You won't, though. Too much paperwork and nothin' to show for it. No, you keep my black ass around to tell you stuff."

"I want the zombie so tell me that."

Do-Rag shook his head so hard sweat splattered off it.

"Can't do it, even if I would do it, I don't know where he be at. No one know. He a fuckin' ghost, one of the undead. I ain't even sure he's human."

"He's not anymore. He's officially dead so I'm here on unofficial business to keep him official, get me, homey?"

Andromeda raised up the Special and kicked the kneeling Do-Rag square in the abdomen. A twenty-two caliber Ruger clattered down to the broken pavement with a hollow bounce. Andromeda beamed.

"A ladies pistol," he sneered, drawing back again and lifting the Special.

"No, wait!" Do-Rag railed.

Andromeda responded with a sigh of professional aplomb. He savaged Do-Rag with the butt of the Special, paying vicious attention to detailed slamming and battering of neck and head until the dope dealer gurgled blood out of his mouth. He knelt down and waved away Do-Rag's limp arm and its loosely clenched fist with token effort, then patted him down hard, relieving him of a tightly wrapped square plastic package looking antiseptic and medical, strangely luminous and white in the unclean shadows of the foul back alley behind Bo Shek's Dim Sum in Chinatown.

"Looks like a good quarter pound of gak there, chief. I can't let you keep the cash you're holding, though. Looks more authentic that way."

Do-Rag tried to warn him. "No, man, he be on you for that fast. Don't know what he use it for? Ain't for clothes or hos, but the fucker loves money."

"You say he loves it. I thought that guy loved nothing."

"He love it like a cat love meat."

"Then make him purr for me."

"You stupid. He gut me out in a hot minute without thinking twice about it. You think I can smooth him down? He a stone seven-thirty nigga!"

"That's right, chief. He's a crazy shit so tell him a story and if he lets you live, then he'll be coming after me."

"You wylin', cracker! He smoke you good."

"Not at all, little man. We'll just see who smokes whom."

"So you say, but he out for the mooga and blood and he don't care which he get. I got the drop on the fact that he get the gak back off your ass and take your scalp for fun."

"I didn't think that dude ever had any fun."

"Not the kind you and I ever heard of."

"Don't worry, Sonny, when he finally gets to me there'll be plenty of fun to go around."

"Careful what you wish for, fuckin' cracker!"

FIFTEEN

"God has a funny way of giving back to you what you lost most."

"Deal with it, Filmore. God is a shadow puppet, a prop for politics and war, but really there's only the chaos we spend our lives ducking. The randomness hits you to no point and purpose, but we whine about a complicated master plan getting knocked off as we go sucking up to the imaginary God to get a better deal."

"No, bro, he real. Love and acceptance and money are zeroing right in on us as if God had always wanted us to have it. Joel Osteen said it on the cable."

"You're a meatball enforcer on the run and I'm an uncredited phony baloney scientific genius with a target on my back for a mook like you."

"No, no, Benway. You honest and true goddamn genius. You got gum that takes down the barriers to human sensitivity, to individual resistance."

"Where's the money, Lumpy? Just when is payday so I can take the Montreal Express outta butts town good and proper?"

"It comin', Benway, you just gotta have faith. God is on our side."

"Which means we can kill anyone who gets in our way with good conscience?"

"Yeah, man. We'll feel bad about it, but not that bad."

"I'm gonna be sick."

"You watch out, Benway. Kids are there."

"I don't care."

"Here, I help you care." With a hard-coiled thrust of his bandy left leg, Lumpy knocked Benway off the polyethylene-studded rock face of the practice wall of the Stalag-Tight rock gym in Somerville.

Benway swung helplessly from his lifeline against the semi-pliant candy colored rock forms of the plastic practice wall looking a nacreous green while Lumpy guffawed as if he had a large cud of the special gum in his mouth, but it was only his thick tongue.

"You a pussy, Doctor."

"I know it. Why I have you!" he sobbed dryly, trying and failing to regain the composure he never truly had as he bounced almost playfully off the face of polyethylene rock wall.

One of the trainers assisted him down with pulleys and carabineer clips; Lumpy chuckled, guffawed, chortled, and snorted every inch of the way down. Benway kicked his legs like an upended insect, limp and trembling. Lumpy looked like he was having a seizure, his face wet with clabber and his wide, flat fetal alcohol syndrome nose turning rose red with effort. He went down only a fraction faster than Benway and pushed away the trainer when the soles of his blue Jordans touched the instep of Benway's blue Crocs at the bottom. The trainer shot a glance at Lumpy, which he shot back all the harder with a pinched little grunt that cut the trainer's intended invective off at the first syllable. Benway cringed, still entwined in safety line, but Lumpy grabbed him, shook him straight. All around them swinging cables, climbing bodies, the shadows cast by the jutting shapes of the rock wall under vacillating fluorescent lights added a sort of cheap science fiction aura to the air. It was movie-like—a ghostly fantasy of something badly imagined.

"We partners, doc. Ain't nothin' gonna stop that but death, and I am gonna make sure we both stay alive. Keep you alive and safe, Doc, believe me." Though his chin and lips were wet, he delivered these words with a heavy seriousness, as if each word were itself a weight. "You don't worry about Ork goons, Doc. They ain't nothin' to me."

Benway brushed him off weakly, but Lumpy acted as if there was some force behind it.

"We're dead meat."

"We were that at the 1270, so them torpedoes thought, but we here now and they a bunch of goo in the I-C-U."

"You know what borrowed time is, Lumpy?"

"Filmore. Not Fill, not Lumpy, not Heap. And I like stolen time better."

"It's not ours."

"Whatever we take is ours."

"They're coming to take it back."

"My Mic-Mac ass they will. Look, Doc, every crew gets tired of dyin' off without a profit. We keep killin', they beat a retreat to something not so expensive as fighting for a drug they think don't work, anyways."

"But it does work—sort of."

"No, man. It work all the fucking way. Even with all that head-crack-backlash, this gum drug got street cred now. Got a big, bad reputation. Too dangerous to use, too hard to get. Nobody know where to get."

Benway clicked. "Therefore, too irresistible to refuse. The hip club kids will want it all the time."

"Beautiful and dangerous, but cheap, like playmate of the year gone crack whore."

"Thrill you and kill you. So these fucking club debacles are like an underground promotion."

"What you mean?"

Benway wiped his crusty lips with his sleeve, his murky gray eyes squinting behind tri-focal glasses. "What they call guerilla marketing."

Lumpy was snorting with suppressed impatience. "What the fuck?"

"The shit's gone viral!" he shouted, grabbing Lumpy by freakishly wide shoulders that felt to his spatulate fingers like outsized knots of wood. Stalag-Tight rock gym patron's and their children's heads both turned toward them and the echoing din of the gym toned down.

They had an audience.

Benway dismissively waved it away.

Lumpy put it together: "On the money! Up the desire—"

"Up the price!"

"We turn that shit over quick soon."

"You don't do much on the computer, but videos of the club brouhahas are all over the Internet, the social networking and sharing sites. Facebook, Instagram, Reddit."

Lumpy blinked. "I don't get all that fidgety-widgety stuff online, but I'm savvy to the computer. I watch videos on the You-Tube for sports, maybe NudeVista for naked celebrities."

"It's everywhere; Google it. They call it "The Boston Beatdown."

"I got a smartphone—don't use it much. Like my flip better."

"You know they can track those phones with GPS, genius?"

"Sure they can. I watch TV. Dead men's phones. Let 'em track away. They won't even know who they're looking for."

Benway spat back: "Fuck the phones. How do we distribute?"

"You the genius, Doc. You don't see it?"

Benway just stood there, craning his neck to the side.

"We give all the low-level gangs like Gangsta Boyz a cheap deal they flock to. We let it out we got the drug what makes you mad sexy rampage-y—club riot death like on the news. Monster cray-cray, but just like ex, all connected and shit. They scream for it."

"It makes an odd kind of reverse sense. I suppose I'm still in."

"You in, anyways, Doc, or I kill your ass, pure and simple."

Standing a head and a half taller than the Mic-Mac Indian, even with his weedy frame in a slouch, his stomach out, his back sloped, Benway nonetheless looked sunken and small. He rubbed the bristling stubble of his angular chin and muttered, somehow loudly, "Did I ever tell you about a man called Null?"

Though he hadn't wanted it inasmuch as he could have plausibly wanted anything at all, even as an academic concept, Null was a great success. A success of enmity. He had made ephemeral paranoia flesh without suffering a twitch of that disorder himself. The muscle of the Ork was out to get him; the cops had him in the system with Identikit sketches of him on every patrol car screen in Greater Boston; Detective Nick Andromeda was bribed and primed and out for his blood and Malek the Mallet wanted him splayed out on a four-point restraint table at Gary Lee Obidowski's garage for a long, sustained session of questioning.

The only ones not directly out to get him were the Gangsta Boyz, who weren't exactly sure if that seven thirty motherfucker wasn't too off the chain to cap or if indeed he was running their whole crew from the outside.

They were all making plans to trap him, triangulate him, get him in their collective sights, and execute him, preferably with a helpful serving of overkill. The essential problem was one they just couldn't recognize or accept: How do you trap a man, lure him to his death if he doesn't want anything, has no goal you can identify? How can you attract a stone? Maybe a magnet if there's iron in it, but what if the iron is all used up—gone? And there was no irony in Null. None. If you don't know what a man wants, or even *if* he wants, then how can you determine what he needs?

And need was the quotient, the sum, the fulcrum upon which to leverage Null into the proper kill zone.

But so far, no one could determine exactly what the son of a bitch needed that he didn't already have or couldn't get without the lure.

Despite the demanding difficulty of this proposition, all Null's predatory antagonists were deeply distracted by other issues and considerations, practicalities, expediencies, by their own needs— overloaded by them in fact—while Null in his brutally simplified pragmatic approach to slicing through Gordian knots rather than untangling them, was not. He could not be distracted, though his focus was lax and un-driven. He could not want, pine, desperately seek, even though his impetus was pure and clear and final. No, as he would tell them, could they but ask, Null only did one thing, just one thing.

That one thing was the only thing beyond eating and sleeping. It was what brought him from point A to point B and straight through to C.

So far in his new history of death, Null did not fail at that one thing—had yet to fail—and by all accounts, few as they were, simply could not fail.

In the undercurrents of rumor that made up the word on the street, this much was the clear consensus belief from the streetwalker to the leg-breaker and even to the housepainter:

He could not be stopped.

This meant Null had inadvertently become very adept at yet another thing.

Fear.

For those who knew most about him down to those who knew the least, especially the police, Null inspired fear.

Fear of that which should not happen, couldn't really happen, wasn't really known to happen, but what if it did?

What if it did happen in that heart-stopping moment of the impossible revealed before widened, transfixed eyes? Housepainters roamed the streets of Boston looking for him, rousting homeless winos and shooting gallery junkies just for him, hunting him down in a sweat. The question now was a new tattoo of the mind:

What if it did happen?

What if he could not be stopped?

What if, while you were coming for him, he was coming for you?

These thoughts all ran through the mind of newly made Detective First Grade Nick Andromeda as Null's forearm creased his windpipe, bending him over backward onto the lip of the central fountain in the sunken granite and marble courtyard of 50 Rowes Wharf on the waterfront by the North End. His grunts and panting echoed below the arched portcullis while Null was almost soundless but for a little wheeze escaping his flared nostrils.

Null right-handed him across the jaw, dragged him up and kneed him in the belly, let him sink to his knees, coughing.

"Where are your friends, Nick? Why aren't they chipping in? Something you said, maybe?"

"How did you know?" Andromeda slobbered.

"The muscle of the Ork taught me they twitch under pressure."

"C-cluster-f-fuck!" Andromeda stammered out.

Null jackhammer punched him in the face, holding him up.

"Not really. Neat as you please, Nick. Nothing sloppy here but you."

"Temporary condition, fucknuts!" Panting and wheezing.

"Life is temporary, Nick. Want me to show you?"

"Do your worst, prick."

"If I could laugh, I would laugh at that, but I really can't. And you can't even see why that's funny."

Andromeda lunged.

Another quick, hard knee to the xyphoid process. Null pulled the lapels of Andromeda's overcoat down to the elbows, imprisoning his arms. He took Andromeda's piece neatly from the shoulder holster.

"Can't have enough nice guns in this town, can we?"

"They're coming for you, you twat!" Andromeda coughed out, "So why don't you blow?"

Null kicked him down to the marble floor, calm as a bank auditor.

"No one's coming, Nick. We made other plans. In case you don't know, in this town, buying off muscle is easy, especially when you got a cocked Glock held to the crotch."

With his Glock set hard to Andromeda's chest, Null knelt down, and neatly, without ceremony, broke his right index finger. Against training and the conditioning of unremitting Boston streets, the detective howled.

"Now it's time for a little Q&A, Nick. Tell me, which one is getting the closest to me?"

Andromeda spat at him and Null clocked him in the face with the muzzle of the gun.

"Answer me, Nick, or I start putting holes in you. Maiming and killing cops is not in my best interest, but at this stage of the game, I think I can risk it."

He started with the detective's left foot and the report echoed loud and menacing amid the marble and granite of the rat-scarred stone landscape. Andromeda screamed.

"Don't make me ask again."

Andromeda caught his breath, rivulets of sweat and tears streaming down his now contorted face.

"I am, you fuck!"

Null shot him again, this time higher up the leg. He had to shake the detective at the shoulders to get him to compose himself afterwards. Then he set the muzzle of the gun hard up against Andromeda's left eye and cocked it. He didn't have to ask again.

"Boyd!" Andromeda screamed into overlapping echoes, the slopping sounds of the brackish bay against the rocks. "Lieutenant Kay fucking Boyd!"

Null sounded almost gentle as he picked Andromeda up from the stone floor of the courtyard and set him floppily onto the lip of the now dry fountain. He spoke in an airy tone barely above a whisper: "And before I drop you off at the E-room, you're going to hand me back my quarter pound of gak. It would simply be bad business to let it get around that you took that off of me and I might have to make some messy symbolic public kills to make up for it."

"You're fucked, zombie," Andromeda gasped. "You just don't know it yet!"

"Oh, I know it, Nick. We all are. And in time, we'll all be leveled at six foot deep. But then again, I would think this 'you're fucked' warning kind of funny coming from a cop on the arm with two bullet holes in his leg and a broken trigger finger."

Andromeda slumped over and vomited.

"We'd better get you down to Mass General before serious complications set in. I don't think it would be a good idea to have to start over with whatever hotshot replacement they have for you waiting in the wings."

Null wiped his mouth, chin and the front of his coat with a handkerchief and helped him up to his one good leg, maneuvering him up to Atlantic Avenue across wide shallow steps.

"I'm not on the arm, zombie fuck!"

"Of course you are, Nick. Every low-life in town except your cop buddies knows that Malek the Mallet put the hit out on me, and you're the hitter."

"Fuck yourself, Null."

"No need to when they're all lining up to do exactly that for me. But I wonder how surprised they'll all be when they get that big O that's coming. Should be something."

Before Andromeda could reply, Null threw him in the back of a sky blue, ancient Ford Escort waiting for them, lights flashing, and obstructing traffic somewhat along the narrow, congested contortion and twist of bleakly filthy urban construction reno-scape that was Atlantic Avenue. Andromeda groaned an unheard retort and Null peeled off toward Staniford Street to get to Mass General Hospital.

SIXTEEN

She rang the bell without hesitation, then stopped when she felt the hard sharp gun sight against her ribs.

"That's right," said Null. "Let's see who answers."

"It's you."

"It is. On that score, you rang and I answered. And now you await yet another answer after ringing. Funny. You do ask for it, don't you, Boyd?"

"I didn't. I don't want you. I don't want anything to do with you."

"But you have me now, and I guess it would be more precise for me to say that I have you."

"Why don't you just go—disappear. Don't you see Boston has rejected you?"

The door clicked open and Boyd startled stiff. Her eyes glazed over when she saw who opened the door. "Benway."

Despite the muzzle of Null's gun pressed into her ribs, she drew her Sig Sauer faster than the man at the door could blink, flashed it and spat, "You're under arrest, Lee."

"Benway," he croaked dryly.

"William "Bull" Lee," Boyd snarled. "Pretty cute your Burroughs joke."

"Who reads anymore?" he said dully.

"Move back, Lee, and let us in."

"Got a warrant?"

"It's a phone call away. Wanna handle it that way?"

"No," he sighed, moving away into the high-ceilinged foyer to let them enter. His hair was wild, a frizzy bush of brown and gray. The house was high-ceilinged Edwardian with oriels and a cupola. There were gables and a widow's watch. There was an ornate fixture of sphinxes and gargoyles that lacked a chandelier.

"You're under arrest, Lee."

"What about me?" asked Null.

"Who's this guy?"

"I'm nobody," said Null. "But you knew me as Joseph Xavier Null."

Boyd turned her back on Benway to face Null. "Drop it," she seethed.

"Ladies first," Null said, barely above a whisper.

"Don't think so."

"Shall we shoot together on three? I think I'll drop you before you drop me. Let's find out."

"You were the fucking *patient?*" Benway asked, genuinely astonished.

"We'll put them both away, Null. You should just walk. Get out of here. Go bury yourself deep."

"No, I think I'll stay for the show. Besides, it's your intent to stop me. And I will not be stopped."

"What do I care? You're a lowlife that preys on low lives. Go to town. Go anywhere. Just go. I don't care." Despite what she said she couldn't shake the pain in her chest that expanded the more she looked at the emaciated, hollow-cheeked figure in the overcoat and felt fedora hat that shaded his bloodshot eyes. She seemed to become the proxy for his own suspended agony.

Benway was halfway up the stairs before Boyd drew a bead on him with the Sig Sauer. "Stand the fuck still, Lee, or I'll shoot you in the femur."

"I didn't want to interrupt what you two had going on. Seemed to be developing into something."

"The only thing that's developing here is a case against you, Lee. Where's the Indian?"

"You mean Lumpy?"

"Filmore Lakeworry." She squinted. "Does he have your mother? Is she a hostage?"

"She's in Boca, staying with her cousin. I have the place to myself."

"You and the Indian are going down for the club riots. I do a search, I find lots of sticks gum, don't I?"

Benway slumped. "Have at it, chief. Sure you will. But you got it wrong. I'm the hostage. I'm a prisoner here. Lumpy's a violent fuck-wit, a goddamn Ork enforcer. I'm just a lowly conman. Get me on impersonating a physician, violating Commonwealth licensing laws, fraud. Get me on assault with intent, but I'm not behind the riots. That fucker Lakeworry is making me do it all the way. Give me a day or two. I'll serve him up for you. Testify as a witness—the whole nine yards. I am really not your man, so I am willing to be your man."

"So, I just leave you my card and you communicate with me and we get Lumpy before he hits another club. I just leave you like that, trust you, you psychopathic fuck?"

"Exactly."

Null had lowered his gun, standing stock still, wheezing slightly out his nostrils, but otherwise frozen.

"You know I'm not going to get much time on what you have to charge me with to date. The gum's not exactly illegal, you know. And when they finally get us—and you and I both know they'll eventually get us—I'll turn at the first given opportunity. Now, you want to solve the case or do I hand it to someone else?"

"I could throw your bony ass into the condos downtown right now and still get the bust. No reason to leave you out on your own."

"Sure there is. Lumpy will bolt if I'm gone. That man is a stone criminal, more paranoid and OCD than a Jewish granny. We're lucky the dumb fuck is out on a gum run or you'd be in a firefight. He wants to connect with the chickadees down at TT The Bears."

"So you want CI status."

"Just like the patient there whatsisface, your guy Null. I want what he had."

"And do you want it to bring you what it brought me?" Null spoke as if from nowhere, hollow voiced and final.

"Of course not. But there's no one as insane as I am to work on me the way I worked on you, and look what it did. It made you better, brought you out of your catatonic trance. So what if you lack affect and emotional reactivity? You can live and—"

"Respond, Doctor? Is that the word you were looking for? Respond? No, I can't do that little thing. My entire life boils down to an a priori assumption of purpose, logical positivism at its most perverse."

"Better than what you had before, bunky."

Null turned to Boyd. "Did you know that he was here? Did you know he was the one who did this to me, Lieutenant Boyd?"

Her head sank along with her stomach, her fingers clenched hard and slick with sweat around the grip of the gun. "Yes, I knew. The gum down at the clubs was more of his neuro-chemical madness."

"Another glorious failure, I might add," said Benway, bowing sarcastically.

Null raised up his weapon and Boyd simply clenched hers even tighter. "I ought to kill him," he announced. "That would be apropos and settle things out."

"Null, you don't want to—"

"I don't want to do anything—ever. I said I ought to kill him, but I just can't think it through."

"Of course you can't." Benway clapped almost laughing. "You can't because there was no evil done here. In a way, you could say my little experimental therapy was a success. A benefit, in fact."

Null's gun was at condition zero, cocked and ready, a hair's breadth away from exploding open Benway's sunken birdcage chest.

"Don't kill him, Null, otherwise I'll have to kill you. And I don't want to."

"Guilty, Lieutenant Boyd?"

"Oh, that and more, Mr. Null. But you already know about that."

"Everybody knows about that, Lieutenant. Not much privacy on the street anymore."

"You can't kill me, Null, because it doesn't comport with whatever academic moral structure you set up to keep yourself alive. It doesn't fit. You have no desire for anything so sense drives you, and it doesn't make sense to kill me. Not right now, anyway."

Null let his arm drop. "No, it doesn't make sense at all. You removed all my addictions, all my emotional pain, my need, and set me out on a purpose, wiping out criminal scum that upset whatever moral balance that can stand in this world—the ethical equation—zero out the balance."

"You whacked out the Family, down to the last man who'll spend the rest of his days at the laughing academy."

"I did."

"I should arrest you, Null. I should end you." Boyd was ready to use her Sig-Sauer and fidgeted with it anxiously against her leg.

"But you won't because you knew it had to be done. Things are better now that it has been done."

"Took a big bite out of kiddie porn with that, didn't it, Null?" Benway sneered.

"I ended it in this town."

"For a while you did, anyway, but the point remains—"

Null finished for him. "That what you did to me—

removing my humanity, my emotions, my fears, my yearnings, my empathy, my very ability to feel anything even physically and know it for what it was, was actually a good thing?"

"That's right, Null. Erasing you actually benefited the world. Something from nothing. How cute."

"So what do we do now?" Boyd drawled with sarcasm. "Have tea?"

Benway cautiously went back downstairs a step at a time. "Excellent idea," he keened. "What kind do you like?"

———

In his mother's kitchen, which was laid out as if it were part of an early twentieth century farmhouse, Null and Boyd sat uneasily at a battered metal enameled table while Benway steeped the tea. For all its appearances, the kitchen could have been in a vegan collective household in Jamaica Plain, not an old Edwardian in Arlington, down to colorful prisms hanging in the windows and ancient rainbow decals still visible on dirty panes of glass, Museum of Fine Arts posters stuck on the cracked plaster wall. "Is that magic mushroom tea, we're drinking, Lee—maybe some psychedelic ergot?"

"Lapsang souchong," he replied, setting the cups down on the table. "We have lemon, cream and sugar."

"Black," they said, nearly in unison.

"He can't poison us," said Null, sipping from his cup. "It's not in his best interest. If he gets you, Boyd, then he gets no deal and remains stuck with Lumpy and me. If he gets me, he gets another mess to clean and again more problems with Lumpy and you. He gets both of us. He gets a double mess to clean and Lumpy."

Boyd sipped with a frown. "How do we even know that him and the Indian aren't still pals? Maybe they're in collusion and this is one big stall."

"You'll know for sure in a few minutes since you're both drinking the tea. I'll join you, in fact." Benway sipped from his greenish brown handle-less cup. "It'll kick in soon, or not."

"This whole thing stinks." Boyd scowled, standing. "I'm taking you in, Lee. Don't struggle or I'll hurt you."

Null grabbed her wrist iron tight. "Think about it, Boyd. Does it look like Benway's happy here? Does it look like he isn't ready to flip?"

Benway fidgeted, setting down his tea. "Truth is, I'll do anything to get rid of that fucking Mic-Mac freak, who up to this minute thinks we're still pals. Just tell me how you want it, Lieutenant, and I'll come across. I need your help like you need mine. Take me in, I'm good—Lumpy bolts, hits Canada, you get a few measly charges against me, I'll say I tried to give up the Indian but you never gave me the chance. Meanwhile, I plead it all down to a couple of years' probation, community service, maybe a five buck a month fine. Upshot is, though, you get no big collar and my problem gets solved, anyway. So do it." He extended his wrists. "Cuff me, take me in. I'll give up everything on the gum down to chemical structure and molecular bonding and you can go chase your own behind trying to get the Indian when he's gone and screwed up North."

"He's right, Boyd. You pretty much get nothing taking him in."

"It's crazy that you're on his side, Null."

"It's all crazy and I have no side. Just expediency and efficiency toward the summum bonum."

"Yeah, and the highest good says I stay at large. But don't worry, Lieutenant. When you pick up Lumpy you can pop me for good measure, whack me around a little to make it look good so he doesn't suspect yet that I'm serving him up like a Christmas turkey. It'll make you feel better."

"I couldn't feel worse than I do now."

"But you got no high from my tea, though, right?"

"No, even that was a disappointment."

"Speaking of disappointments, I think Null should try some of the gum."

———

Lumpy was rolling.

In the dingy, rank shadows of T.T. The Bears Place he was crush dancing hard with a recently post-teenaged collegiate babe who was all over the squat, older street criminal—her meta-bad boy phase on meth, which Lumpy had also thoughtfully provided. Meanwhile, his mouth was chock full of gum, and he lolled a large cud of it with his thick tongue bopping sloppily on his heels to the chaotic shrieking of Death Cab For Cutie, which scourged the monitors and big stack speakers to the point of cracking.

He grabbed her and held her close into the pooling sweat of his body against his saturated "Kill 'em all—Let God Sort 'em Out" tee shirt. She squirmed, halfway to get away and halfway to get further into it. Lumpy licked her ear and whispered with a grating rasp, "We connecting, you and me. *We connecting!*"

She followed his body to the rhythm even as he caromed into other dancers, grabbing each one for a few moments with his thick free arm, holding them each for a moment as he danced in short spastic motions, jagged kicks and gyrations, then set them free as they themselves caromed into yet other dancers. Lumpy wailed into the distorted, clashing din, *"We connect—we connect!"* And with each wail, the girl's heart palpitated with dread and fluttered with increasing anxiety.

Her eyes darted about the dingy, shadowy expanse of the bar, now referred to in the profession as a "toilet," whereas once-upon-a-time it was a macramé and pottery hippie restaurant and folk club, looking for a clear way out. There was none.

Darkness, distortion, and bodies barred her way.

The girl bolted away from him, anyway, freeing herself from the muscled arc of his arm with a quick knee to the groin and lunging through other dancers into the slouching crowd, knocking cigarettes and drinks this way and that. Lumpy grunted, danced and wailed plaintively, but did not give chase. He planted his feet and screamed it loud enough to make chicken-wired windows shake:

"We fucking connect!"

He didn't find himself bounced out into the street; he didn't get into a semi-professional brawl with the bouncers or the flack-jack-eted gel-haired naïf with the earpiece working security. He was swallowed up by the cacophony of Death Cab For Cutie and the boisterous crowd spurring them on to greater depths of atonal debasement. He was ignored, no mass of struggle and violence to attract a nexus of young lockstep college mavericks to witness his recklessness and extremity.

Muscles pumped, veins pulsating and protruding, Lumpy was ready for more. The drug of the gum was rushing through his circulatory system and his brain was flaming red—he could feel it behind swollen eyes. They began to tear.

Neural misfiring into a harsh echo.

Lumpy wanted love, intimacy—some way to breach the barrier of skin, to connect and be joined—

To someone.

To something.

But the night was cold and bitterly damp as was the smoking crowd of twenty-somethings, tweeners and twinks clotting up the entrance to TT's, bleeding out slowly onto Pearl Street, and cutting up. He glared at them, and in a limp, swaggering way, they glared back. Lumpy smiled, his thick palms sweaty, stunted fingers clutching tight in the pockets of his unfashionable boot cut jeans. He spit out the cud of gum which then stuck to the curb.

Lumpy had a knife.

Lumpy was no longer rolling.

Some jock voice volunteered: "The midget Hiawatha wants to party!"

Another adolescent cracking voice volunteered: "Fuck him up!"

Lumpy beamed, eyes wide and gleaming in streetlight. He flashed both middle fingers, turned and walked off down Mass. Ave. He stopped and jerked like a puppet in the damp air as rushing cars and croaking voices swirled about his storm-affected head. He screamed, straightened himself up a short second later and marched down Mass. Ave. with purpose.

He hit Libby's Liquors.

Quietly, and in the full fluorescent lighting amid a bunch of customers, he demanded the money, smiling at the camera in the corner of the ceiling above the cashier, adjusting his shirt for a moment in the convex, anti-theft mirror hung on the opposite side.

The clerk, a sideburn sporting gaunt faced rocker with a dangling unlit cigarette between his lips, pulled a forty-five Ruger revolver out from under the counter. "Not tonight, chief," he said, pressing the button (also under the counter) that would bring the Cambridge cops *toute de suite*.

"Too much gun," Lumpy sighed, clicking his tongue.

"Fuckin' don't move ya little hard-on!"

"For way too, little man."

"Listen, dwarf, you're fucking done."

The blue lights flew through the plate glass and there was the lowing siren, moaning down to a toneless bleat.

"There ya go, chief."

Lumpy held his breath, checked the scene.

The cops just sat there in the front seat, talking, fiddling. Jerking to and fro for a long two seconds, Lumpy stomped and screamed, "Too much gun for too little man!"

The clerk moved backward, his gun arm trembling, but he was too slow.

Lumpy vaulted the counter neatly and gutted the clerk in a

single sideways motion with the knife quick across the belly, then crossed back with the hilt and ran it straight up to the sternum. The clerk clucked, then buckled to the ground. Lumpy stood over him for a moment and blinked, then grabbed down and stuck the Ruger in the waistband of his jeans. He savaged the register for cash as well as the skim box that the clerk had been running under the counter shelf by the alarm button. Customers had long minutes ago gravitated to the back of the store in a confused gaggle of fear. He checked himself for blood, found it wasn't too bad on his clothes, then let himself out from behind the counter, trundling toward the rear security door as the small crowd whispered, creaked and shrank away from him into the furthest corner of the store. In a violent motion, he thrust up the flat red fire-alarmed bolt of the door, which set off a loud electric bell, and lurched out into the back alley, walking fast toward Green Street.

As the long, street-light given shadows fell and blended in the street, he slowed down into them.

Two uniformed cops entered the scene at Libby's, guns holstered, lurking.

The older supervisor of the two with the gravid pot belly protruding from his uniform squinting hard under mirrored aviator glasses asked commandingly, "Alright. What the fuck is actually going on here?"

SEVENTEEN

The brain was clear and cold, the mind hard and sharp as ice.

He was clean, lying in bed. Even though his body was conspicuously rotting, he was freshly soaped and showered. He probably even smelled good, though his body was wasted, his mouth thick and white with candida, his neck and limbs dappled with the sad purple of Kaposi's Sarcoma, his eyes cloudy. Tense, yet at the same time sustained within a kind of calm, Kenny Embers ran over in his mind just how hospice care for him would end that night. Despite the lax security, he would have to be quiet and precise—no wasted movements or disease impeded clumsy motions allowed. He would have to be directed and clinical, swift and sure.

This was no easy demand to meet, since he had the shakes tolerably bad.

His mouth watered uncontrollably, which put him on the edge of drooling and his brain, though clear and steady in its thinking as he lay in his main ward bed, felt slow and staggered.

It should be easy, he told himself, lying there. This was a hospice —death care for the doomed. Security was all about preventing break-ins, not break-outs. Who on his last legs would want to break out of the gentle and cozy care of the hospice? Who wanted to bleed their disease into the street?

He did.

It was a simple matter of what he owed to God.

His God needed him; it was evident in his not appearing to him as he was wracked in agony on protease inhibitors, interferon, ribavirin, Incivek and other retrovirus drugs that it seemed were far too late to do him any good. The disease was eating him alive even as he methodically and systematically was vomiting his life away. He was a quarter of the size he had been when he was superficially healthy, when he glowed with the awkwardly energetic bloom of youth. He was light as a bird, cut apart by pains and weird occlusions of energy that rendered him a trembling twig of a human clutching at the sheets of his bed, shivering and prone.

Even now he was sweating in rivulets.

Nevertheless, he could have escaped at any time.

Even in his sickened state, the staff were all weaker than he, they lacked resolve. They may have had conviction, which he was actually grateful for, but they lacked the hardcore isolation of dynamic need. And such was his need for god.

His God had deposited him there, a victim of the ministrations of Mrs. Coelacanth. They had taken away his half-rotted clothing, his two handy buck knives, his ragged wallet and gave him a plot in the room of the dying. No private rooms in the Medicaid funded hospice wing of the Dapper O'Neil Shelter and Service Group. He had started out in one, but that was just for transition's sake, to calm him down and orient him. It was all "intake," wherein predictably enough they had taken him in.

Yet they were persistently nice to him, kind to him, fed him, medicated him, helped him bathe. The nurses were sympathetic yet professional and his counselor, a dork named Dworkin, overweight and a little sloppy with his wraparound beard, had conversations with him that made him feel continually attached to life even as he knew he was losing it.

He did not hate the hospice as he was so initially assured that he would, but the overarching bitterness and anxiety beneath all good feeling for the conscientious care he was receiving was the argument that kept screaming in his mind at the forefront of many others:

God had forsaken him!

But he had known from all the church-going crypto-Catholic religious training he had received before his parents booted him out on the street with nothing but the clothes on his back and fled to a paradisial place called New Smyrna Beach in Florida, that all of this was merely a test—a trial provided by the deity to set him right at the end of his life and to guide him to an afterlife reward where he would be united with the late Jimmy Blue Eyes and his grandparents and Goldie, the one-eyed boxer dog. It would be a place where the care and kindness of the hospice would both be extended and continued and yet no longer be necessary at all, just a by-product of essentially unquestioned love. His body yearned for love and connection like a cure.

He had to—find God. That was the simple edict that made him clutch at the sheets of his bed in anticipation of action.

He had to save God, for his deity in his human incarnation was set on a path of destruction no one person could tolerate for long without going under. And God, as human, had sacrificed infinite miracles for his own skin. It had all been engineered that way in order to save Kenny Embers, in fact, which underscored his importance and gave him a flush feeling of ego. After all, in his doomed effort to exact retribution on the Muscle of the Ork, he found himself at the scene of the slaughter of an angry God who yet managed to need his help in order to survive the very cataclysm that he had caused. It was all God's plan toward an elaborate salvation.

It was excruciatingly simple: Null was God and Null needed his help. Therefore, he was essential and godly.

And the rat bastards that slew Jimmy Blue Eyes and tricked him out as a whore needed to die, as much by his edict as by God's.

It was excruciatingly simple: he had been elevated by God's law. And God's law was the violence of dying for a vengeance that benefited no one within its own enclosed and self-sustaining purpose. Vengeance without purpose, without practical protection, or benefit to anyone living was the honor and purpose and law unto God. It was the essence of the divine.

Set the penance, punish those who believe in nothing, sanctify the faithful willing to die purely for the deaths of others to protect the influence and power of God, the righteousness of the afflicted, the tortured, the victims of unclean death; those crushed under the jackboot of unbelief. This was the will of God. This was the incarnation of Null.

So now, all he had to do was hold himself together without entering into a coughing jag, vomiting or shaking so badly that he would clumsily fall over some piece of furniture or bed frame and get the hell out of Dapper O'Neil into the biting cold of the night. All he had to do was sneak out of a place where there were few, if any, measures meant to keep you in and find Null.

He threw himself out of bed and wound up on the floor, shaken but not panicked. The tiles were cool against his sweat-soaked clothing. His head throbbed with a slight bump he had received hitting the floor. His limbs ached. In the stillness, all he could hear was the humming buzz of the servers and routers in the office and of the fluorescent lights in the hallway and the uneven breathing of the other now sleeping residents.

All he had to do was unwind the sheet from his body, pick himself up and make his escape from a place that, unlike Assault 'n' Stall juvie, wasn't meant to keep him in at all.

All he had to do was to find his fucking knives.

————

"It's utter junk," said Yonah Shimmel, who sat slack in his metal chair, wiping his mouth with his sleeve. "Crap."

"I ask you for a report, everything you could work up on the shit, and this is what you have to give me?"

"In general, yes. Lieutenant. I've already submitted the formal version for your review, but here's my précis: After enough doses, the agent proves toxic to the limbic system and to the amygdaloid nucleus of the brain, then ultimately to the whole cortical structure of the brain itself. Just another brain-fry designer street drug, not even a good one."

"And the gum is the delivery system. So why the hell do they chew it?"

"It tastes good, for one. For the other, monster dopamine and serotonin reuptake properties, much more so than MDMA, which gives a greater release of serotonin and norepinephrine than of dopamine or bathsalts, which just send everybody to the moon on a one-way trip. "

"Molly," she mumbled, leaning back in her chair. "How much more?"

"By maybe a factor of four, enough to kill you if you keep chewing the stuff, which you want to do."

"What stops them then? We don't have that many corpses to count yet."

"Violence stops them."

"This is what they call 'Chaw?'"

"This is what they call death knell. Just the fact of its wearing off can bring on emotional lows so intense—"

"I know—it drives them to violence."

"There needs to be more testing, so I can only guess. But the frustration and lower-brain response is such that a wild lashing out could be expected. Chaw has an amphetamine-type effect when it slides further into the brain and disperses. It's fat soluble, meaning it works its way permanently into the neuroganglia. It's another phenethylamine, like bath salts, gravel, Molly or flakka, α-Pyrro-lidinopentiophenone, an artificial cathinone."

"So what does that mean, layman's goddamn idiot terms if you please?"

"Damage it causes is permanent and it's out-and-out poison. Imagine Molly so powerful you feel a connected euphoria to everyone and everything which then gets ripped away abruptly, no nice easy gradations of coming down, no slowly diminishing effect, just a great gash in reality. Imagine the emotional amygdaloidal response when heaven's torn away replaced by hell. One word covers it."

"Rage?"

"Berserk is more like it. Excited delirium. Hysterical psychosis and aggression. When those club kids rioted, they were trying to rend each other to bits, tooth and nail. Kicking and screaming improvised mayhem. The most common wounds from all the scenes so far have been nail scratchings, some of them inches deep Then we have knife wounds, shoe-heel wounds, teeth marks, marks on faces from rings, keys, cigarette burns—it's been the whole gamut."

Shimmel adjusted his woolen bobby-pinned yarmulke along his hairline. It itched madly. "People tried to batter each other to death just with their knees and elbows."

Boyd sighed and lit a cigarette in her "no smoking" office, blew a ring, and cursed. "So what's the bottom line?"

Shimmel spat back: "Get it off the street. The damn Chaw is a health hazard coming and going. And it's legal! Just like gravel or flakka. Bath salts."

"Good opinion, not that I needed it, and not that the powers that be will want to do anything about it. I meant, is there an antidote, a counter-agent?"

Shimmel rose, knowing that he'd overstayed his welcome. "If there ain't one for Molly, then there ain't one for this. You can only hope that those who take too much of it fry their brains out to a coma state quickly enough before they do much harm. So far, that doesn't seem to be working."

"I'll get LaCuna to authorize the issuance of a public warning."

Shimmel hitched up his corduroys as he left. "Not that my opinion really counts for much, but you better leak it."

Boyd filed her report on the 1270 massacre, highlighting the suspected involvement of the Ork crime crew, met with Inspector Phil LaCuna who genially laughed her out of his office at the mention of issuing a public service announcement warning of the depredations of "Chaw." She made sure to leak details of Chaw to the Boston network news affiliates as well as to the dailies and handouts, The Globe, The Herald, The Dig and Tab. It was a press conference done in shadowy, whispered installments.

It echoed fast down to the street—the whisper campaign hit the bars, clubs and after-hours enclaves with the vengeance of an urban myth. Soon every friend-of-a-friend-of-a-friend on Facebook had tried Chaw. But no one could find any.

That's when the undercurrent of demand began to roil and rumble as cable news ran national feed story segments about the deadly gum.

Such a dangerous high, it should be avoided—so dangerous you had to feel it, to taste it.

You had to try it—to roll hard with it, harder than Molly.

And if you wanted it, and your intention was to score a supply, then all roads led to Boston. You supposedly couldn't even get a knock off in New York, which made underground New York entrepreneurs swoop down hard and fast on Bean Town streets to scoop up the drug. Gypsy dealers were combing the catacombs and enclaves in packs for product, but there was none save what had gone loose at the clubs. And that had all been cleaned up and confiscated by the police as evidence. What was worse, no one knew where it actually wound up—none was in evidence in the evidence room despite bribes and juice and extortion brought to bear to glom onto it.

The usual cops couldn't help because someone had hoarded it all.

Boyd and Shimmel, they did it. The remaining public supply of gum was stuffed in a corrugated box at the bottom of the closet in Boyd's office.

Regardless, demand was only ramping.

They were sitting on the mother lode without knowing it.

Lumpy was about to drag Benway upstairs, sit him down at the wrapping machine and set him to work. The overly industrious Benway had already made too much gum cut into flat sticks before the Ork realized its failure and apparent lack of value, but he had neglected to wrap it. And now that Benway seemed diffident and lazy, almost defeated in fact, even as the apogee of their success was about to be reached, rather than punish him, Lumpy was exultant, even ebullient.

He did a war dance of delight, catching the first inklings of national coverage of his and Benway's special product while Benway, the strained grin frozen to a harsh rictus on his face, cringed in discomfort.

Filmore whooped and warbled, mocking the cliché of old time Hollywood Indians but strikingly right somehow for a rave dance. Benway made tea and dreamed of freedom. He was conniving a time and a place to arrange for that bitch Lieutenant Boyd to take Lumpy and stick the gum mayhem on him so that he could flee peacefully to Canada and make in-roads, maybe in Montreal, to begin another business. The problem was how to keep the Muscle of the Ork from following him after they killed Lumpy in lock up, because that's what they would do. Lumpy had done far too many enforcements for the crew for Malek the Mallet to let him live and just serve time, plus he'd murdered crew members in good-standing down at the 1270. Not really an allowable offense, even if he had had something to offer in trade like a big stash of the bad gum or a hot million bucks worth of meth which had gone missing after some wildcat fuck held court with Ork housepainters down at a defunct safehouse in Alston.

And now the wildcat fuck somehow was running the Gangsta Boyz crew, and just about nobody had seen him, reasoned with him, spoken to him and the few who did had nothing to say about it. Some of them were now corpses. Nobody knew who he was, where he came from, even his name, or if they did know they weren't saying it. They only knew what he was. When pressed, one of their lieutenants called him "that 7:30 motherfucker." He translated it with a backward hitch of the shoulders to mean that the man wasn't just crazy but had taken psychopath to a new level.

Talking about him was considered bad luck on the street, and the lieutenant shied away from it. It was as if the wildcat fuck who now ran the Gangsta Boyz, which they would not deny, embodied some sort of tribal curse, something Voodoo, Santeria or *Ordo Templi Orientis*.

Benway had never seen one of the Gangsta Boyz scared before and he deeply envied whoever could have had such an effect on them. He wished he himself had that kind of street cred—could put fear in their faces, respect in their manner, caution in their attitude in the way that just the mention of the anonymous wildcat fuck could.

He didn't make the connection.

He didn't see it glaring back at him from the shadows; it was too fleeting an idea. Benway was trying so hard to counterbalance the concept of turning his stock of the defective gum drug into quick riches, despairing of selling off his formula and services to such a quick hit numb-nuts crowd, dumping Lumpy for good and all while managing not to get himself ripped off and killed in the process that he could not see it. It was so tempting a prospect, yet so grim he could not notice at all the long and unobtrusive figure of Null lurking over the whole process.

He could mutilate Null's brain function, have tea with him in his kitchen, but could not imagine that murderous, ineffective specter being key to his scoring ample drug money to flee. Benway couldn't just see the enveloping shadow of Null.

And neither did Lumpy, now lounging alone in an extra bed in the highest tiny room bundled in the gambrel attic truss of the Edwardian house. He was lying on his back, one leg crossed over his knee, fiddling with his smart phone. Gray light poured in from a single shadeless window, a flock of starlings cast a large dappled shadow briefly over him as they flew by.

He lay on his back looking at figure model selfies and lingerie pics on Instagram. He didn't really know quite how it worked—the phone app and the website—but he let the phone guide him through, which more often than not was successful, and when it wasn't, he had no time for it. His eyelids were languid, as if he was about to drift off to sleep, but he preserved beneath a canny under-current of wariness.

He was thinking about masturbating, licking full lips.

He wanted flesh and the urge swelled inside him, still, a quick tug and that would be that. Or maybe go to the trouble of a whore. He was sure there was an "app" for that somewhere on his phone, perhaps several in fact. There was a whole world of hookup sex apps that he had barely scratched the surface of, and any one of them would likely have worked, even if he had to conscript Benway into doing all the smooth talking, but the problem was, despite the animal of lust that he was, Lumpy required something other than flesh. Intensity, yes, certainly flesh, but something other, something more profound and transcendent. It troubled his brain and made his head pulse with the sheer difficulty of apprehending it, of defining it —it was connection, yes. He wanted to connect. But in connecting it was to achieve something bigger, deeper, like the transubstantiation he had learned about the bullshit of Christ being cheap red wine and a cracker long ago when he was being educated by volunteer nuns at Assault 'n' Stall. It was like the memory of a name on the tip of his tongue; a butterfly on a hot summer's day he caught a glimpse of but couldn't fix in his vision for long enough to be grasped from the air. An ephemeral image.

Mercury through the fingers.

Love, maybe.

But no, that was a tawdry, overused term.

It was a word from deep, subverbal childhood, from toddler days.

Affliction—that's what it was. It had come from his mother, a word she had used once. Lumpy wanted expansive, extreme *affliction*. That was how he conceived the word, dismissing mere *affection*. It was such a reverent term to him he couldn't even do a search for the word to confirm its meaning with his phone—as if getting the correct definition of the word would violate its power and meaning.

It was a kind of oneness that occurred in enthusiasm and intensity, exploding into that violent rush of intoxicating rage, subsiding into a peace that soon was subsumed by isolation and disconsolate woe.

The rumble and thunder of the drug.

Lumpy thumbed his way through more nudes on his screen. These images did nothing to stir him; if anything, they were like a momentary pacifier, a pleasant view, those vistas of feminine flesh, somehow soothing and hopeful. He lay there drinking them in, their breasts and shaved vaginas, the sloping curves of shoulder, waist and back, the floods of lush hair. He was waiting there, flat on his back on the attic bed in Benway's family hideaway for the calls he knew would come—the emissary of the Ork inveigling him to meet somewhere to be quickly and cleanly dispatched; the Gangsta Boyz negotiator angling for the remaining supply of gum, either to broker a deal with the New York gypsy traders or to rip off the gum themselves for quick Boston street resale and shoot Lumpy in the face. Either way, no doubt Benway had gotten the message he didn't want to deliver; it was time to blow town and give up the gum, hopefully for a tidy sum. He entertained thoughts of taking Benway to Montreal and setting up shop there, dismal companion though he was. He also thought of killing him efficiently, maybe in a sacrifice play to either Ork, New York or Gangsta Boyz. It would be easier, but then goodbye gum. Albatross around the neck that he was, the fucker was still useful, and he promised a lifetime supply of the gum. Even now Lumpy's brain was jonesing to be tossed about and shuffled up by a chaw or two of Benway's flawed product; his brain felt shriveled-in at the edges and saliva ran down the dry insides of his cheeks in anticipation.

The ring tone bleated as the phone vibrated in his hand.

"Time to play," Lumpy grunted, and swiped his thumb across the smartphone screen to answer the call.

"Motherfucker," he spoke into the phone.

EIGHTEEN

"Are you soft or what?"

"Easy, Nicky," said the short, paunchy, salt and pepper-haired man in the wraparound amber visor and gray off-the-rack suit. Malek the Mallet. "You'll open your stitches if you get too rambunctious."

Typical ward floor of Mass General Hospital—not an empty bed in sight. Moaning and groaning adding to the ambient sound of the machines monitoring and sustaining life. Nurses, residents and an attending or two flurried about ignoring the two of them as they spoke. Nick Andromeda was flat on his back, his leg in traction.

"You being here is like an admission," Andromeda complained. "Kiss of fucking death."

Malek stood pat chewing gum, calm as a mortuary attendant. "Warm this afternoon. Looks like some good sun to help us out of the late winter gloom."

"Fuck the weather report and get lost before someone sees you here with me and tells a friend down at One Schroeder." Andromeda made a pained sound at the back of his throat having thrust himself a bit too far to the right.

"I think I have more friends down at One Schroeder than just about anyone else. I got a big payroll, Nicky, which is why you're on it."

"A little louder there, Malek. I don't think they heard you at Internal Affairs. And what's that gum your chewing? You rolling?"

"It's Juicy Fruit and no one gives a shit, Nicky. It's an open secret who's with me and who isn't. They make jokes about it but no one's going to do anything. Well, except maybe the ones working OC with that *strega* bitch Boyd."

"That would be me, Malek."

"Well, you're not in much of a position to do anything."

"I'm in a position to bleed."

"Better the dead friend should be the one who's bleeding, but instead he's got my fucking meth."

Andromeda grunted, making a thwarted effort to shift himself. "Shut up, Malek. We're in a fucking crowd here. Are you trying to get us charged or what?"

Malek spat on the floor, frowning. "Nicky, I don't have time to play spy games and like I told you, no one gives a shit."

"If I have to go to a hearing when I'm ambulatory, I'll put a bullet in you."

"If you have to go to a hearing, you won't have to worry about that."

"Like I have to worry now?"

"Exactly, Nicky. We're in the middle of Mass General, where everybody's talking and nobody pays attention to anything. Just swallow your fucking pain meds and focus."

"I got a morphine drip," Andromeda stated emptily. "Shattered femur, thanks to that zombie fuck. Fucked up metatarsals."

"He got the best of you, Nicky. I'm thoroughly disappointed."

"It doesn't take much to see you don't need me in this anymore."

"Can I really use you, Nicky, like this?"

"You're using me, anyway."

"That can change."

"Gonna cut my pay?"

"Cutting you may be expedient."

"I'm making no plea, Malek."

"Where's my fucking hot million bucks of meth?"

"That Null fuck has it all, but you know that."

"I know it. You let him have it."

"He took it off me after he shot my legs out from under me."

"You were supposed to do him, Nicky. Not add vaudeville to the street."

"The dead friend is better than we thought."

"He wants us all to be his dead friends, just like the Family. He wants to cut me out and run Boston like he already runs the Gangsta Boyz."

"Nobody knows who runs the Gangsta Boyz—some shadow man."

"It's that zombie fuck, Nicky, and you know it. And we both know we got to kill him again. Make a grease spot where once there was a shadow."

"Not for nothing, Malek, but when I can get up, he goes down."

"Not for nothing, Nicky. He's already down."

Andromeda's eyebrows both rose with irony. He spun the wheel on his morphine drip. "I see—he just doesn't know it yet." This was snide.

"No, he don't, but he'll get his education soon enough. School's in session."

"You're triangulating him. You bought off some Gangsta Boyz."

Malek mopped the sweat off his brow. "I don't get it, Nicky, but no. Can't buy 'em off no matter what, superstitious damn jigaboos. They think this wildcat fuck is some evil demon from beyond what they can't kill. They freaking *believe*."

"He's coming for you, Malek."

"He's already been to see me and I got a collapsed lung for my trouble. Hey, why don't you got any fuckable nurses fawning all over you fluffing your fucking pillow?"

"I'm in maintenance mode here. They just ignore you between meals. Besides, they're almost all fugly."

"Nobody's coming for you, Nicky?"

Andromeda went under his pillow, pulled a thirty-eight Ruger, unsilenced.

"Let him try. I'll hold court from my freaking hospital bed."

"Why didn't they get that off you? This is a hospital, for Christ's sake."

"And I'm a cop. We get away with murder these days." He blew on the muzzle of the gun, then stashed it back under the pillow.

"He's got us both marked and made, don't he?"

"Sure, Malek, but he don't fucking want me. I'm just a cop he took off the game board. I don't mean anything to him. You, on the other hand—"

"Jerk me off with the other hand. He's got too many problems to worry about me."

"How do you know?"

"I'm creating them," Malek sighed.

"Better alert the media then. Put the creep to bed already and stop bothering me about it. Nothing I can do about any of it for a while." Andromeda grunted, squirming slightly where he lay.

"Sadly true, Nicky."

"So what am I, fired? I have to expect some goon in my car in the backseat with a garrote? A long-range sniper shot to the neck while I'm getting coffee outside? A shiv to the ribs in an elevator? What?"

"No, Nicky, you will be useful in spite of yourself."

"Oh yeah, well, how'll that play?"

Malek spat out his wad of juicy fruit so that it stuck to the wall. "I want you to get my gum out of One Schroeder."

———

Null might as well have been sleeping. His pulse, respiration and blood pressure were all an even, solid normal. He was sweating slightly, but his face was smooth despite scarring, untroubled-looking, no creases of effort around the mouth and eyes. He was almost smiling, and there was something tickling in the depths of his brain that almost made him want to smile. It was an unaccountable dream-like impression of satisfaction, a faded ghost image, a suggested outline of something once felt that might have been present at the physical act of remembering in a stream of acetylcholine but was really no longer present in Null's abridged lexicon of responses.

His attitude for anyone would have simply been out of place, a situational mismatch, as he was being pounded in the stomach by more of the muscle of the Ork as he was being held tentatively and insecurely in a full nelson from behind. Ork muscle behind him and in front of him, straining his arms, hammering his abdomen. They let him go and opened fire, not one took a head shot or a kill shot, but enough rounds hit his flak jacket at the center that the force knocked him to the ground, knocked the wind out of him, left him wheezing at their feet. Null struggled but could barely get a lungful of air, let alone rise to his feet.

"Bullet in the head," one pock marked, thick lipped assailant called.

"Kill the mook," was the response,

Null seethed air through his teeth as the sound of wheels on the red brick and concrete of the Lindemann Mental Health Center street alley off Cambridge Street and the scraping of heels reached his ears.

"Blow out what's left of his brains but let me get a look at him first."

Null coughed blood as the muscle of the Ork up-ended him, clumped around him so hard that his feet couldn't touch the bricks. They had him grabbed hard from behind, good and tight.

The odd sound was quickly revealed: A wheelchair.

The Lead Muscle Thug wearing casual Khakis and a La Coste shirt and jacket grabbed Null by the throat and spoke up: "Take a good fucking look, zombie fuck!" His hair was in a neatly trimmed pompadour.

One of the three thugs behind him, the one in the center, directed his head toward the object. Null stared forward fish-eyed, unblinking.

"It's a present from Nicky Andromeda. Know him?"

Null breathed evenly.

The three thugs picked him up from behind. It seemed that when they did that his legs should have kicked, but they didn't. The Lead Muscle Thug hammered him in the abdomen such that saliva bubbled up on the outer rim of Null's mouth. "Well, he knows you."

"Fucked with the Ork for the last time, mutt."

He creased Null's windpipe with his forearm.

"You put him in a wheelchair, now he's gonna put *you* in a wheelchair."

Lead Muscle Thug motioned for the ones behind Null to let him down.

"Funny, I don't see him around here enjoying the show."

Null then took a shot to the face that should have broken his nose. It didn't.

"We can do this all night," Null said nonchalantly. "Or do you have something else in mind? If you do, then would you mind getting down to it? Otherwise I might fall asleep."

"They say you're pretty good at taking a beating there, zombie fuck. Maybe the best at it ever."

"Dubious distinction, I assure you."

"Ten-dollar words, I like that. You're an educated corpse, ain't ya?"

Null spat blood coolly. "Not a corpse yet. Close, but not yet."

"Yeah, you ugly fuck? Well, tonight you're going all the way, you smart-mouthed fuckstick. You're going to make a wicked ugly corpse."

"Wicked pisser," said Null without irony. "But all I hear is you talking poetry to me. I don't see anything else happening, much less feel it, not that I really feel anything at all anymore, of course."

"You're cute for such an ugly fuck."

"You trying to suck my dick, or what?"

"Suck on this," Lead Muscle Thug snarled and hit him full on in the chest with a stun gun that hummed and crackled menacingly. There was a faint burning scent, smoky in the chill night air.

Null went rigid and jerked hard into a seizure before hanging limp and slack from the arms of his captors. His pants dripped urine from under his topcoat.

"Fuck," said the center thug behind him. "He fucking peed!"

"Pissed his pants."

"Hold him hard, motherfuckers. Don't loosen up corpse boy an inch," Lead Muscle Thug called out. "He's full of tricks. I hear he's slid out of deals like this before. But this is my deal and he's not sliding out no matter what. This contract is sealed and delivered."

"He's still peeing!" whined the thug to the left, shoring up his grasp on Null's shoulder and arm.

"What do you expect, giving him fifty thousand volts to the chest?"

"You're not supposed to do that," said the thug on the right. "You mighta killed him."

"Is he dead? And no, do NOT loosen up!"

"I can't tell."

"Well, check on it."

"Not when I'm holding him like this I can't."

"Don't under *any* fucking circumstances let him go! Goddamn it!"

But they did. It was the way the dead weight of Null's body lurched forward, which hit a reflex in them that caused one of them to let go entirely, causing the others in turn to follow suit, dropping Null completely crumpled to the shadowy pavement.

Then the gunfire came that made the Muscle of the Ork disperse, leaving Null lolling akimbo like a crash test dummy thrown from a car to the pavement. Lead Muscle Thug returned the fire with a mini AR-15 semi-automatic pistol as he went back to Null's dark and desolate figure that stained the bricks of the pavement. "Fuck you, niggas. I'm finishing the fucking mook! You can't do shit about it!"

A spray of semi-automatic rounds miraculously missed him. None of the Gangsta Boyz were firearms qualified, licensed or trained shots, and it showed. They were good at close range or for spraying bullets into a wide field, not so great at accuracy. So they did what they were best at. For added measure, Do-Rag popped his head up from behind concrete.

"Smoke them ofay motherfuckers!" he shouted.

Lead Muscle Thug produced a long switchblade, the kind you hardly see any more with the blade jacking up steady and firm from the center of the pommel and hilt. It gleamed in streetlight. "Finally I'm gonna turn you into a real corpse, Pinocchio," he sneered.

The wheelchair came rolling toward Null and the Lead Muscle Thug backwards.

Lead Muscle Thug looked away from the dark figure on the

pavement for a moment, distracted. The chair came close, stopped, then spun around abruptly.

Came a hoarse, whispered voice, "How about dealing with a real boy, first?"

Lead Muscle Thug rose up, surprised, knife in one hand, automatic in the other, arms outstretched like Christ and Kenny Embers with a grunt, ground both of his knives just beneath his solar plexus when he lurched forward from the chair.

Then he pulled his arms apart hard, virtually splitting Lead Muscle Thug up the middle before he slumped over into the spot where Null lay. Or where he once lay, because Null, unsteady on his feet and cocking his head groggily, was up and grabbing at the waving semi-automatic.

He was grabbing at the semi-automatic even as he watched Lead Muscle Thug's last move go down: a perfectly arced stab into the chest of frail and coughing, half-dead looking Kenny Embers. Lead Muscle Thug bled out where he lay gurgling softly on the ground while Kenny Embers, switchblade buried in his chest up to the hilt, hissed piteously.

Do-Rag approached with three Gangsta Boyz crudely carrying semi-automatic rifles several paces behind him in tow.

"You gonna make it, Cap'n'?"

Without taking a breath, Null replied: "Tell those idiots to either lose or hide the goddamn Bushmasters or whatever they're carrying and get back to home turf Dorchester before I kill them *and* you."

"But we had yo' back—"

"Do it now," he said flatly, sliding the bolt back on the semi-automatic, loading the chamber. He raised the gun up. "And I am not a lousy shot."

"You gonna provide us more product to sell?" Do-Rag asked weakly.

"Do or die, little Do-Rag. I have no patience. Get them out now."

Sweating heavily, Do-Rag obliged. He quickly impeded the other Gangsta Boyz from approaching Null and parried their questions with the order to get back to sacred Dorchester turf. They were full of questions, near innocent curiosity and fear when they got a straight look into the dark disaster and calamity that was the face of Null. They could see it in him, even in his current diminished state, he was a stone righteous killer who would not be questioned or reasoned with. He exuded a naked purpose which would cut through anything to reach its end. And it was clear from where they stood in relation to Null that they were expendable and he was quite willing to expend them with a blink of the eye and a flick of the wrist.

They left in a noisy huddle and Null contemplated shooting them all for a moment, then slowly lowered the gun.

"Take the knife out of me," Kenny Embers croaked, lying back and sunken into the wheelchair.

"If I do, you'll bleed out."

"There's a lot of pain." This was followed by a whimper.

"It'll hurt more if I pull it out."

"Not fair," Kenny sniffled.

"The pain will be gone soon." Null intoned.

"Dead soon, Lord God."

"That's right."

"Fix it for me, God, bring me back. I have things to do."

"I'm not God, Kenny. I'm just a man and not much of one."

"I have to make it right. Can't let the Mallet get away with it, get away."

"Don't worry, kid. Malek will never get away. I'll see him soon."

"You'll kill him?"

"He'll be wishing for it—beg me for death."

"Jimmy wants him to suffer—Jimmy Blue Eyes. I'll see him soon too."

There was a crackling in the back of his throat and his eyes rolled back in his head for a second.

"Maybe," said Null blankly, "and again maybe not. But I will see Malek and when I do, you can be sure that if Jimmy is anywhere around, he will be pleased."

"They killed me long ago and you let them. Why, God?"

"I'm not God. You saved my life again tonight. And you can't save God."

"They're going to get away with it—with everything. With

Goldie. They killed her you know, skinned her alive, nailed her hide up on the side of the house. Took her eye. For protecting me. My dog."

"She was just a dog."

"God knows better than that. You know."

"If there was a God, maybe."

"But you know!" he shrieked.

"I don't know anything," Null muttered.

"Raped me, hid it, threw me away like trash."

"That I do know."

"They're getting away with it. They're getting away. No one left to save. No one to tell—free and clear. They're getting away."

"No, Kenny. They're not getting away. There's been a change in plan."

"They're getting away."

"No, I promise they're not. I swear to you they won't get away with it."

"Lord God!" he screamed.

"No, there is no God. Just me. And if I could wish anything, I would wish to trade places with you right now at this very instant. I would wish to be you. But I can't make it happen. I can't even wish. I can only do the things that I can do."

Kenny lurched back in the chair, arms spasming outward. "Help me, Lord God. Help me! He pleaded.

Null said gently. "I can do that." He jerked the knife out of Kenny's chest in a single motion, causing him to sink down like a deflated balloon, quietly bleed out in deep, rich, dark gouts of blood, and die.

He did so without further sound.

Null blinked, dropped the knife with a clatter, reached into his topcoat pocket for several pieces of gum, tore them out of the wrappers clumsily, and popped them into his mouth in a wad. He turned away and strode off evenly, purposefully into the night air under the gleaming streetlights down Cambridge Street, past the Harrison Gray Otis House, chewing the gum with his mouth open.

NINETEEN

There was a sobbing.

It was just outside the door to her condo, like the scratching of a dog, which is what it sounded like at first. Easy to ignore, at first.

But then it got louder, followed by a skidding against the door, then a soft thud.

Boyd got up from not really watching C-Span on her forty-two-inch flat screen TV that dominated her living room, picked up her Sig-Sauer from its resting place on the arm of the sofa, and went toward the sound.

"Get the hell out of here!" she barked.

If it was anyone legitimate, they would have used the intercom, dialed her unit number. This sounded wrong out of the gate, and whoever it was wouldn't be getting in, that much was sure.

She slid the bolt back on the Sig-Sauer.

"I don't have to call the cops, sonny!" she shouted, her cheek flat up against the door. "I *am* the fucking cops!"

The voice on the other side of the door wailed, thin, high though decidedly male. "I feel death! I *feel* it!" There was panting.

Boyd shook a bit and put the Sig against the door. There was something in the voice that hit her, penetrated her bones like a chill. She let silent seconds tick, sweating.

"Shut up and get the hell out of here!"

The voice keened, "I can't! This is the last place I have to go.

Death is everywhere and life is killing me. Life has me on fire—can't think!"

"I don't know you, so go away," she replied absently, emptily.

"You know me," countered the voice tremulously.

Boyd slid down too and crouched by the door, still clutching the Sig.

It was ear-spitting, the amalgam of a screech and a wail rattling off at the end: "I can feel—life!"

Boyd abruptly sprang to her feet, unbolted the door, yanked it open and stood in a defensive posture, the Sig raised.

There was no one there until she looked down and saw a dark, crumpled clump at her feet.

A small voice pleaded: "Help me."

She knelt down and tugged aside some of the dilapidated topcoat. Breathing was rough and ragged. She nudged the clump on the floor and a limb flopped over.

Boyd said it on the inhalation, suffused with wonder as soon as the word escaped her mouth.

"Null," she mouthed for a second time at the figure on the condo hallway floor.

And a debauched moment in time opened before her.

———

The door opened, and the gang walked through into a blistering light.

"The Fuck?" said the one at the front.

"What's with the fucking lights?" asked the one behind him.

There was a delayed, near unison cocking sound of semi-automatic weapons that came in answer.

What could be made out of the room spoke of a rumpus room in disrepair; matchstick furniture and wood veneer fixtures atop a filthy, discolored mauve carpet shadowed by groups of figures. In the quiet after the cocking sounds for a moment, there was only breathing. Gun barrels quavered.

Lumpy, in a white tank top stained by sweat under hot lights and baggy black cargo pants, spoke up. "Who are these motherfucking guys? I thought everybody who was going to be here, was here."

"Everybody but the boss of the Gangsta Boyz," chimed Benway.

"We don't got no, boss, fucking cracker," spouted Do-Rag.

There were yet more weapons cocking.

"Listen up. This is a clusterfuck," said a boy-man with tousled sandy hair in a leather jacket and khakis. "Any one of you motherfuckers fires off a round and we all get shot up to pieces. This is a goddamn powder keg situation, so chill already. No one's gonna get shit wounded or dead."

"Why the fucking lights?" the first speaker spoke again.

Do-Rag answered. "We wired 'em up to make sure you ofays couldn't hide no bullshit on us."

"Too late for that," huffed Lumpy.

He spoke again—the first thug. "We want your boss."

"Listen up, you fucks. We're here for the Chaw. Got money all counted and waiting. We came from New York in good faith to do a little transaction. No blood, no bodies," said the young New Yorker, standing pat.

"Who the fuck are you?" said the first speaker. "I'm fucking Ork muscle here to press the rights of Malek the Mallet. Know who he is?"

"I'm from New York—I don't know from no fucking Ork. Call me Ed."

"I'll call you fucking corpse, you don't give us the money and the gum."

"Try taking it, genius, and we all die in this little over lit room."

"We just here to guide the transaction," said Do-Rag breathing heavily. "Make sure it go smooth, take a fee for insurance and get you asses out the door."

"They call this an Epic Fail on the Internet," yawned Ed. "If we don't have a deal, then we leave."

"You can go bright eyes, but leave the money."

Ed chuckled and shook his head. "No can do, buddy. My guys are outside with it. They need a call from me on the cell to tell them to bring it in, which, under the circumstances, I'm not going to do."

"We can make you make that call."

"You can try wading through the corpses to do it, but you may not make it," Ed sneered.

One of the men behind the first came up fast beside him and piped up in a nasal voice. "Parley, there ain't nothin' coming for us here. Everybody's out in the open, jacked up with guns. There ain't no advantage."

Ed beamed at this. "Listen to your little friend, Parley. He's right."

"Maybe," said Parley. "But this little fuck over here ain't carryin' is he? No, little pissant!" And he strode over to where Benway stood sheepishly next to Lumpy and shoved his semi-automatic directly under his chin. "You're too chickenshit to carry a gun, ain't you, Benway?"

"I'm civilized," Benway grunted softly.

"You're about dead as it sits," replied Parley.

"Careful," Ed intervened. "You're about to light the powder keg. Explosion imminent."

"This fuck made the Chaw for Malek and the Ork, but he didn't deliver on it, did he? Now he and his boyfriend, a fucking renegade from our ranks who has yet to get dealt with, wanna sell their fucked up product to New York? It ain't gonna happen."

Lumpy brought out his blade, let it glint in the light. "Take the gun off Benway."

"I should put the gun on you instead, Chiefy."

"Okay," said Ed. "This deal is tainted. Nothing is coming from this. We're out!"

"But we got the gum," Lumpy nearly whined. "All packed up and ready to go. You just give us the cash, we take you to it."

Parley shoved a trembling Benway back at Lumpy. "That happens we'll take the gum and the cash for our trouble. Don't put up a fuss, leave and then we can do these two boys quick out back before we go."

"Get the fuck out," grumbled Do-Rag. "Our guy gets back, everybody die."

"We want your fucking guy too while we're at it."

"You only think you want him. You won't when you see him." Do-Rag laughed.

"When I see him, I'll shoot the fucking eyes out of his head."

Ed gestured for his men to move toward the door. "It's been fun, but this deal is a big fat no-go."

The muscle of the Ork raised up their guns. "Nobody goes anywhere till we're done."

"Look around you, Parley. Are you really going to say we're not done? Either we go with casualties or we go without casualties. Any way you slice it, we're going, and that applies to you and your guys too."

"We don't need anyone else to show up, ofay fucks," said Do-Rag coolly. "One o' you takes one shot, one gat triggers off, and everybody die pretty fucking fast."

Benway's face exploded into a smile. "That's right," he said, pushing his way toward the door. "Since nobody can do anything without hitting the morgue, everybody can leave. Bye-bye!"

Lumpy helped clear the way and pushed in behind him. When they got to the door, Lumpy kicked it open into the coldly sour Boston night air. Voices rose on the inside when they hit the street.

"Fucking run!" cried Lumpy.

"Fucking way ahead of you!" Benway panted, striding gawkily.

They were not much further down Dorchester Avenue when they heard the first squalid pattern of shots ring out.

———

The office was sparse but well appertained with leather chairs, imposing oak desk and apparent shelves of book veneer. Malek the Mallet smoked a thin cheroot, one of his eyes drifting off to the side. His lips were curled into a frown, his brow furrowed, and though he sat back in his chair, his body was tense.

"So, I got no fucking gum, and I got no fucking money."

Parley stood before him, slouching disheveled. "We got out alive."

Malek stood and exploded. "To what point? Spending more of my fucking money coming up empty? You fucking goons don't get nothing done. I'm down a hot million in meth, I got a renegade Indian enforcer what whacked out I don't know how many soldiers on the loose, a maniac chemist what ripped me off holding a stash of drugs I can't sell and a fucking zombie trying to whack us all out who now runs a rival crew. This is a shit storm of major proportions and you just stand there whining that you're goddamn alive—a situation I would like to remedy!"

"There's a way out," sighed Parley. "We got the means to do it."

"There are several ways out, fuckstick, and I can figure them all. Without you. In fact, I don't really know what the fuck to do with you." He spat a fleck of tobacco from his tongue.

"Patch it up with the Indian and the geek," Parley rumbled deep from his throat. "Buy them off. Their sale to the New York crowd fizzled—they're hungry for cash."

"Genius!" He clapped. "Pay off the guy what whacked my crew and the chemist who ripped me off. Perfect."

"Yes," said Parley, running his fingers through thinning hair. "Give them the money, tell them all is forgiven, let 'em relax, then blow their fucking brains out. Take 'em down to Gary Lee Obidowski's garage and have a specialist rearrange their internal organs for all I care."

"What about this Null fuck?"

"Make terms with him and do the same. Get him down to Gary Lee's. Fuck, I'll work on him and he'll tell us where the meth is stashed and anything else for that matter—we won't be able to shut him up but for the screaming."

"I don't know, the fucker's tough."

"Ain't we all."

Malek smiled, his eye drifting back and forth. "We'll make him beg for death, then?"

"Sure. Any tune you want, we'll get him to sing. We can make him die real slow."

Malek waved his hand dismissively. "Nothing I haven't thought of."

"I'm sure," said Parley. "But we're on the same page. I know what you need us to do, and I'll get it done."

"You're saying I shouldn't whack you out for that fucking Gangsta Boyz screw-up, then?"

"It's what I'm saying."

"You could take me out with the 38 you got holstered and make a pass at running the crew, you know." Malek spoke this almost musically.

"I could, but I'd never leave this suite alive."

"Just as long as you know that."

"I know it."

"But I can see the one hitch you didn't tell me about, right?"

"Of course you can. You're going to have to meet with them all before they die."

"Yeah, the first is a handshake deal. A meet and greet, let 'em know all is forgiven and everything is hunky dory."

"Yeah. Necessary shit that. What about the second?"

"I thought you knew."

"Well, I had an idea. But I'm not sure."

"Simple." Malek sat back behind his desk and crushed out his dying cheroot. He spoke nonchalantly: "I want to be the last thing that Null fuck sees when I stick a red-hot poker down the center of his chest."

———

"I've got enough money, Filmore. I'm getting out," said Benway, in his childhood bedroom, packing.

"You called me Filmore instead of Lumpy, Doctor—means no good."

"Means I quit."

"Quit nothing. You stay put or I will quit you of life."

"Listen, Lumpy, I got enough cash for the both us from the box of gum I delivered to the Ork the last time. We got to admit this is a bust. We ain't got nothing coming." He needed to get him interested in leaving. He had no intention of sharing his stash of money with Lumpy. He would dump him fast at the first opportunity—leave him flat without a nickel. He just had to keep him on his side somehow until then.

"We got money coming and lots more from New York," Lumpy insisted.

"That's blown, Lumpy—done. They won't touch the gum. They

don't want to ignite crew conflicts going up the eastern corridor. That was a one-time score, don't you get it?"

Lumpy grabbed him by the arms hard, reaching up to the shoulders. "Don't ever say a deal is done when I say it's not! They was gonna buy that gum, sell it out quick and take you and me on in the city. You'd be the chemist making them more product, and I'd be the manager. Simple."

"Manager of what?"

"Of you, Benway. I know how to make you behave. We make it work in New York."

Benway squirmed out of his harsh grasp. "You can't really believe that."

"But I do."

"You're right about one thing. We gotta get out outta here before they whack us out good and proper. We're a pride thing now —a street cred deal. We live and Malek is over and he knows it. He has to show us a messy exit to the next world or he'll wind up going first."

"The Ork wants the gum, make money from the drug as originally planned. We can sell it back to them, then you be their chemist."

"I'll be their trophy down at Gary Lee Obidowski's garage. You'll be several night's entertainment on a meat hook before they burn you down."

"I know they'll make an offer—it'll be all over the street. They want the gum. They were gonna spill blood for it at the Gangsta Boyz." He was almost pleading.

Benway sat down on the bed. "You know, you're right. They're gonna put it out on the street so we hear about it, make us an offer on all the gum we got, a generous one."

"Now you thinking positive, just like Joel Osteen says—feelin' that holy spirit." He slapped Benway on the shoulder and Benway flinched with pain.

"Lumpy, they're gonna lure us in with money and whack us out hard as soon as we meet them—no matter where we do it, no matter who we bring along for security. We're too important dead to

Malek; our being alive makes his life worth less every second we breathe."

Lumpy got it and gulped down. "Trap us and skin us alive."

"So much for Joel Osteen."

"No, no," Lumpy said pacing, "through Jesus we overcome all adversity, let the strength flow through you. Jesus wants us to succeed."

"And what does Jesus want us to do?"

"Jesus wants us to whack 'em out before they get a chance to do it to us, take the fucking cash and hightail it to Montreal."

"I never knew you were such a devout Christian," Benway said with parody sarcasm.

"I don't know about devout," Lumpy replied flatly. "I just watch the cable."

———

There was a low moaning in the dark.

"I feel!" a voice keened.

"You're hot," said Boyd, placing a cold blue washcloth on Null's scarred forehead. "Christ, it's a bad fever."

"I feel!" Null cried again, louder.

"Quiet, Null. Of course you feel. You're alive. Everything that's alive feels."

"Not me—except—for now!"

She sat at the edge of her bed where Null lay squirming, fully clothed although his topcoat had been removed. She had also removed a machete on a lanyard, a sawed-off Remington shot gun, also on a lanyard, and a Glock nine-millimeter. And at the end, an ounce of brown sugar-like crystal meth tumbled out of his pocket to the floor. She took a fanny pack chock full of sticks of Chaw off him too. He had acquiesced and didn't fight her. In fact, he could barely make it to the bed.

"I am alive," he confirmed. "Of course."

"Why did you come here?"

"No one else would take me in." For an instant he thought

about Missy, the nurse, and it was as if he could see her blinding hatred like a red explosion behind his eyes.

"How did you know I would?"

"I just knew." Blue behind the eyes when he thought of Boyd, though. Blue, or was it just the washcloth?

"That was a guess," Boyd murmured.

"Everything I do is a guess," he replied, his tongue thick and agonized as if stuck full with shirt pins.

"What did they do to you?"

"It wasn't what they did to me. It's what I did to them. And it wasn't enough."

"Why wasn't it enough?"

"Because," and he gulped down hard on a clump of shirt pins and could not swallow, "they killed the kid."

"Who's they?"

Null spasmed in obvious pain. "The muscle. "His throat crackled. "The muscle of the Ork!"

"They did this to you."

Wracked with pain, he nearly screamed, "No—the gum!"

"You're on Chaw? You idiot!"

"Chaw and meth," he croaked. "Benway said I should try it— saw no reason not to. Scored a bunch at the murder scene down at the 1270."

"You were there?"

"Only afterward."

"Idiot!" she sighed.

"Meth kept me going—energy."

Boyd replaced the washcloth on his forehead when it fell off. She tried to hold him still.

"And what has the Chaw done for you?"

"Made me live." Then Null stretched out taut across the bed, his mouth gaping open as if to scream, but stayed silent.

Boyd got up and paced, as close to being desperate for a drink as she had ever been.

Null made death rattling sounds.

She came back and sat with him on the edge of the bed. She

shook him at the shoulders and asked, futility clear in her voice, "What is this doing to you?"

Then Null shouted, "Making me feel!"

"And this is a crisis?"

"Everything hurts," Null grunted, "everything. The pain is its own crisis."

Boyd went up in the darkness to the bathroom medicine chest, came back with Vicodin and water. She force fed him four tablets. "That might make a dent."

"How do you know?"

"Never underestimate the ability of human sensitivity to be numbed by drugs."

"My problem is it went the other way."

"I need to sleep. You do too, once the Vic kicks in."

"Got meth for that!" His eyes scrunched down and his lips contorted.

"That'll kill you."

"So far, like the Chaw, it's only made me live."

"Null," she said gravely, adjusting the cloth on his forehead and stroking his cheek. "What you don't understand is that none of that is living."

———

As Boyd slept in the living room on the sofa, Null was up and showering, trembling as the water hit him—first too cold, then too hot and all of it like a violent explosion throughout his body. With tentative hands, he clumsily adjusted the temperature. He moaned when he got it right, his eyes closed and colors playing before his brain. He soaped up and scars writhed under his fingertips.

As the water cascaded across his face from the massage head, he came to the conclusion that he was not himself.

Fluctuations in temperature and water-forced vibrations goaded forth another thought that he was more himself than he had ever been.

His emotions had returned, and he was in greater inner pain than he had ever known; each jagged, fractured recollection was like a knife wound cutting deeper with each image and past sensual reflection into whatever it was that constituted his life. It was the life lived cutting hard and fast into the life that was actually living.

Null needed to scream but stifled it.

He stood directly under the stream and felt vibrating rays of water wash over him.

Every joint hurt.

Every muscle.

The entire area of his skin.

His groin ached.

His back throbbed thick and menacing beats.

His fingers clenched and cramped.

The backs of his knees were like wild animals gnawing at his legs.

Tears spilled in rivulets from his eyes, washed away by the shower spray, but continually refreshed.

He embraced himself and stood flush under the vibrating spray until the water began to cool.

And then there was another pair of hands.

He startled and jerked back at first, then allowed himself to experience the touching.

It was Boyd, naked next to him, her smooth skin sliding up against him beneath the diminishing heat of the stream. Null refused to turn at first, smashing his eyes shut.

"I don't know why I'm doing this," she said, childlike.

"I know why," answered Null, finally turning and facing her.

They kissed with steady abruptness.

The embrace was full—limbs entwined even as the shower grew cold.

They slid out, wet and tumescent; Null breathing husky and deep, Boyd's breaths fluttering.

It was, quite literally, a waltz to the bedroom.

They parted for a moment.

The light of the room was unkind. Ropy scars snaked up and behind Null's body, which had large bruises all over it, purple spider webs in some places, scabbed-over wounds in others. Boyd was pear shaped, heavy in the legs with a bit of a belly, stretch marks and a little cellulite. Her skin was pale and otherwise unmarked. Her wet brunette hair shone a reflection of the window. Her breasts were pert and pointed up.

She stroked Null's shoulder softly, tracing scars almost hesitantly. "How much pain can you take?" she asked with a hollow voice. "How can anybody take this?"

He drew her to him. "I can't take it. Not anymore."

She rested her head against him. "No, you can't, and you shouldn't."

"But I did. Apparently, I wasn't very human." Their breathing together was heavy.

"No, you were not."

"But I am now."

"How human are you?"

"Let me show you."

The waltz resumed and continued several steps to the bed, whereupon it ended and they fell into it.

There was a struggle between the two to break through the barrier of flesh and somehow merge to become something splendid and transcendent, and if not to break through to end entirely, once and for all. It was a struggle against death and isolation, decay and loneliness.

Resistance in panting breaths and straining muscles: a wild energy blistering between them.

A clinging, wrenched in spasm.

He slid into her, marveling at the ease of it.

She sighed and grabbed the small of his back.

Mouths joined, lips pressed close, tongues entwined.

They got into a rhythm that was sustained despite sliding against each other, wet, sweaty, determined to force their way through the barrier—

To defeat isolation.

To end the terrible oneness.

To reach that unassailable point of communion that would reign over death and pain like light over shadow.

Boyd cried out something unintelligible, which made perfect sense.

Null simply grunted, low and guttural.

Like some cosmic nova, an urchin of light burst between them and they were sure that they were winning—that it could be done, that through the flesh they could breach the flesh.

It was a laugh, simple and easy.

Why had this not happened years ago? Why could this not have been?

It was the answer to the lonely questions for so long left abandoned.

It was the thing, the point of contention, the hope against fear.

They were lost in a fog of sweat, although they were sure that they had been found.

There was no doubt.

There was no question.

The surety had been made, the bond solidified more durable than any transitory flesh.

And it was all certain in the mists of bodily fluids and commingled breathing, the sweat and the castoff sheets of the bed.

It was all set.

Until they broke apart and it wasn't.

Success had crashed blindingly into a whole and perfect blackness of failure, an event horizon of loss and disappointment that came from nowhere but within the harshly defined boundaries of the flesh, each defining each.

What had been tried and been so promising had failed.

Death had overcome life again, even though life still lived.

The shadows returned without a word.

Without a sound they knew they had been defeated, without a word, their surrender was in the connection of their glances as they lay apart and facing each other.

Hope had declined with every breath, despite reaching, despite longing, despite the repeated effort as they clambered together in doomed defiance.

But they had broken apart with the greatest finality when Boyd gasped at the fact that Null had somehow at last fallen asleep.

She sat there watching him, her fingers tracing scar after scar.

And what had the world done to him? she wondered to herself, knowing all the while.

And she mouthed the question to herself, knowing the answer to that as well.

Just what had the world done to her?

———

A silent screaming came through his brain. The soundless music boomed.

He was bolt upright in bed, sweating, holding his temples as the need within him rose.

He got up and got dressed with jerky desperation.

It was simple. He had to get out.

It was a miserable and low need to connect—with anyone at any moment, but the immediacy of it screamed in his brain, played on all senses with a hushed noise surging through his body.

As he hunted with jagged desperation for her spare keys, Boyd startled him.

She stood there naked, a pleading look on her face, not betrayed in her words. "Where are you going?"

"I don't know," he said, pausing in thought, looking her over with appreciation and fondness. His eyes were fixed upon her.

"I don't know either," she said.

"But I have to go," he replied in a familiar, blank tone. "I have to."

"Fine," she said with some disappointment, then added before he could speak, "Can I go with you?"

Null experienced something close to shock for a moment, then cooled. "Sure," he said. "You should come with me. You may be the reason I was going out to begin with."

"To get away from me?"

"No, to be closer to you. I don't have any other way to say it, but the point was to be closer to you and to the rest of the world. To humanity."

She shook her head, confused and somewhat moved, standing naked in the sunlight pouring into her condo living room through the cheap Levolor Venetian blinds. She tossed back her still damp hair. "Well, we can do that, I think. We'll start small."

"Starting with you is not starting small," he said, searching for his hat.

"No," she answered, "but beginning where you ended might be a good start."

"Our ends never know our beginnings," Null quoted.

"But in this case, ours do, don't they?"

Null assented, shakily lighting a cigarette.

She dressed, and they left together, and as they left, she took his arm and wouldn't let go.

TWENTY

They were lovers for a few days that seemed to last weeks or months.

Boyd hoped for years.

Null hoped for moment after moment.

Boyd had dropped herself and what remained standing was something as new and vulnerable as a fresh, green insect nymph. She felt flushed with sickness and renewed with possibility, that played across her mind like candy across the tongue.

Null was hyper-vigilant, electrified with a vital sense of his own energy and force, his strength a palpable sensation of renewal, and he was subsumed by sensation. The breeze, the warmth of the sun on his skin, the voices of passersby, the touch of Boyd's sweat-slicked fingers, the cadence of his own breathing nearly paralyzed him.

She pressed into him close as they walked, which steadied him.

They walked in contact in bright, early spring afternoon sundown Newbury Street, where the shops and the cafes were touted to express what was Boston's finest, a coeval to parts of Fifth Avenue in New York City. They sat at an outside table at an overpriced Eurotrash bistro and had lunch.

Null broke out into a sweat, enjoying his food, taken aback by it.

Boyd could not help but laugh.

He was so gaunt and vulnerable, a walking shambles of a man.

Scars were everywhere visible upon him, everywhere.

Could you describe him as handsome?

Maybe not, but in the cold light of day Boyd could. There was something in him that came out almost violently, if you were on the west coast you might call it "an energy," on the east coast maybe "chi," but it was a vital urgency that bordered on passion that may have actually been passion banked like a fire. In Boston you could say "he had a thing."

Handsome? In that he was compelling, a void of need and a surfeit of undirected emotion, you could say this was a condition beyond the flesh that transformed its aspect.

Yes, to Boyd, he was handsome.

And at that moment, over a table of food in the warm sun and unremitting breeze, he was everything that there was to Boston Police Lieutenant Kay Boyd.

His shadow against the sun blotted out the other shadows.

Her dead husband.

The murdered children.

The wounds laid upon her by criminals.

A knife in her side.

Detox.

She resisted ordering wine.

It was easy as she realized she didn't want the wine in any degree as much as she wanted Null. Null, who actually crackled a raspy laugh at one of her jokes.

Null, who could now laugh. Null who could now be called human.

Null, on fire from within, with a need for every sensation, every possible slaking ease of emotion and who when he looked at Boyd saw only contentment and fulfillment.

This blocked out the shadow of her betrayal, when she led him on to be a CI against The Family while using him to be a decoy against yet another CI. The whole thing had failed and led to the main CI being tortured to death and Null being tortured into something less than human.

Something distorted and wrong.

Something rent and bent into a relentless monster of cold,

unemotional retribution—a biased and predetermined justice that found its conclusion in a perpetual sentence of death.

But Null now had been changed yet again.

He was raw emotion, cluttered and obfuscated into the jerky parody of a paramour.

He wanted everything that Boyd could offer him—

everything, even the implicit pain of the connection. And she wanted him. It was as if the vacuum that he had been, now filled the vacuum within her.

Boyd was on the verge of weeping since the advent of Null. She, too, was possessed of raw emotion.

In a thoughtless way, she wanted him to replace all that had been damaged and missing—substitute good experience for bad memory, pleasure for pain, hope for fear.

Null was prepared for a relentless sentence of life.

When she clasped his uncertain hand, he accepted it, and clasped back.

They did as lovers do—practiced as lovers, behaved as lovers.

They held hands strolling in sunshine through the rose path at the Public Garden. They window-shopped the antiques on Charles Street. They ogled the massive representations of world religions at the Sargent Wing of the Boston Public Library in the old McKim building.

They made a lighthearted promenade through the pretty parts of Boston—the ends of Boylston Street and the Back Bay—the long way to Cambridge along the Esplanade.

They bonded at night in Boyd's bed, in her place after sex that whispered like a dream.

And in dreams, Null walked the streets of the South End, shadowed by the old brick rehabs, looking for trouble. Worse yet, he was looking for trouble in fact.

His dream had, in fact, become reality.

Gum chewing Null, gum addicted Null, meth infused Null was looking for trouble.

They saw him limping, the roving street gang, and instantly took him for a mark. He was easy to surround and intimidate. They crushed in on him, hard. To their amusement, at first, he crushed back. It wasn't a difficult calculation to make—five against one. They were going to have some fun before beating the mark to death.

Null sized them up in the brooding shadows of Columbus Avenue amid the rehabs and basement boutiques.

They sized him up, and laughed unanimously.

They were all white young twenty somethings—the usual Boston Irish Jewish Hispano mix from the projects or driven down from Lynn or Dorchester. They had personalities and individual quirks and crochets, charm and even an uneven a kind of charisma. And none of that mattered. As a group, all that was annihilated. As a group, they formed an entity of hungry violence, a wrenching yet frivolous need.

Null limped toward them and faced them, shaking.

He was not calm, nor cold, nor unaffected.

He was sweating and his lips were white and pulled back into a grimace of contempt.

The leader taunted, "Little bitch wants to get by."

"Little bitch ain't never gettin' by again!"

The leader, tall in a distressed bowler hat, slumped in denim and a torn high school varsity jacket, walked up to Null to push him over, counting on the injured leg to buckle, grinning happily.

But that's not what happened.

Null reared back his head and screamed.

This took the leader aback, stopping him in his tracks, but only for a moment. He regained his composure with a laugh and muttered just loud enough to hear: "Crazy fuck."

Null screamed again, but in words carefully articulated, defined by rage: "You're absolutely right!"

The bowler-topped leader pushed against Null to knock him backwards and Null instead gutted him like a pig in a single direct motion. He sank to his knees and fell backward.

They barely saw the blur of the knife.

Null screamed again and the remainder of the group tried to break, but they failed.

He descended on them like an eclipse, like fast falling darkness, a shadow of calamity and hatred.

Null was not detached nor machine logical, yet he was electric, connected. And he hooked up and patched in with each of the gang, solely using fists and the blade of his knife.

They fell even faster than Null upon them.

The short one with the red bandana around his neck managed to get up and turned to run, then turned again, squinted his flushed, pimply face and drew down on Null with 38 Ruger semi-automatic, firing too many rounds to miss.

But of course he missed.

Null pulled the Glock nine to respond in kind and blew up his chest and throat.

Sirens and blue lights followed and Null sat down, cross-legged, looking tired.

Two cliché cops, uniforms emerging from a newly detailed patrol car, one young and tall, the other equally tall but paunchy and gray-haired, came for him crouched and determined, police specials drawn. They screamed consecutively and in a round at Null to get down on the ground, even though he was already down on the pavement, sitting cross-legged.

Null spat.

The younger cop shot first—one round from the revolver—but didn't get to shoot again after Null blew his ankles out from under him. The older cop was a better shot and just about nailed him with two rounds, but Null shot him in the throat before he could adjust his aim for a third. Then he got up from where he was sitting reluctantly, smashed their holstered radios, then drove the squad car home, lights off, ditching it in a landfill tilted on a mud pile six blocks away from Boyd's condo.

Breathing hard, shaking and covered with sweat, he made his way awkwardly up the stairs, ignoring the elevator, to Boyd's condo. He entered, locked the door and stripped off his clothes, unburdening himself of every weapon, went to the bedroom and stood over the sleeping Boyd. He slipped into bed next to her and spooned himself against her hard, trembling.

This was the first of what was to become a nightly routine.

In a contravening compulsion against the need for affectionate bonding, the deep transcendence of the love and romance paradigm that had swept up Null and Boyd both like an irresistible, irrefutable tsunami, it was now an even more paramount imperative that Null violently beat the heads in of anyone he could find once it was assured that the gum was wearing off.

Null was caught up in the violent backlash riot of "The Chaw."

And even as he thought of the blood suffused knot of the white gang on Columbus Avenue and their tangle of desperate limbs, he allowed himself an easy blanket of pleasure to cover the recollection with a twilight state of numb fatigue. Just before sleep took him, he smiled.

———

When Benway opened the front door, he was immediately smeared with blood.

He recoiled as Lumpy blundered in and nearly fell over.

"I dumped the gum!" he cried.

"What the fuck?" sputtered Benway.

Lumpy lunged toward the sofa in the den of the ancient house and plopped down on it. He tore off what remained of his shirt and mopped sweat with it. "We fucked up!"

"What do you mean, *we?*"

"Yeah, while you were drinking tea, I was getting my ass kicked."

"You're getting blood all over my mother's sofa."

"Towels!" Lumpy growled. "Get me some fucking towels!"

Benway obliged and Lumpy stuffed them against himself to stanch various wounds. "Drink!" ordered lumpy. His lips bled. *"Drink!"*

Benway shakily did as he was told, pouring four fingers of cheap whisky into a tumbler from one of his mother's fancy decanters.

Lumpy took it all in a single swallow and panted a bit afterward.

"So, we're fucked," Benway observed glumly.

"Fucked out of the gum."

"Time to leave, then, I think."

"You could be right. But we need to leave with a stake."

"I got cash reserves—enough to get us to Montreal."

"No, we need a wedge to get in the game there—the gum."

I don't have the set-up to make more. And it's only a matter of time before they find us here at my mother's place. The cops and the zombie found us already.

"The fuck you saying?" Lumpy's eyes were wide; his face flush.

Benway explained in the kindest, most palliative, most unrealistic way possible, which Lumpy immediately translated as betrayal.

"You were going to serve me up to that Boyd bitch?!" he cried, lurching toward Benway, who stepped away and flinched. Even wounded and spent, Lumpy was dangerous.

"It was a backup plan. I just needed to stall them while we did what we had to do and blew the hell out of here."

"You should be dead, Benway, get me?"

"The idea is becoming distressingly clearer over time."

"It's clearer than you think, Doc. I almost got my own damn clarity tonight."

"I thought you were coming at them hard, kill shots at the ready. Jesus was on your side and all."

"I did come in hard, but they were there first, and they came *harder*. And Jesus, well they didn't have Jesus like me, that's for certain, because I may be shot up but only in two places, just the meat—no bullets stuck in me, praise the lord. But I'm fuckin' benched for a while."

"They followed you here."

"Nah. Ones that got closest fell hardest. I got away dirty, but free of those McGoons."

"You're sure."

"I know my business, Doc. Malek never hires quality muscle. Too cheap. They're all a bunch of clueless doofuses. I should have killed them all and got our grubstake off them."

"Why didn't you?"

"Too many, too fast—too damn ready for me. You were right. It was a whack-out waiting to happen. It's a damn Jesus miracle I'm not all shot up all to pieces."

"Might be due to the flak jacket you were wearing. Praise that."

"I had to ditch the thing for speed. Fucking McGoons were right on my heels."

"Listen, Lumpy. The cops know where we are, waiting for me to dime you out. The Ork has pull down at One Schroeder—they got cops on the arm—just how long you think before they get this infor-mation? How long before the housepainters come and make a mural out of us?"

"We under some pressure and that's a fact."

"No, we're already in arrears and about to be foreclosed on. They're *all* coming and before we can make any good plans to do anything about it. We got to go tonight, no time to recoup! We got to bandage you up and get you strolling."

Lumpy sat back, released some of the blood-streaked bleached white towels he was dabbing himself with, and pulled down on Benway with an old Colt 45 semi-automatic Combat Commander that he took off one of the muscle of the Ork. "We go when I say so, Doc—or I go alone." He cocked it, *condition zero.*

"You're suicidal."

"Think you not, Doc, with this gun in your face? Right now it's 50/50 whether I use you or blow you away."

"Back at you," Benway thought to himself silently, struggling not to hyperventilate.

"Right now, we got use for you."

"Okay. Great. So lighten the fuck down on that gadget there and clue me in. You're not going to shoot—that'll be yet another problem for you to solve. Right now you got more problems than solutions."

"You're gonna solve one."

"And what about you?"

"Ain't it obvious? I need a few days to heal up. Then we blow this popsicle stand for real."

"You got people in Montreal?"

"No, but I'll get 'em. People come cheap or ain't you guessed that by now?"

"I'm out," Benway mastered his breathing.

"You're whatever I say you are."

"You're not in much of a position to prove that."

"I think at this angle, if I shot you in the shoulder, there'd still be enough left of you for me to get out of you what I want.

"It's stupid."

"No, what would be stupid would be if I got up off this couch and started hurting you the way we used to do down at Gary Lee Obidowski's garage."

Benway caved and slumped into that fact with a wince. "Okay, whatever. What the fuck am I supposed to do while you lie in bed watching Fox News—sell my blood?"

"It ain't worth anything."

"What then, genius?"

"The cops—that Boyd bitch you told me about—they got the gum off the clubs, right?"

"Yeah. I guess. So?"

"So, that's enough for us to start selling hard in Montreal off the traveling reputation of the Chaw. News is out all over about the gum by now."

"But the cops got it, and we have no way to get it. We can't take it off the cops."

"Yeah, we can. I got a way. Think you can whip us up some good drugs. You got enough of a set-up for that?"

"Sure. What do we need?"

"Downers, tranks—something to put someone out—then maybe something hallucinogenic for when he wakes up. That'll do."

"For when *who* wakes up?"

"You'll see." Lumpy yawned, settling back and dabbing at himself again with more bloody towels. "Now, go get me some more of your mom's shitty whisky!"

———

"Don't tell me it was you," Boyd pleaded over coffee at a little brioche shop off Clarendon Street in the South End.

Null's hands shook, mishandling his cup of espresso.

"I don't want to lie to you."

"How does it feel to want?"

"I cherish it."

"Then tell me."

"I think it's failing me."

"What are you talking about?"

"The gum, the drug, it's a wash. The limbic system, the amygdaloid nucleus—they're crapping out on me."

"So you did it."

"I *had* to do it." He leaned into her, ferocity in his eyes, his lips drawn taut.

"I don't get it. You did them all? Every one of them the past few nights. How many deaths?"

"I didn't count."

"You're a mass murderer." She dropped her coffee and the cup shattered. The cashier hustled over to help clean up the mess, but Boyd grabbed his stack of napkins and waved him off.

"Even now it's true, what I told you before. I really only do one thing. Just one thing."

"No! It's no longer true! That was different. You're different now and you don't have to do these things."

Null was resolute, intense, yet somehow resigned with a hollow laxity in his voice. "Now more than ever I have to do them. And that's the change. Before, when I did them, I did them for expediency, for necessity, for a kind of justice. Now, I do them like an addict, desire and need combined. I'm compelled to do them not by any outside requirement, but from inner urge. Out of selfishness, not out of situational construct, the only necessity now being these new, raw feelings. I do them for myself—a self I don't understand that must do these things to avoid unbearable pain. But up till now, I never did them out of pain at all but only as a consequence of pain. The effacement of pain is what caused it all then and ironically, is what causes it now. Only then it was the solution and now it's the problem. There's only one way I know to solve this problem."

"No!" cried Boyd. "No, that doesn't work at all."

Getting up briefly to toss away the coffee garbage, then sitting down again, Boyd started sobbing. Null just sat there, tense and waiting.

When she was finished, she looked up at him with watery eyes and said, "I should arrest you."

"You should probably just shoot me here and now. Get it done. I'm fucked as it is."

"Don't say that. You need a hospital, tests, some kind of anti-toxin."

"I need a bullet in the brain."

"Don't make that be the only answer."

"I can't make up the answers any more than I can make up the questions."

Boyd sprang up again, stepped over to Null's side of the table, and dragged him up from his seat. He didn't resist.

She embraced him, breathed into his ear. "Just be with me, Null. Just be with me as long as you can."

"I want nothing but that, nothing but that and an end to the night terrors."

"Night terrors? Is that what you call them? Is that all they are?"

Null grabbed her back abruptly and pulled her into him. He kissed her hard and deep and then said in a raspy half whisper, "What else would they be?"

———

Yonah Shimmel, senior forensic specialist for the Boston Police Department, was indulging his vice for comic books at the Million Year Picnic in Harvard Square. He had scored several graphic novels, some underground porn comic books called Horny Biker Sluts, and a few crucial issues of the X-Men for his collection. Weedy, slight and small with a woolen yarmulke bobby pinned to his baby fine hair, his posture formed a small "s" when he walked. He never made it to the parking garage on Garden Street. Benway, his rented panel van parked awkwardly by a Thai restaurant, stabbed him hard in the neck with a syringe of fast acting solution of Dilaudid and plunged it down sweatily. He made a scene of struggle and grunting, dragging Shimmel off to the back of the van, but these incidents went mostly ignored in Harvard Square and were reported slowly when reported at all.

All along the way back to Arlington, Benway plotted the demise of Lumpy to offset the terrific fright of kidnapping a police official, trussing him up in the basement of his aunt's house in Arlington and drugging him out of his mind. He drove with nervous slowness all the way back, stopping short one time too many. "Another Jesus miracle," he said to himself, parking the van by backing into the driveway so the hatch would face the basement bulkhead.

It was a bad lug for Benway to carry the slight frame of Yonah Shimmel to the basement through the filthy bulkhead, down crumbling steps.

Even worse, it was a long, awkward process to strap the flopping, unconscious body of Yonah Shimmel to a hastily constructed pivot board with Humane Restraints, and Benway kept getting hit in the face by a wayward arm and kicked by an aimless leg. He would have laughed uproariously if he were outside himself watching, but he wasn't. He cursed and grunted and found none of it funny.

Getting a line in for the IV was also a bit of a struggle. He had to hang it just right, adjust the drip, make sure drugs, lactate of Ringers and fluids were all routed in. He was also clumsy with the needle, going through two of them before getting it right.

The black, mossy clumps covering an approximate hundred years of neglected tools and shop equipment made him filthy and clung thick to his sweat. He couldn't get out to the fan fast enough.

Shimmel was groggily waking up, but Benway wasn't concerned. The kid was so whacked out on custom acid and ergot concoctions, with a little mescaline mixed in, he wouldn't be sure if he was alive or whether death was either dream or reality. He drooled a bit from his mouth and his head lolled. Benway took pains to strap down his skull against a headboard, wet his mouth down with a clean rag soaked in fresh water, then went out clumsily up crumbling steps, securing the bulkhead behind him.

Benway stowed the Dodge Econoline white panel van at the far end of the driveway in front of the ancient free-standing garage and hoofed it back to his mother's house, still in the name of Freddy "Boom Boom" Cannon, off Mass. Ave. where Lumpy was recuperating in the gambrel attic room

Lumpy lay naked in bed on his back, cruising his iPhone for porn.

"You fuck it up?" he mumbled.

Benway was resigned, craven. "I think I did it right. He's in the land of Oz with the munchkins in my aunt's house basement."

"You hooked him up?"

"But good. He doesn't even know if he's conscious or not."

"He could be a cop then."

"That Boyd bitch is on top of it, though. You contact the cops the way you say, and she'll be on both our asses in a day or two."

"We just need the gum, then we blow."

"You need stitches and antibiotics first."

"I know, Doc, nothing you can't handle, though. Right?"

"Right."

"We contact the cops anonymously, do the meet and drop, then send them their boy back in the Econoline. They'll waste days tracking down the origins of that beast to some dead men in lockup that know squat." Lumpy shifted positions, hissing with pain.

"This plan is whacked, Lumpy. We should be on the move now."

"The cops are clueless and slow. I'll text 'em from my deadman's phone and they won't come swarming here—not unless you tell that Boyd, which you wouldn't do, right?"

It was a thought, and it appealed to Benway. He'd have to work it just right to escape intact. "Right," he echoed.

"You need to get the goods to sew me up and dose me up, Doc, unless you want me to go bleeding into this mattress all night."

Benway was beginning to feel hopeful. "You know, Lumpy? Maybe there's a clean way out of this thing after all."

"Of course there is, Doc. Jesus Christ and Joel Osteen both gave me the lowdown."

"I see."

"And get me some pain pills too, while you're at it. I hurt like a little bitch!"

TWENTY-ONE

Null was sweaty in bed and lunged to get up, but Boyd grabbed him and pulled him down hard.

"Not tonight," she whispered.

"It has to be tonight," he breathed. "Tonight and no other time."

He jerked up from the bed and she followed him. Boyd put her hands on him, smoothed him down by the shoulders tracing ropy scars. "It has to be never again."

"It can't be that. And yet you might be right about never again."

"What do you mean?"

"I mean that my neurons are firing crazy and that in my brain I can't feel what I need to feel."

"You're telling me you don't love me anymore." She inhaled this, trembling.

"It's gone. and the rest of me is going. I don't know how far it goes."

"Going too far will determine how far it goes."

"And you think I've already gone too far?"

"Well, haven't you? Violent crimes, mass murder—now the word is you're the one running the Gangsta Boyz crew, or someone like you. And how could there be anyone like you? They call you a zombie."

"I'm dead in name only."

Boyd grabbed him, kissed him, held the back of his neck tight. "But you were alive with me, in love with *me!*"

"The gum failed me, failed you, like all Benway's experiments."

"He's a criminal."

"Well, so am I. And he made me this way, for good or for ill. And there have been benefits. He's not on my list."

"Who is on that list?"

"Just a few. Just a choice few."

"Well, he's on mine. Him and his partner flooded the clubs with gum and I don't know how many died and how many are permanently messed up."

"Does it matter? The street exacts a death toll."

"Yes, and you and Benway and the Indian collect it."

"So, you'll pick them up."

"I'm waiting for Benway to serve him up to keep the body count down."

"You'll be waiting a long time."

"Seems the pressure's off, I think they're out of gum, so the club incidents have stopped."

"My incidents may have stopped, too."

"May have? But I thought you were hot to trot. You had to go out and do in a few more gangsters and line cops."

"They make the cops look pretty on the news, though. Thugs, not so much. Besides, I thought you loved me."

"I do, hence your not being in lockup this second and my being out on extended sick leave."

"Well, that's all over now."

"What is?"

"*My* sick leave. I'm no longer sick."

"Get back to bed." She made a feint to drag him down.

Null acquiesced. "It won't mean anything, anyway."

"When does it?" she asked, tears welling.

They embraced and Null spasmed stiff, different. Lights played behind his eyes. "How much time do I got?" he said in a low voice.

"Until what?"

"Until you arrest me for my crimes. There's been more than a few."

"All the time you want and need. Never, in fact. Never again, as we said before."

"Why?"

"Would it matter about love?"

"Not anymore. Benway's gum was a bust. Even the impulse need for violent aggression and delusional satisfaction is now only a ghost."

Tears were flowing slowly down both her cheeks and Null seemed not to notice. She sniffled a bit. "Well, then, you can't arrest a dead man, and as far as I know, Joseph Xavier Null, you're legally declared dead and no one's undoing that any time soon."

He kissed her remorselessly with senseless lips. "Death benefits, you're saying?"

"That's what I'm saying."

She had become frozen under his deadening kiss.

"Good, because I have steps to take in order to put things in order. There are accounts to balance out. More than settling them, they need to be zeroed out completely.

On the nightstand by the bed, her Android phone tolled angrily.

"Called back to work already?"

She played with the phone, looked at its screen intently, then pouted.

"Emergency text."

"About me," he drawled.

"No, but maybe something to do with you. Maybe not. It seems one of my guys, criminalist Yonah Shimmel, was kidnapped earlier today."

"How do they know he was kidnapped? Could be he played hooky like you."

"They know because someone sent a ransom note from a dead-man's phone down to One Schroeder. They were asking for the rest of the gum."

"Better move the Indian up on your list," he said emptily, then pushed her aside, got up and got dressed.

———

It was a cookie box house in Billerica, whose motto calls it "America's Yankee Doodle Town", twenty miles outside of Boston headed north on the way to Lowell at the bottom of a cul-de-sac called Curley Lane. It had a small, fenced-in yard overgrown with grass and shrubs, untended and unkempt. The fence was wire, rusted and bent. The gray and brown trim paint of the façade was weather-beaten, cracked and splintered. The houses were all cookie box and far too close together. Null had hotwired a 90s Datsun on Clarendon Street to get there. It was a car not to be overly missed. It was brick red, flat and dented by bumper and fender. The suburban North Shore greenery seemed tawdry to him somehow, salacious as a lie.

The house was boarded up, not just vacant, but abandoned.

The address of the Embers family, such as it was.

Twisting open the gate, Null walked around the one story house twice. He stopped at a discolored section of a wall marked by wide peg holes.

"That's where they hung the dog," said a voice behind him.

Null turned and saw a stooped and wrinkled man in glasses, beige windbreaker and matching soiled cap holding a spade. He grasped the Glock in his coat pocket.

"Who are you?"

"Neighbor," the man said with resignation in his voice. "I knew you'd come."

"You did. How?"

"Someone had to after what they did to the boy. Somebody should have done something long ago."

"But they didn't, did they? And now it's too late."

"The kid dead?"

"Yes. Dead as they come."

"They killed him a long time ago anyhow." His eyes were set hard behind the glasses. His lips were pursed.

"They?"

"The parents. I watched it for years, heard the screaming at night. The father was a monster. The mother not much better. She gave it her blessing, covered for hubby. Helped them live in denial."

"And you did nothing."

"That's right. I had a lot of excuses I could give you, but none of them make much sense now. I'm guilty too. I could of stopped it. I was too interested in myself and my own problems. I thought someone else would do it. Someone would come, like you."

"But I'm too late."

"Yes, you are. They're long gone and you say little Kenny is dead."

"And he is."

"I can tell what you're about, mister. You came for them, didn't you?"

"Yes, I have. I am here for them."

"So, it's about revenge, justice."

"I say balance."

"Whatever, they're history. I'm all that's left." He crinkled up his eyes and sneered. "You here for me too?"

Null's sunken eyes narrowed. "That depends."

"Depends on what I tell you, right?"

"Could be."

"Well, they're off nice and safely retired to Florida. It'll be a trip to catch up with them."

"I can travel."

"You know what they did, right?"

"I know all of it, and I know death won't be enough to satisfy the need for balance. There will have to be more."

"More?"

"You know what I mean by more, don't you?"

"I was in the Vietnam war. I know all about more. You know, I've seen brave men and cowards and the bravest are never the ones you think are going to do it—to get it done no matter what. I've seen men die who knew what they faced was impossible and one of the bravest things I've ever seen was a little boy standing up to an angry, violent full-grown man to protect a dog—a dog who lost an eye protecting the boy from his father. That boy stood his ground and let his father punch him into the dirt on the ground where you and I are standing now. A sixty pound little nothing up against a 200 hundred odd pound man flailing his fists at him. He didn't run, and he didn't shy away, but fought back hopelessly, defiantly, knowing the outcome but doing it, anyway to save the dog that saved him."

"And you did nothing but watch."

"I did nothing."

"You know what happened, don't you?"

"Yeah. Emmett Embers killed the dog, skinned her alive and hung her hide on the side of the house for his son to marvel at."

"Goldie. The dog's name was Goldie."

"I think so.

"You did nothing and let it happen."

"And I'm ashamed of it." He cleared his throat. "So, you're here for me too, I take it? Factoring me in?"

"Yes, you're all factored in."

The old man suddenly brightened. "I have some leftover mail, one piece has their new address on it. I mean in it. Maybe that will help."

"It will help."

"And when I bring it to you, you'll let me go."

"Could be."

"If I don't, then what?"

"More," said Null quietly. "More."

"They're down in New Smyrna Beach, Florida. Don't know where that is."

"I'll find it."

"Well, you found me."

"No, you were waiting for me and I just finally came."

"Yes," he said nervously. "You came for me too." He shifted from foot to foot.

"I did, I think. But go get me the mail and you're off the agenda for today."

The old man slinked off at that and Null didn't have to wait very long for his mail.

———

It wasn't very subtle and it made local affiliate 5 pm cable news.

They used a battering ram on the front door to Benway's mother's house in Arlington, the over-militarized Boston Police blocking off a section of Mass. Ave. as they surrounded the place, covering all sides with semi-automatic tactical weapons. Boyd in a flak jacket led the charge just as old standby Bim Hundertwasser handled the ram.

When the door cracked open, Boyd discharged her Sig-Sauer. Other weapons followed with crisp reports, then abruptly died. Boyd stood aside as the squad poured through the house and piled upstairs and down into the basement. The attic gambrel room was breached. There was brief shouting, which died off to grumbling conversation quickly. The verdict was in: *nobody home.*

Boyd bummed a cigarette and just shook her head.

After the squad ganged up around the collapsed front entrance, the old aluminum screen door with an Italic "L" in the center still propped open, Boyd hollered, "We ain't done yet, boys! This is going to turn into one motherfucker of a household and street canvas, so break off into pairs and start humping before you get back into those fucking Humvees!"

She declined to speak to reporters presiding over the canvas, blocking the street, longing not for a drink, but for Null.

And Null had been there earlier looking desultorily for Benway, stalled when he couldn't do a clean break-in and settling instead on boosting a local vehicle as the Datsun had begun to die, so, moving a few houses down, he picked out a badly concealed Dodge Econoline van half submerged in overgrowth at the end of a long driveway, not realizing that Lumpy and Benway were in that very house lying low and were the ones he was trying so carefully not to arouse as he stole the car.

Null had been looking in vain for Benway, not only for more gum, but for other considerations.

Could he make the gum work again?

Could he just give Null just the raw chemicals directly to restore his humanity?

Perhaps he could finally answer Null's fate—validate that he actually had one.

Or maybe he could do nothing at all and the gum was his limit.

Saturation point.

Null gunned the van. which had a full tank of gas down Mass.

Ave. to Route 16, then fought bumper to bumper with inhuman patience down the Southeast Expressway to the Mattapan squat. He was going to need to stock up for a little trip. But first he had a local visit to make. After all, he was now more than titular gang leader of the Gangsta Boyz, and they had work to do for him. Do-Rag needed a reminder of his precarious position in life as, in fact, they all did. They needed to have the fear of God put in them without subtlety, but with the good effect of a boot heel crushing down on a human face.

There would be music he could almost feel—dark blues on the iPod, "Howlin' Wolf screaming "I Asked For Water And She Gave Me Gasoline;" Robert Johnson wailing "Hell Hound on My Trail," Sonny Boy Williamson II blowing his harp to the edge of human nerves with "Mr. Downchild." He was like a deaf man enjoying music, the vibrations somehow got to him.

There would be meth to keep him going.

There had to be a lot of meth to keep things going.

And Null knew he could not crime crew drug run for much longer than his meth would hold out, but that could be time enough to claim the streets, which he was already pretty sure he owned. He just needed to apply a little pressure. Petty cash, gossip, data, fencing, vig—all of it would trickle up the atomistic pyramid of Boston crime to his steeple as lord of the Gangsta Boyz.

There would be as many rounds for as many weapons as he could hold: two side arms—Glock and Walther PPK—and the sawed-off 12-gauge shotgun that would hang from a lanyard under his coat. On another lanyard around the neck was a shortened machete that was still straight-razor sharp.

There would be money. He needed one of his hefty prepaid debit cards to make the trip. And Gomez Gomelsky's dead-man smartphone, topped up for months in advance, he needed that for the GPS mapping if he was going to get to New Smyrna Beach, Florida efficiently.

He bumped up on several lines of meth and noticed a sense of gleaming clarity; it was almost as if he could feel it.

Moving swiftly, he secured the squat, then made his way in the Econoline to the no-name crib where Gangsta Boyz piped up and did business in Dorchester. They were assembled eating take out and watching NESN sports reruns on dilapidated living room furniture. Two of the chairs had loud houndstooth patterns. Null blasted in with the Glock to get their attention. One lower soldier made a move and Null blasted down at his feet, missing them deliberately.

"I don't mind a little attrition if you don't," he said flatly.

Null tossed a tightly wrapped broken block packet of small bricks to Do-Rag—the rest of the meth. "Sell it all," he said. "Cut it efficiently, portion it out efficiently, sell it efficiently. Don't fuck up or I'll come back and clean up—efficiently. Efficiency one way or another."

Null shot the biggest one of them in the thigh for emphasis.

"Shit man, you just shot Buggles the accountant! If he die, how we track all yo' cheese?" Do-Rag was hysterical to the point of tears.

"He won't die. But get him down to Carney Hospital to make sure. Mass General would be too far."

Buggles rocked himself praying in whispers on the floor.

Null fired more rounds into the ceiling. "I'm going to Florida, boys. Make me rich when I come back or make a good job of killing me. I expect you to try to kill me, so either reach that mark of efficiency or reach mine. But bear in mind that every one of you in my book is a cipher to be erased when you don't add up. So, either make sure you do or zero me out. Whatever the choice, though, you had better commit, no in-between. It's fucking binary: No gray zone. Zero or one. Black or white. Life or death. Figure it out and get it done."

Then he was swinging his arms out the door in long strides, tweaked up high on meth, sweating, assured in articulated purpose and a state that mimicked conviction but which contained no belief. Do Rag was running after him, but he wrote him off, getting into the Econoline fast and gunning past him as he vainly called out his name.

Null shouted back, unconcerned as to who else might hear. "Carney fucking hospital. And watch my fucking meth!"

Then he entered that long lingering state of Zen that occurs driving straight down the long highway. Blues shouting down for all the 19 hours of the 1258-mile bumpy ride, stopping only for cheap burritos and gas: Blind Lemon Jefferson's "Black Snake Moan." Elmore James's "Dust My Broom." Howlin' Wolf's "How Many More Years." All screaming high at top volume.

He started out on the Southeast Expressway's existential commuter torment, then went west on the Mass. Turnpike to Interstate 84, south on Connecticut 15, then south on the New Jersey Turnpike and I-95 south to Florida 44 east in New Smyrna Beach. He GPS'ed the house right by high wire and concrete fencing an eighth of a mile from the ocean. Null could smell it when he left the van like a slap in the face, a salty scent of decay. He had seen this ocean before—garlands of dead seaweed all along the shore.

Beautiful tableau.

The house was a modest-seeming one-floor cottage with more rooms than the cookie box back in Billerica. And he watched the house for hours, from morning until late afternoon until he was sure they were home, the Embers. Fifteen minutes after they got home, Null moved toward the house, approached the door and rang the bell.

Filthy, sweaty, dark topcoat, pork pie hat, mottled aspect, gaunt cheeked face; Null was not a welcome sight at the door.

The elder man opened the door and tried to shut it in a hurry.

"Go away," he coughed.

Null pushed his way in calmly past the man, then just as calmly shut the door.

He looked tired and non-threatening—maybe even a little sick. The elder man relaxed. "Okay, but don't try to sell me nothin'."

"I won't."

"Take a seat." And the elder man sat on the corduroy sofa, which Null thought should have been encased in plastic. It was an old-time Boston sitting room transported to Florida, paisley wallpaper, bric-a-brac hanging sconces, needle-pointed foot stools. Predictably enough, no portraits of children on the walls or anywhere in sight.

"Thanks, I will." Null brushed off his coat with his hands and sat in a pink fuzz upholstered chair with prominent bronze rivets.

"Sort of warm for a coat and hat like that, you know." He was right. It was in the mid-eighties outside and the inside central air conditioning was barely perceptible. The man was dressed in khaki shorts, argyle socks and Hawaiian shirt with dark oranges, blues, greens and yellows—some sort of lagoon scene.

"I came a long way. No time to change."

"Well, I'm not drinking, not that I'd offer you, anyway, and I'm not buying anything and you say you're not selling—"

"That's right. I'm really not."

"Then we've really got nothing to talk about."

"Your wife is home?"

"Yes, she's in the kitchen, but she won't be making us any sandwiches."

"That's okay. I had a burrito a few hours ago."

"Those things'll kill ya, ya know."

"Over time, almost anything will."

"So, why don't you just fuckin' blow. You ain't got nothin' comin here.'"

"I've heard that before. It's not always true."

The wife emerged, a prim pear-shaped woman in a nacreous blue blouse and matching skirt below the knee and harlequin eyeglasses. "Is this a friend of yours, Emmett?" she asked airily. She paused to look at Null, then pursed her lips to offset a frown. "Can I get you anything?"

"He's leaving," Emmett spat.

"No thank you," said Null, appearing relaxed.

"Call the police, Phyllis. This jamoke won't go. I don't even know how he got in here."

"You let me in."

"Against my will. You muscled your way in."

"That's true. I did."

The wife threw up her hands and froze. "Oh my God. He's a home invader!" She made a move to go back to the kitchen.

"Sit down, Phyllis. No one's calling the police."

"Emmett, where's the smartphone?"

"Do you really want me to stop you?" This was quiet and severe.

"Get the phone, Phyllis!"

"Phyllis is thinking it over. Emmett, do you really want me to stop you? Don't you think I could?"

"You got a gun or something?"

"Or something."

The wife made her way to the corduroy sofa and sat down next to her husband.

"Well then, what the fuck do you want?"

"Emmett, language!"

"This shit heel is holding us hostage, and I want to know why."

"I'm not holding you hostage. Not yet. So far, I really haven't done anything but pay you a visit. I just have a little something to do here and then you'll never see me again."

"Please, leave us alone! What do you *want?*"

"To have a little chat. More formally, an informational interview."

"Ask what you want already and get the fuck out!"

"Fine. I'll ask. Do you know where your son is now?"

"We have no son!" piped up Phyllis.

"That little fuck causes nothing but problems. You want him, you can have him. We have no idea where the little shit is."

"I know where he is, don't worry."

"Well, good, keep it to yourself. I can't help you if he owes you money. You're on your own, chief."

"I don't want money."

"Then what the hell do you want?"

"Tell me about Goldie."

"I don't know who that is."

"Sure you do. Friend of your son's."

Emmett looked exasperated and exhausted. "Lookit, mister. I don't know anything you want to know. Just tell me what I can do for you that will make you leave already, for Christ's sake!"

"The dog. Tell me about her."

"You want to know about the dog."

"Just tell him so he can go," whined Phyllis.

"Yes. Tell me."

"Okay. That bitch bit me—"

"Goldie."

"Yeah. That bitch—Goldie!—bit me when I was disciplining the boy. So, I disciplined her too."

"And what happened?"

225

"Nothing."

"Nothing? Are you sure?" Null's eyes narrowed.

"Fine." Emmett's face was red, but he wasn't blushing. "If it'll satisfy you, I beat her in the face until she lost her left eye."

Null stood, stretched. "It doesn't satisfy me."

"No, fucko? Then what *will* satisfy you?"

"Let's start with *your* left eye," Null said genially.

Emmett looked puzzled for a moment and pouted.

Then, in a single lightning motion, Null took it.

TWENTY-TWO

It took three long days for Null to accomplish what he had set out to do.

It took three days for them to deny.

It took three days for them to confess.

It took three days for them to beg.

It took three days for resolution.

It started out clean and orderly. Null bound up Emmett with handy zip ties from the garage, had Phyllis make phone calls, warning off friends and canceling appointments. Then he bound her up too. He was generous and patient, making sure they were watered and fed, released at first at intervals to go to the bathroom. He even dressed Emmett's wounded eye appropriately from how Missy once had shown him. These decencies did not last.

Day One was for explanations, and Null patiently listened to them all, not laying a finger on them as they agonized without sleep and bored of telling the same lies over and over. Yet they continued to tell them. "He was a difficult child. We were the best parents we knew how to be at the time. He fell in with a bad crowd at school. He was disobedient and turned his dog against us. His father never beat him and raped him. His mother never covered it up. She would never have allowed it—it was all a lie to gain sympathy. It was nobody's fault, really. He really was just a bad kid."

"I was tortured once," Null replied. "And it ended much worse for me than it will for you."

Day Two was for atonement, and Null worked on them with tools without relent, but taking little breaks at contrived points to let the magnitude of the pain sink in. There were clippers, calipers, knives, hammers, wrenches, pliers, various irons. They quickly confessed, shouted confessions loudly and desperately, though Null explained that it didn't matter if they confessed—it simply wouldn't affect anything. They begged to confess, anyway, to be allowed to tell the truth. He let them up to go to the bathroom, blood draining everywhere, but not too much. He had calculated that it wasn't to be too much. There needed to be time to fit everything in. Before they could resume their bound positions, Null offered them a task.

He had them write their confessions on the bedroom walls in their own blood, at length. He told them there would be no reward or punishment for their performance, just more of what they were already getting. It wouldn't affect the outcome.

They went the extra mile to do a thorough and exemplary job regardless, taking hours to do it, painstaking and slow.

Null bound them back up and resumed torturing them, anyway.

No one slept.

Day Three was for forgiveness. Null explained he had none to give, that it wasn't in his power to forgive them and that their son was dead and in dying he couldn't forgive them either. "In fact," he said. "I am here honoring his last request."

"What was that?" came from the bloody, torn mouth of Emmett Embers.

Phyllis sobbed in incoherent pain.

"That you didn't get away with it."

Emmett coughed and spat.

Null went back to working on them until Emmett screamed out for God to help him. Phyllis whined for God in echo, too. They had invoked God all along the torment.

Null stopped and stood over them both, assessing them.

"I guess at this point your thoughts would turn to God," he stated blankly. "Good. You may well ask why he isn't intervening in your torture, saving you. There are two answers. The first being the most salient and sensible: There is no God. However, if you choose to believe, then you must conclude that God approves of what's happening here. Since you believe in God, you no doubt think that what you did to Kenny—raping him, brutalizing him, letting it happen, covering it up, mind fucking him until he could barely function then tossing him out on his ear when you were through— was perfectly fine. You must have thought that God approved of that, letting it happen just like Phyllis, nodding along, sometimes looking the other way. Or again, maybe there is no God."

They together screamed for God and mercy again.

"But let's grant the idea that God exists as you believe in him, micromanaging all life everywhere. If that's true, then you can be sure he sent me. Am I an angel then?"

They groaned pathetically. Mercy again was begged for.

"You might think of me as one, because your belief makes me one. It would make sense in that scheme that I'm here to exact God's vengeance, to right the moral wrong as part of the judgment of God. Though it might bother me, if I were you, that your precious God allowed it all to happen in the first place. Yes, it must surprise and perplex you that God would approve of the horror you commit one day then, years later, ensure that horror is enacted upon you in payment for that. You thought God was on your side one minute, but were then betrayed by him the next. A believer would say God moves in mysterious ways. A non-believer would mark it as the pure contradictory absurdity in believing in any God."

They cried again for God, sobbed and begged for Null to stop and think about what he was doing.

"Oh, I've thought about it," he said. "And I'm here to settle the question. For my part, God had nothing to do with it. Chaos brought me here—chaos and a dying breath. That, mixed with the bad chemicals in my brain that make me what I am, brought us to the exact point of where we are now. And where we are now, is at the end. A few more touches and you'll be able to die slowly from your wounds and no one will be coming to save you. You'll simply peter out and die in agony. It won't take years of suffering to kill you as it did your son, but it will feel like years. And when you're found inevitably, and it will happen, though it may take a week or two, what you have done will be plainly readable on the bedroom wall, and God's mystery of who tortured and killed you may never be solved."

He was ignoring their screams all through that.

"Maybe you'll find forgiveness in heaven, if you still believe on the off-chance that there is one."

The scent of human despair was palpable, thick and dank. They whined between screams with more begging.

"I'll have to gag you now—just in case someone might hear you. You are kind of loud for two half-dead old people."

As he approached Phyllis first, she cried with surprising lucidity, "No, please! I have something you need to know about Kenny. Something important!"

"How important?"

"Important enough to let me live?"

"What about Emmett?"

Phyllis gurgled, drooling blood, and coughed. "You can have him. It's all his fault, anyway. He was the one who had to use Kenny like a whore. I tried to stop him."

"No, Phyllis!" Emmett cried, then went back to sobbing and muttering.

"We both know that that isn't true. And we both know that I'll make sure you both die, no matter what you tell me."

"But I have information you really want!" she screamed.

"Tell me then or we continue."

"First, tell me that if I do, you'll stop the pain."

"I can do that," Null said with something that sounded almost like compassion. "Tell me and I'll make it stop."

"You'll do it fast if I tell you?"

"Quick as mercury," said Null in a whisper.

"Kenny has a child," she gasped.

When he broke her neck, she barely let out a sigh.

———

Benway was sweating, pacing around the drab mauve den and Lumpy was hunched over intently, obsessed with porn on the aunt's obsolete PC at an old writing table.

"This place sucks, Benway," he grumbled, ogling nude glamour girls that were beyond him.

"I said we should go," fumed Benway. "You're the one wants us to wait on the gum ransom for the dweeb in the basement."

"You should be more respectful of our man in the basement. He's doing us a good turn."

"He's peeing into a bucket through a catheter whacked out of his mind on my homebrewed hallucinogens and probably slowly starving to death. Not much need for respect there."

"Ya made him comfortable, right? Probably a sensitive little guy."

"He wouldn't know it if I stuck needles in his eyes. He's too far gone. But what about you, Filmore? How you doin' on the pain meds?"

"Your stitches itch and I'm crazy bored. Can't even use the smartphone for entertainment."

"No, it was your great idea to send a ransom text to the cops from it. Deadman's phone or not, whenever it's on they can pinpoint our location by GPS. Just checking for responses alone is a risk."

Lumpy cleared his throat with a growl. "Doc, I got to party. Get into Cambridge and hunt up some trim. I got to *ball!*"

"You gotta lay low until they set an exchange of the guy for the gum."

"And I need more gum too. I feel sick without it. Maybe withdrawal."

"You acted sick with it. I can't help you. There's no lab set up here, and you went through whatever we had."

"I need it to *connect*. I'm isolated now, trapped in myself."

"Now who's the sensitive little guy?"

"Watch it, Benway, or I isolate your motherfucking teeth."

"Keep moving around like that and you're going to get blood all over my aunt's den. You can't go anywhere. You seriously believe there isn't a manhunt on for you? If the Ork doesn't finally kill you, the cops will pick you up now for certain, thanks to Boyd making the connection."

"How do you know she has?"

"You want to risk that she hasn't? She found us at my mother's house last go 'round. You really think it's going to take her that long to connect you with the dweeb kidnapping and find us here at my aunt's?"

"Maybe you paranoid, Doc?"

"Sure, but can we really afford not to be? How much luck you think we can ride for how long?"

"I got the news, Doc, that Joel Osteen and the Christ both say our time is coming for all good blessings to be bestowed upon us if we just believe and choose faith over facts."

"And I got the news that cops already raided my mother's house looking for us. And I'm going to have to explain all the damage when she gets back from Florida, which is going to be a bad scene."

"Bullshit. They couldn't of done it so quick!" He got up from the couch and counter-paced Benway.

"Lumpy, you can work it out with God later and send a donation to Osteen after we get away clear, but before that we have to recognize that we may not get away at all, much less score the cops' supply of gum before we even get to that."

"We can hold out a couple a days before they get a clue."

"Are you fucking kidding me? They already raided my mother's house. It was all over the news and blocking traffic on Mass. Ave. They were only two blocks away. They're coming for us Lumpy, Ork or Cops and we'll not survive either when they get here."

"We hold out for two more days, then we blow. Fine. Gum or no gum. We get a response yet?"

"Not unless you count a bunch of missed calls from One Schroeder a response."

"You didn't answer?"

"You want to invite them in right now—send 'em an invitation?"

"Jesus, this is a fucked-up situation. Just text them our time-frame If they don't come across with the gum, sensitive boy gets sent to la-la-land permanent."

"Sure, Lumpy. Fine. I'll text them now. What the fuck are you doing with my aunt's sofa?"

Lumpy looked up and beamed. "Hunting up some change to take the 77 bus to Harvard Square."

———

Boyd had just finished getting a long, firm dressing down from Captain Parseeman and Chief Inspector Phil LaCuna in unison and disharmony. They had called her every name in the book, including the "C" word. So, in addition to clearing the mass mayhem and murder case of "The Chaw," she also had to deal with the Shimmel kidnapping, which was about to hit the news in a major way in less than a day, if not that very afternoon, but which still had yet to be leaked.

She had received the text from the deadman's phone that two days was the limit for negotiations. Two days before they slit Shimmel's throat and bailed. It was obvious to her that Lumpy was the kidnapper, and that Benway was involved, which is why she couldn't find them. Meanwhile, Nick Andromeda, potentially her best street asset, was laid up at Mass. General with mysterious gunshot wounds acquired off-duty, and her reliance on available squads of bodies was going to be cut painfully thin by dictum of the new commissioner.

Her greatest hope was that Benway would call and give up Lumpy so he could get off with some light probation. Her next greatest hope was that Null had had nothing to do with it.

She had prayed to God to let her have something with Null—a relationship if you had to call it that—a love affair—anything! Prayed to let it go on until she realized when Null had left her that God said "No!"

The realization went further: God said nothing. There was no God and she had once again been left hanging without resolution, satisfaction or closure. The absence of God spoke loudest of all.

The end had come hard and yet everything else had kept right on going.

Her need for Null kept right on going. Of course she hated him, and of course she prayed into the nothingness and between bombardments of chaos that somehow throughout all the horrible things he did and was going to do that he would remain safe. She wished him dead, and she wished him alive all at once.

Then she went about recruiting from the willing and available crew of detectives to patrolmen on down those who would help her clean up the gum and nail Lumpy and Benway.

———

Null had left Emmet Embers in the expanded cookie box cottage in New Smyrna Beach, Florida to die of the wounds he had inflicted upon him he knew to be eventually lethal, trussed up good and tight. Phyllis was already gone, but before she had left her body with the broken neck behind, she had given Null a story, a picture and curt directions. She told the story in gasps and sobs of pain.

When Kenny was in high school, due to his sexual confusion, he had a fling with another student, a girl. His last-ditch effort at heterosexuality. She got pregnant and was determined to have the baby, so the Embers, before kicking Kenny out, supported the birth as the mother had no family to speak of but a drunken grandfather to help her during the pregnancy and after. After the birth, they got rid of her and they got rid of Kenny. And when the boy, Rudy Embers, was old enough to be trouble, they got rid of him too.

They moved to New Smyrna Beach, took the kid with them in a seeming compassionate move and then *sold* him to something called "Boys Farm." It was in Ocala in the middle of nowhere and with state and federal checks they fostered boys until they were "adopted" by the right men. What was odd was that they actually sold him outright, were paid a fee for delivering him up, which was because it was in reality and fact a holding pen for rich pedophiles, "chicken-hawks" and their fresh "chicken." A preferred clientele of old men would pay for a boy, use him and discard him. It was an open secret, but not open enough for the state or county to intervene or investigate, as plenty of the right bribes went to all the right officials and shut off any interest in right action.

Boys Farm had existed for years under the radar, and no doubt would probably still exist, at least until he visited it.

Even if the boy was delivered, deflowered and dead, Null made a quiet resolution regardless on the open road, the chorus of "Muddy Waters' "Mannish Boy" screaming in his head—to simply kill them all.

He would kill them all and make sure Boys Farm stood as an example in memory for what became of those who would make sex slaves of children, then snuff them out.

He would snuff Boys Farm out.

He would snuff them all out.

It wasn't a long ride to Ocala. He took the picture of the five-year-old Rudy and the directions with him.

Null stopped along the way for provisions, burritos, water, bedding—pillows and sheets—and over the counter sleep drugs, just in case Rudy was still alive.

He was going to take him.

Null drove carefully, heading southwest on Washington Street toward the North Dixie Freeway, went down I-95 North and Florida 40 West to Florida 326 West in Marion County, Ocala. It took, with stops, about three hours, so it was still daylight when he arrived at Boys Farm. There was no sign, but the address and description were matched. He was immediately greeted in the gravel parking lot of a low, rectangular and "L"-shaped building like a long, rustic barn by a short, squat, swarthy man in overalls. He looked Hispanic.

Null leaned out the driver's side window.

"You lost?" asked the man.

"No, I'm where I need to be."

"You don't need to be here, man. This is private property."

"Not even if I want to buy a child?"

The Hispanic man pulled a Smith and Wesson 38 revolver. "You've made a mistake, sir. You had better pull back out and make your way back to the highway."

"No," said Null, sounding almost tired. "You made a mistake." Before he had finished speaking, he had blown a hole in the man's neck with the Glock. He waited a moment in the quiet aftermath where the only sound was the man choking and gagging until the death rattle and was nonplussed that no one else had come out to greet him.

So, he went in to greet them.

After an empty ante-room with a rustic reception area, Null entered a large, high-raftered work room with several work tables. Another man with his pants down was thrusting himself into a boy who was bent over a table, his face flush with it, yelling. The man was making cooing sounds as he took the boy. Null tore the man off of him in a single jerk.

The man said with a southern honking drawl, "What the fuck you doin', dude?" in shock, void of embarrassment.

"Quiet you," said Null evenly. "And pull up your pants."

The boy was sniffling and in tears, his face red and smudged with dirt. Null waited for him to pull up his pants, then from nowhere hit him so hard in the jaw that he passed out on the dirt floor amid strands and tufts of hay. He must have been a bit younger than fourteen.

Null commented on this to him. "You're too young to have to see what's going to happen."

"What the fuck you doing here, man? Didn't they pay you not to show up?" asked the man, who was somewhat obese with a gray stubble beard, bald, gleaming pate and thick features. He looked like you didn't want to get close to him as it was likely he stank of some sort of corruption, even though Null smelled nothing near him but the fear-sweat.

"They missed me, I think."

After a full minute of tense silence, the man screamed, "Help! We got a vigilante here! We're being invaded! *Hey Rube!*"

Null had the sawed-off shotgun in his hands with the speed of a magician and methodically pumped two rounds into the fat midsection of the man, knocking him back to the table..

He went down on his back, grunting and groaning, bloody gray viscera exposed from the front of his overalls.

Null wiped spatter from his face and hands.

He swiftly loaded two more rounds and made them count when two more men, both white and lanky with straw colored hair, also in overalls, came running into the room. He downed both of them with the shotgun and they writhed bloodily on the ground just like the man who had been raping the now unconscious boy. Null got out of him that his name was Ephraim. He then strolled over to the two men on the floor and put a single round from the Glock in each man's forehead. They immediately quieted.

"You killed Manolo, Scott and Stewart!" Ephraim sobbed and wailed.

"I've killed you too. You won't survive that wound."

"Fuck you, cracker!" he grunted.

"Yes, but no more fucking little boys."

Ephraim spat.

"Where are the rest of the boys? Where are they kept?"

"We got more hands coming to kill you, cracker! You ain't got nothing coming!"

Ephraim shrieked in pain when Null inserted his foot into the wound.

Null bent down, showed him the picture. "I'm looking for this one in particular," he stated.

"You could have just bought the stupid kid through channels," Ephraim sobbed.

"I'm not good at politics," replied Null.

"Just let me die!" screamed Ephraim.

"I'll help you along if you tell me where he is," said Null. "Kill you clean."

"He's in the hotbox in the next room," Ephraim panted. "Discipline problem."

"Of course," Null assented, and then blew his head off with a single round of the sawed-off shotgun.

There were no more bodies manning the farm, but there were cages like dog crates full of filthy boys of varying races, ages and states of undress crowded into the adjoining room which looked like it had once been used for assembly line production of some kind with one long table going down the center of it. This room delivered on the stink that Ephraim's aspect had formerly promised. The stench almost knocked him back. Null opened the cages fast by breaking the padlocks with rounds from the Glock and fired a single round of the shotgun into the ceiling.

"I don't know where you're from, or where you can go or will go, but you had better get going now. I'm calling the heat and if you don't want to be delivered into their hands for whatever reasons, then you'd better leave quick!

The hot box was easy to find, a padlocked airless square of wood under the long table. Null shot the lock off and extracted a skinny, dirty, spindly little boy with runny nose and eyes from it. He squinted at the photo and at the boy, even as he struggled vainly to get loose from his grip. Null couldn't feel any surprise when they matched, but he thought it was extremely unlikely. He kept the struggling boy by his side as he strolled through the farm's physical plant looking for more cages. Other than a crude kitchen, there was nothing but old junk and rusted mechanical implements in the other rooms.

He didn't start a fire but left the building standing, calling both police and the Marion County Sheriff's Department on his dead-man's phone to alert them to the strange and criminal goings on at the Boys Farm—not that they didn't know already. But the recorded call, even though it was anonymous, had to be responded to. And they would certainly find something as he had propped up the corpse of Manolo in a seated position to greet them.

He actually felt a physical itch to burn the place to the ground but instead peeled out on the gravel heading back to the highway, a shrieking, struggling boy of perhaps seven held unstably restrained with his right arm.

Null thought it would have been more efficient if he had had an opioid to tranquilize and knock the kid for a loop, but as it was, he offered him over the counter sleep medications and was violently rebuffed. The only choice left was to stop the van and knock him out with a surprise punch. Then he tucked the boy into the bedding in the back and gunned the van down I-95 North.

It was going to be a long drive back to Boston.

Maintaining legal speed, obeying traffic laws scrupulously to avoid overzealous Florida State Patrol, Null cranked the iPod loud playing Slim Harpo's "Moody Blues."

He wondered whether or not the kid would be out long enough to give him some distance. Fracturing his jaw was not a good option.

"We need to kill that wildcat fucker, Null" said Malek, sipping single malt scotch he had no appreciation for from a fat tumbler.

Franchot and Parley, looking tired and haggard in overcoats, shoulder holsters exposed, assented.

"What about the Indian, Padrone?" Franchot asked. "Ain't he urgent?"

"All our guys are lookin' for the guy. We put up a bounty. He'll be trunk music soon enough."

"Forget it," said Malek. "He's low priority."

"He whacked about ten of our guys and he's low priority?"

Malek smashed the bottom of the glass down on his desk. "That Null fuck killed just as many, maybe more, and he has a hot million bucks of my meth! Now he thinks him and the Gangsta Boyz crew, which he's plainly taken over, are running the streets. He's cutting into business and territory and needs to go right fucking away!"

"But what about the Indian?" whined Parley. "I got a personal beef with that mutt."

"We forgive that shitbird," said Malek. "Get the bounty off his head."

"And Null?" asked Franchot?

"Him too."

"You're giving him a pass? The Gangsta Boyz are selling your gak out on the street."

"I know—it's a dead loss."

"So we whack 'em."

"No, I'm killing both of them." Malek shook his head and poured more scotch into the fat tumbler. "With kindness."

"With kindness?"

"You could say. I'm going to set them after each other. See who kills who first."

"What about the survivor?" Franchot protested.

"We spoil him. Make him happy, take him back into the fold, give him back our love and trust, make him content and feel safe."

"And when he feels safe, we whack him!"

"Exactamundo!" Malek exclaimed, draining his glass. "He gets a ticket to Gary Lee Obiodowski's garage."

"What if it's Null?" Franchot posited.

"Then we negotiate for the same result. We work with him, strike a compromise, then we work *on* him."

"What about the Gangsta Boyz?"

"Cowboys and indians, Franchot, cowboys and indians."

"I don't get you."

"We go in big and scalp them. Take back the streets."

"You want a war."

"It won't be a war. A few heads on pikes will turn the trick. Then they will come to Jesus!"

"They're too fuckin' wild to do that."

"When they come to worship the crucified Null, we'll take them all. We'll offer them what's left of their leader and when they show, keep taking them out until they get the message. Every one of the Gangsta Boys'll be on the list to be kissed until we get back what's mine."

Franchot was sweating and for once visibly nervous. "You're talking a full-out bloodbath, Padrone."

"No, no. Just a good old-fashioned Boston beatdown. The way it used to be."

TWENTY-THREE

Their eyes met and stuck that way until the boy tore them apart.

Null thrust him through the door while Boyd stood before him, shaking slightly.

Rudy, the boy, screamed as he was thrown into the living room of the condo.

"This is what you wanted," said Null coolly.

"I don't want anything from you!" she cried.

Null pushed his way in as the boy, sweaty, dirty and panting, sat down on the rug. He slammed the door and for some unknown reason, despite being red-faced with emotion, maybe even anger, Boyd acquiesced. It was late, edging on 10 pm, and Boyd was tired, distraught, taken aback. She was full of need and confused repulsion.

"Can I have a burrito?" Rudy whined. "I'm hungry."

"Not now," said Null. "Later. But not much later."

The boy slumped down, disgruntled.

"Who is this kid?" Boyd stammered.

"His name's Rudy, and he'll keep you busy."

"I'm busy enough. Get him and yourself out of here—"

"Before you call a cop?"

"You know I won't do that. I can't really. What do you want from me?"

"It's what you want from me that I can't give."

"So you say."

"So I do, but you know it's true."

By this time, Rudy had gotten up and was foraging for food in the kitchen, which he found moving from room to room.

"Get back here!" shouted Null.

"Let him go," said Boyd, grabbing his shoulder. "There's not much food here and what he finds he can have. There's not much for him to steal—what harm can he do?"

"He could set fire to the place."

"But he won't."

"No, he won't."

"What do you want?"

"You know I don't want," he said icily. "It's what *you* want."

"I don't get you. Really, you and him have to go. I have work tomorrow and I can't handle this!"

"You need a drink."

"I always need a drink."

"Maybe you don't really need it. Maybe it's not a physical addiction. Maybe you need something else."

"Like what?"

Null's brow wrinkled. His lips were dry. "Love, of course. Love I can't give you. But more importantly, love that you have to give. You need to love. And stupidly enough, you love me."

"That can change," she croaked. "It already has. I know what you are."

"Yet you still love me. But I can't love you back. I can't love anything. Whatever the drug of the gum had given me has collapsed. Whatever sensitive humanity of feeling and grace that was there for you has crumbled away to nothing and left me with nothing. Bereft so much I cannot even grieve."

Boyd plowed into him, hit him with her fists. "But there must be a way, a therapy, some method!"

"No," said Null, grabbing her wrists. "Benway burned the bridge. Whatever was there just isn't anymore. And I am left what I was after the treatment, crossing in the fire."

"A zombie." She sniffled, forcing back tears.

"Something like that. I'm not really dead, but I might as well be."

"If a dimwit like Benway could come up with something, maybe the real geniuses can! You can't give up!"

"Benway was an idiot savant. He came up with something no one else has. I don't think therapies exist for my particular syndrome, whatever it is."

"Please don't give up." She kissed his impassive face. "Please."

"It's done."

She pulled away. "Fine," she said. "I can't argue you into having human feeling. I can't make you be with me, even though it's the best thing for you and maybe for me. Just destroy everything, kill it all dead. It's what you do."

"I only do one thing," said Null in a dull, near whisper. "Just one thing. Remember that."

"What about the, boy—where's he from? "What's he doing here?"

"He's from a farm for pedophiles in Florida. His father is a dead man who saved my life a couple of times who was dying of AIDS, anyway, but was killed because of me. His name is Rudy, no real last name, no real records, a John Doe foster/adoption case if ever there was one. Look at him, sitting on your kitchen floor eating Ben and Jerry's ice cream from the tub with his fingers. Desperate and pathetic. Full of need."

"I can't do anything for him."

"Sure you can. If he were a dog, you'd take him in. He's worth as much as a dog, maybe more."

"There's nothing I can do, Joey—I can't. My life won't permit it."

"Your life demands it. You're wracked with the need to love, isolated and lonely, deprived of intimacy. Here's your answer. No-name Rudy. If he stays with me, then his lifespan gets very short. If you don't take him in, I'll have to leave him to the street where he'll have a better chance but will still wind up worse than his father. Either he'll grow up the kind of criminal you'd put a bullet in in a New York minute, or he'll be fodder for the freaks until they fuck him to death. You are the final stop-gap. You're the last chance to take this mutt and turn him into a person. You can do it. Further, I know deep within you that you really *want* to do it."

She turned away from him with more tears. "I can't handle it. I just can't."

He grabbed her, shook her. "You can and you will!" This time he shouted such that it made Rudy put down the ice cream for a moment. "You want to love something, don't you?"

"Yes!" she screamed at him. "Yes, alright I do!"

His eyes looked at her, glassy, unblinking, beady yet liquid, and he spoke softly, "Then love *him.*"

———

Boyd looked into the cold, dead eyes of Yonah Shimmel bound to a pivot board in an ancient Arlington basement as she pried them open. He was tripping his brains out. Tactical had canvassed the house, clearing each and every room. Just as Benway had said, he had left his aunt's house for greener pastures and renegade Mic-Mac Indian Filmore Lakeworry, ace button man for the Ork gone rogue, was nowhere to be found, yet might return, running out of places to hole up while figuring out his own exit. She put Hundertwasser and another uniform cop on stake-out off Mass Ave. and had the team gingerly put the house back in order while removing the uncon-scious Shimmel to the awaiting pizza wagon.

She had a bigger dilemma than just daycare for the unruly Rudy, a five-year-old ball of madness, rage and pain, unpredictable and wild, who had been sprung upon her like a trap, or like an epiphany.

She had to decide about Null.

Boyd had told Null that Filmore Lakeworry, a.k.a. Lumpy or Heap, had contacted her directly from his deadman's phone asking that Null deliver the gum for the release of Yonah Shimmel. She prevailed on him to do it, giving him the deadman's phone number for time and place. Two quick texts and it was all set. Of course that was before Benway called in to give Lumpy up and surrender Shimmel as further good faith. As for turning himself in, well, sadly no. Benway was going to go on a long vacation and he hoped Boyd would never hear from him or of him again. He explained that

Lumpy was likely to return to his aunt's house and Boyd and company could catch him there, stake it out. Regardless and coldly, she let Null go and work his magic on Lumpy rather than see to it with Boston Police. She was sure it would be worse for Lumpy that way.

Typically, Null refused to take the gum. "I won't need it," he said. "And soon, nobody else will need it either."

Did she think Null risked death heading after him?

She did.

But he agreed in an instant to do it, anyway.

"I only do one thing," he had said again. "Just one thing."

But she couldn't bring herself to stop Null, especially now that the meeting was superfluous as a means to arrest the Indian, and that there would be no one there to do that. Just Null, stopping him in his own inimitable way.

She resolved not to go there, not to bring backup, to flush all knowledge of the impending incident away.

She was not going to help him.

She was not!

Yet when it came time, she was there in the shadows.

It was late that night on Atlantic Street past the North End at one of the waterfront construction high rises, a skeletal mass of girders and scaffolding. She was tempted to call for backup,

She didn't.

She could see them at the top of the structure by a service elevator, two silhouettes, one short, one tall.

They collided into one another in what looked like a modern dance ballet against the moonlit, cloud-streaked sky.

There were gunshots and she couldn't see them clearly amongst the distant shadows for a moment. Boyd held her breath, watching the mass of slow shifting shadows.

They were up and dancing again, clearly colliding against one another, yet seemingly reaching out for one another.

There was yet more dancing, again more shots, but none of the two fell. She grabbed her Android phone, ready to make the call, but didn't. She was sweating, feeling stupid, feeling guilty, feeling hatred.

Then a scream, a loud muffled word, and a silhouetted figure went over the side of the girders and scaffolding—

And just hung there from a chain or a rope. Just hung, motionless.

The word escaped her mouth loud into the night. "Null!"

There was no response.

She started walking toward the structure, her Android phone clutched tightly in her hand.

This is what Lieutenant Kay Boyle, Organized Crime Specialist for the Boston Police, missed at such a remove from the semi-constructed high rise off Atlantic Avenue. She saw the two figures; could not really distinguish one from the other and could not certainly hear them. It went like this:

Null, late for the appointed time, took the scaffold elevator up ten flights to meet Lumpy at the pine board landing, supported by girders, plywood, joists and indeterminate scaffolding. He emerged at the final flight, unsteady and cautious regaled soon enough by Lumpy's loud, jovial voice.

He said, "Hey, Joe, you got gum?"

"I should find that funny, but I don't find anything funny anymore."

"You're carryin', right?"

"I'm carrying, but not gum. You Filmore Lakeworry?"

He was breathing hard, feeling tired from his wounds and lack of sleep, but he could still handle this straw man. "Call me Lumpy. Everyone else does. Or Heap. Nobody calls me Filmore."

"Not even your mother?"

"Never had one of those. I'm a child of the state."

"Tell me where the criminalist is."

"Gimme the gum and I'll tell you where to collect the mope."

"I'm empty. No gum."

"Then tell me where I can get it."

"You ain't got nothin' comin," said Null evenly.

"That's okay. You're gonna give me the gum, anyway."

"And how am I going to do that?"

"I'm gonna trade you for a box of Benway's Chaw, a wad of cash and a ticket back in to the good graces of the Ork."

"And how do you think you'll do that?"

"Easy, Bro'. You ain't too steady on those girders. When I come to do you, you'll likely fall before I gut you like a pig, anyway. I'll take a photo of you afterward with my phone."

Null lunged forward and almost stumbled from his uneasy purchase on the girder.

Lumpy danced over to him mirthfully in a balletic parody and gestured at Null with his knife. Null fell backward onto a plywood board precariously situated between joists. Lumpy stomped on the board and Null fell one full story onto a narrow girder. He wheezed hard. Lumpy followed him down, easy and precise, swinging from a girder to alight on the main girder. Null fired at him with the Glock and missed. He fired again, but Lumpy gingerly ducked with athletic timing. They stood at opposite ends of the girder.

Null motioned to fire again and Lumpy knocked the gun out of his hand with a hanging winch on a chain.

They collided as an awestruck Boyd watched them below, visualizing it as a dance devoid of the actual struggle that couched and defined it. It was an awkward wrestling, a conflicted knot and Lumpy cut his sides with smooth knife strokes several times in vain, angling each time for an organ shot but deflected each time by a surprisingly agile Null. They broke apart and Null pushed Lumpy with everything he had to the edge of the scaffolding and Lumpy wavered, waving his arms frantically to keep his balance, jerked, then stopped. He said, "Whoa."

He stood at a seemingly untenable angle, jerking about in spastic parody then dancing back and forth at the highest angle of the edge, ultimately making fun of Null. He made it plain that he had faked losing his balance.

"Try this, you wildcat zombie fuck, and you go over like a pancake. You can't survive up here, but this place is my meat and potatoes." He spun about, secure on one foot. "I'm gonna play with you before you die, like I did with the toads when I was a kid back at Assault n' Stall." He pseudo tap-danced on the edge for good measure, never missing.

Null tried to approach him and nearly went over. So he paused, drew the Colt .45 semi-automatic, and fired twice. Lumpy was suddenly nowhere.

Then he was behind Null, giving him an arm bar to the neck and the Colt fell far below while the Glock was only one story down resting on plywood. "How you wanna go, bro? Down to the street or by my knife, set you up like a scarecrow to meet the working stiffs tomorrow in the A.M.? "Tell me you zombie fuck!"

Null felt hot moisture by his side. He thought he might already have been stabbed.

But no, it wasn't him. He wasn't bleeding that much. It must have been Lumpy.

And then he knew.

Even as Lumpy reached with his free hand to draw his knife out again and slice Null up the gullet, Null located Lumpy's unstitching wound with his finger and with a single punch reached in and drew out his liver, casting it down to the street. Lumpy stumbled, released Null and drew back, stunned and pained. The knife clattered down to the sacks of concrete at the foundation. Lumpy cradled his belly like a baby drenched in blood and moaned when he realized he was also cradling his viscera.

Null grabbed a rope swinging from the above story dead-ended to a winch and threw it hard against Lumpy's head, whereupon it rebounded. He threw it again as Lumpy stood swaying, dismayed and almost tearful, with blood covering his arms and midsection, and wrapped it around his neck.

"You've lived a wasted life. You were thrown away like garbage from the very start and this is where your ending was marked, whether it was going to be me or someone else who gave it to you."

"Shut up zombie fuck!" Lumpy wailed.

Null grabbed him firmly and opened his wounds further with his hands. Lumpy screamed.

"You're a tragedy," Null intoned. "A walking causation and cavalcade of death. How many did you kill Lumpy, since a child?"

"I don't know, he shrieked, but you're *tearing me apart!*"

"I am, yes, but life did that long before I ever laid eyes on you." Null stuck his arm into the wound on the opposite side near his back and clawed deeply.

Lumpy screamed like a teenager being raped.

Null rattled it off: "Fetal alcohol syndrome, abandonment, torment, bullying, sodomy, survival and crime, you've had it all, Lumpy, and now you have this."

Lumpy gritted his teeth, struggled to fight more, but Null just yanked a kidney out of his side, dropped it on the plywood and Lumpy sagged, crying pathetically like a child.

"If I could feel anything at all!" Null shouted to him. "I would feel for you!"

"Please," Lumpy whimpered, buckling so as to be held up entirely by Null, vulnerable yet cringing. He flinched as Null moved.

Null whispered softly to him up close. "Death is for you," then threw him over the side with the winch rope wrapped around his neck, wondering if it would hold strongly enough against the ragged scaffolding to break his neck.

He heard him call out one word as he went down.

In a curious moment to Null, it seemed to him that Lumpy had cried out loudly for the mother that he had never actually known.

EPILOGUE

It was ill lit and mostly dark in the office section of Gary Lee Obidowski's Body Shop, Service and Tow in seaside Revere outside of East Boston. The chiaroscuro was a dim paisley of moody shadows and obdurate flames of muted light. A fluorescent tube swung and flickered from the ceiling. Malek "The Mallet" Turbot sat warily at the ancient, scarred wooden desk smoking a cigar and scowling. His shirtsleeves were rolled up, amber visor glasses steamed up, and he was sweating. He was going over accounts on an iPad tablet while oddly checking items off in a little notebook. The tall, craggy button man Franchot was standing before him, looking tired.

"You ain't heard from him, have you?" Malek sneered.

"Just what I get from those that traffic with the Gangsta Boyz—that he's coming for you."

"But no contact? No approach, no wish to make a deal? That makes no sense. He knows I'll eventually find him and string him up, then get him a set of new rims down at this very fucking garage!"

"Not a peep. He's a determined fuck."

"Wildcat fuck's got a hot million of my meth and is selling it on the street while running a vicious crew that rivals mine. He wants a war without even trying to make terms first? He's fucking stupid."

"I don't know what he wants, Padrone. One thing's sure—he don't act like he should."

"Fucker's too damn wildcat for his own good."

"In which case, you should just turn the heat back on, get the bounty back on his ass, and we'll deliver him back to you in pieces. Simple."

"I thought sure when he got the word that the heat's off he'd want to go the amnesty route, talk business, make an accommodation, maybe even give me an apology so we can welcome him into the fold."

"You mean to slaughter him like a sheep."

"Well," said Malek, puffing away intently. "Yes, but I wanted to make him comfortable first. Make him feel all warm and fuzzy."

"I don't think he does warm and fuzzy."

"So you think he's on his way?"

"For my money, I find it hard to believe he hasn't gotten here already."

"If he were here, you'd be dead."

"Or close to it, Padrone. Maybe we are as things stand and don't know it."

"He's not fucking here."

"Maybe not yet."

"So I'll have to be babysat until you guys find him and kill him. I'll have to be surrounded by muscle until somebody makes a grease spot of this wildcat zombie fuck!"

"Padrone, there just ain't no other way. Nobody knows where this mook is and even the Gangsta Boyz are too scared to talk about him, not that they even know."

"Fine, then you and whatever boys want extra cash'll be watching over me when I leave."

"That's the way it is. Right now, I'll watch the front entrance and have a couple of guys walk the perimeter and around back until you're ready to go."

"You think he's that good?"

"Seems to be, Padrone."

"I'll let you know then," he said, grabbing up the tablet and working the screen with his finger. "I'm just finishing up." His cigar puffs were sibilant.

Franchot bowed out and slammed shut the entry door that led to a side service area. His footsteps echoed in the quiet.

Maybe an hour passed. The only sound after that was the buzzing of the flickering fluorescent light tube hanging unevenly over the desk, looking damaged and in need of repair and Malek's sucking on his cigar. Malek paused from his accounting notation and considered the problem of Null. Just how did this nonentity suddenly emerge as such a problem, even as he realized that Null must have come to the same conclusion that he did?

Simply put, Null had to die.

This was why there was no accommodation—no olive branch translating to a cooperative deal. He'd already reached the endgame.

Malek heard an untoward sound that startled him—a sloppy gushing and splashing.

It jerked him to his core, and he raced up from his ancient wooden swivel desk chair and went to the source of the noise.

It was from a sludge barrel in the back.

Malek stood before the barrel, which was only footsteps away from the area where the muscle of the Ork would work over subjects of their "enhanced interrogations," being Republicans to the last. It was where the late Filmore Lakeworry plied his trade.

Malek went limp, seeing what he refused to see.

Splashing up from the barrel with a long straw in his mouth, saturated with filthy oil and grease, old blood and unspecified offal was Null, drawing his Glock still covered in a lunch baggie. He spat the straw to the crumbling floor.

"Fuck this!" muttered Malek.

"Fuck you, I think is the proper response."

"Hey Rube, get in here! I've cornered the fucking mutt!"

"Seems to be your rubric, Malek. You ain't got nothin' comin'."

Null sloshed out from the barrel, dripping indescribably wretched goo onto the broken concrete floor, brackish and tinged with old fetid blood. The Glock hardly moved.

"Hey Rube!" Malek screamed again.

Null just stood there, dripping.

Malek looked toward the door. Null shoved him back with the Glock in his solar plexus.

"They're not coming, Malek. Haven't you grasped that by now?"

"What the fuck?"

"A guy I call Do-Rag and a few of his friends did a little clean-up for me around the edges of this place. I don't think any of them will be coming in here to bother us."

"How did—?"

"Your guys are detained."

"You were in that fucking barrel for how long?"

"Maybe a day or two before you came back here. I had to do a lot of counting and there was some wild estimation as to how long the Gangsta Boyz would be waiting for your friends outside, but they tend to be an obedient lot once disciplined."

He shoved Malek down into the ancient wooden swivel chair by the scarred and equally ancient wooden desk, put the Glock to his forehead.

"So fucking kill me already, because you know if you don't at the first chance, it's exactly what I'll be doing to you."

The light buzzed and flickered.

"I should kill you, you're right. But that might be redundant. You're already post mortem, Malek. The streets are mine."

"Put down the gun, you fucking faggot, and we'll see who owns what."

"That's dramatic. You watch a lot of movies, Malek. You like the British Crime ones, lots of daring action in those. Very tough stuff."

"I'll shove that gun up your motherfucking ass."

"Is that an invitation?"

Malek stood up. Null placed the Glock on the desk between them and held up his hands. "Go for it," he stated.

Malek lunged for the Glock and Null belted him hard in the jaw, making him flail backward. Null leapt across the desk, ignoring the gun, grabbing up Malek by the shirt, tossing away his wrap-around amber visor and beat him repeatedly in the face to cool him out. Malek struck back hard, but he felt like he was hitting a bird. The blows felt light and insubstantial on contact. He managed to wrench away.

Malek made a low lunge for the gun and Null kicked him in the face with a single easy movement. As he struggled up from the grainy, crumbling floor, Null kicked him back down and actually stomped on him repeatedly with his right foot, then dragged him up and uppercut him just under the jaw.

Malek sagged and Null had to help him back to the wooden swivel chair.

Null dragged him up again and for five long minutes gave him a brutally procedural beating, precise and debilitating, careful not to break his nose. He then let him slump semi-conscious back to the chair. He put the muzzle of the Glock into Malek's mouth.

There were no sounds other than the buzzing of the light and Malek's stertorous breathing. Null produced another baggie and looked at his deadman's phone. "I think they're still outside, the Gangsta Boyz, waiting for me. Shall I keep them waiting, Malek?"

"Just do it already," he panted. "You fucking *choratsats ookhti poots!*" He sprayed flecks of saliva in his defiance.

"No, Malek, I'm not going to kill you. I'm going to give you a gift. I'm going to give you back your humanity."

"What the *fuck?*"

"How many guys you have tortured to death here in this garage? How many women beaten, raped, tormented, murdered? Can you even count?"

"What does it fucking matter?"

"They screamed in pain, begged for their lives, but you barely listened and ate a sandwich while Filmore Lakeworry and his friends yanked out a man's teeth and fingernails, cut him slowly to pieces."

"It's what we do when we have to," spat Malek. "What *men* do."

"No, Malek. Men cry. They beg for their lives—they whimper, snivel and beg under great pain and threat of more pain. Their sensitivity makes them vulnerable and prone. They're like babies, subject to kindness or cruelty, whichever may be imposed. They're boiled down to the essential value of human feeling, which is what we are at best—sympathetic, empathetic, feeling entities marked by the caring that what we feel others can feel. Our misery can be theirs and vice versa. In this delicacy of sensation, we become careful, respectful even of the suffering of others, it becomes something that matters."

He whipped Malek across the face with the butt of the Glock abruptly.

"What are you gonna do?" heaved Malek. "Put me out of my misery?"

"No, Malek. I think you need to get better acquainted with it. Your misery."

Malek grunted and gurgled spittle in his throat. "No need to acquaint me with pain," he announced. "We're old friends. Pain is my enforcer. Pain obeys me, not the other way around! So, go ahead, finish me already! But stop trying to bore me to death!"

"No, Malek, I'm not going to kill you."

"Then, what then?"

"You have to live. That way, I still control the streets. I don't want to have to break in a new replacement for you and have to break him all over again the way I broke you."

"Pussy. You haven't broken me yet, pally!"

"Give it time, Malek. I'm not done."

Then he paced back and forth in front of Malek, practically inviting him to make a move, but Malek just sat there in a slump, wheezing and bleeding. Null spied an old wooden-handled axe propped up in the corner of the room by the exit to the main garage and he stepped over to pick it up. He tested it for weight and balance, then strode back to the desk quickly. He was expecting something from Malek, waiting for him to draw some hidden pistol or to make some other pathetic move that he would have to put down hard.

None came.

Null took a breath. "I'm going to restore your humanity to you now, Malek," he said. "One day you'll thank me, I think. It's a great gift, you know, the understanding of being human. The basic feeling that one human being can have for another. The knowledge and understanding of sensitivity and vulnerability—how weak and fragile we are. So easy to hurt."

"Oh? And what's this great gift going to cost me, pray tell? An arm and a leg?

"*As a matter of fact—!*" said Null, hefting the axe.

He took the right leg, and the left arm off cleanly, with a

modicum of mess, called 911 and went outside looking for the Gangsta Boyz who were still lying in wait for him as if he were their master.

———

Rudy was screaming.

Boyd was giving the boy a bath in her florally decorated pink bathroom, and he was splashing water everywhere. Red faced and squalling, he struggled in vain. Boyd held him close into her, soaping his head. She didn't care about his resistance; she was determined to get him clean and hugged him tight in his defiance, though it sopped water through her clothes. She wasn't sure whether she could ever love this foundling boy, but for now his need for someone like her was paramount and somehow his need, as Null had pointed out, fulfilled a need of her own.

She drugged him to get to sleep, using her own prescription for trazodone to do so.

Watching him in her bed, tucked in with clean sheets and bedding, made her feel at peace, under control and purposeful.

She got herself a different gun.

It was a clean piece with a taped-up handle and the serial number filed off—completely illegal despite her living in the land with the most permissive gun laws on earth, though admittedly Boston took a hard line on guns with a hardass one-year mandatory sentence for possession of a firearm without a license. She had clipped it earlier that day from the evidence room down at District A-1 and A-15 by Government Center and no one batted an eye, though she did it clumsily enough to be seen.

She accepted that it would be brought up again, then buried in return for a favor. She was prepared for that. No one stopped her. No one said a word.

It was almost a half hour drive to the old Edwardian house in Arlington deeded on the books to one Freddy "Boom Boom" Cannon. She didn't have to break in, as the front door had yet to be repaired from the onslaught of the police battering ram. Lights were on and there were faint sounds of movement coming from upstairs.

She went up the steep staircase to the second floor, moved open a door left ajar and heard a yelping scream.

Benway.

He stood there under the light, frozen for a moment and very much slack-jawed. His upper lip was covered with sweat and his frizzy hair was wilder than usual.

"You're not supposed to be here," Benway sighed. "Didn't you already search this place and come up empty?"

"It's a cliché about returning to the scene of the crime."

"This is my mother's house. We don't commit no crimes here."

"But you and Lumpy did. You wrapped up the gum."

"The gum's not illegal. It should be, but it isn't. So, packing up legal recreational gum's about as illegal as bath salts or flakka."

"You're splitting hairs, Benway."

"Did you get him?" he asked, wide eyed.

"Get who?"

"Lumpy. I served him up to you on a platter, and your criminalist, too."

"I didn't get Lumpy. Your science project did."

"Null arrested him? I didn't know he could do that."

"Don't be funny. You knew what would happen. You played it great. Manipulated Lumpy right into the ground."

"He was headed there, anyway. I just helped him along."

"You set it up for him to go after Null."

"Sure. Everybody did. Have the two negatives cancel each other out."

"Null is the one doing the canceling."

"You see? All's well that ends well."

"I'm placing you under arrest." She took out her Smith and Wesson handcuffs, ready to secure Benway. He demurred and drew back toward the closet where he had been removing and packing clothes.

"What for? What are you really going to charge me with I won't be out in twenty-four hours or less on once I lawyer up?"

"Suspicion of kidnapping—"

"Are you kidding?" Benway suddenly looked relaxed, good humored. "Lumpy kidnapped *me*. I was doing his bidding under threat of bodily harm, and I informed on him and where you could find the victim. I fucking saved the day and you're going to charge me? Try again, twinkle toes."

"Malicious mischief and mayhem in the matter of Joseph Xavier Null. impersonating a physician, distribution of harmful drugs."

"Good luck proving the malicious mischief and mayhem. Do you think Null will testify, sign affidavits? I bet not. Seems a reach, Lieutenant." He paced back and forth nonchalantly, eying his suit-case. "Impersonating a physician? That's a hummer too. No traction there. I'll get a slap on the wrist, maybe. Probation if I stay around for it. And what harmful drugs, for God's sake? The stuff's not illegal nor medically proven to cause harm. Maybe in a few years it will be, but until then, I was just giving the kids a good time. How was I to know there was anything amiss with the goodies? Besides, I was kidnapped and doing Lumpy's bidding. He called the shots, I was just a slave. I doubt I'd make accomplice—it's a case of Stockholm Syndrome. I'll beat it."

"Creating a disturbance," she said, lowering her arm and jingling the cuffs nervously.

"You're joking."

"No, I'm not."

"Well, whether or not you are, I'm headed to Montreal. The scene's a bit more forgiving there."

"You're going nowhere."

"You're going to shoot me—really?"

"The thought had occurred."

"Forget it. How will you justify it? And you're guilt-ridden enough as it is. You'd never shoot an unarmed man who really isn't clearly guilty of anything."

"You murdered Filmore Lakeworry and I don't know how many died at the clubs."

"Prove it."

"You destroyed Joseph Xavier Null."

"No, I brought him back from a psychotic catatonic break he would have never have recovered from otherwise. I did him a favor, and I didn't charge a dime for it. I'm a fucking good Samaritan."

"No, you're something else."

"Temper, temper, Lieutenant."

"You made him a monster."

"He doesn't care. He gave me a pass. Even that wildcat fuck knows I'm a hero. Hell, he's gangster number one in Boston as things stand. I don't think he'd say a word against me." Benway went over to the suitcase with a nervous grace and continued packing items from the closet. "Now if you'll excuse me, Lieutenant, I got a hot bus to catch to get to Montreal. I don't know how they handle a late check-in there."

Boyd slumped her shoulders a bit, lowered the gun, then looked up at Benway, her eyes narrowed, her nostrils flaring. If the iris of the eye could truly burn, both of hers would have. "Well, Null did teach me something—something you're going to want to know, Benway."

"Yeah? Well, what is it?"

"He taught me one thing. Just one thing."

Boyd moved quickly.

"So, tell me what it is, for fuck's sake!"

She said it in her loudest whisper, and the sound of the word was drowned out by the blast, which was louder than she had thought, and Benway didn't even know that he had heard it at the exact moment when the back of his head was blown out and its contents splattered against the closet's back wall:

"This!"

―――――

Don't miss out on your next favorite book!
Join the Melange Books mailing list at
www.melange-books.com/mail.html

ACKNOWLEDGMENTS

The author hereby wishes to acknowledge his small band of supporters:

Nancy Pepin, nee Durocher, who's with me in all things and in everything that matters.

Scott Oddo, for his friendship and keen intellect. Marc Songini, for his wit and his literary japing; Huntley Dent, for all his support; Steve Dooner, for his astonishing breadth of cultural literacy, abstruse and not; Kate Nicholas, for her sharp wit, bordering on slight insanity; Susan Gambrell Reinhardt, whose sweetly acid commentary is always inspiring; Glen Dansker for being a mensch and Joe Schatzle for always knowing how to crack me up.

This parvum opus is for you all.

ABOUT THE AUTHOR

Gary S. Kadet has been a journalist, covering various beats for the Boston Herald, Globe and even Playboy Magazine, which also published his fiction. He was a contributing editor for the nationally-read Boston Book Review where he covered crime fiction in his "Trouble is Their Business" column. In the 90s, he was a trailblazer on the Internet, running the 10th largest adult website in the world, appearing on MSNBC commenting on the future of adult material on the web. His novel "D/s - an Anti-Love Story" was the first novel to portray the real-world BDSM scene without prurience or sentimentality and was a Book Of The Month Club main selection.

GarySKadet@protonmail.com

facebook.com/CleverNovels

twitter.com/GaryScottKadet